W9-BFC-218

GRAYSON COUNTY LIBRARY
INDEPENDENCE, VA 24348

DISAPPEARING MOON 殘月 CAFE

月

楼

SKY LEE

The Seal Press

Copyright © 1990 by SKY Lee

This U.S. edition first published in 1991 by The Seal Press, 3131
Western Avenue Suite 410, Seattle, Washington 98121. Published by
agreement with Douglas & McIntyre, Vancouver, British Columbia.

All rights reserved. No part of this book may be reproduced in whole
or in part, except for the quotation of brief passages in reviews, without
prior permission from the publisher.

All of the characters and experiences depicted in this book are fictional.

Library of Congress Cataloging-in-Publication Data
Lee, Sky.
    Disappearing Moon Cafe / by Sky Lee.
        p.   cm.
    ISBN 1-878067-11-7
    1. Chinese--Canada--History--Fiction.   I. Title.
    PR9199.3.L393D57   1991   91-22580
    813'.54--dc20   CIP

Printed in Canada

First printing, September 1991
10 9 8 7 6 5 4 3 2 1

To Mother

81064

Acknowledgements

I offer my thanks and appreciation to those who have shared in the realization of this dream. They include Saeko Usukawa, Ginger Lee, Philip Wong, Jim Wong-Chu, May Lynn Woo, Lorraine Chan, Jamila Ismail, Viola Thomas, Paul Yee, Frederick Lee, Agnes Mui, Leila Chu, Shirley Chan, Albert Lee, Nathan Wong, Dennis Lee, Cao Xiao and Don Poy.

Special acknowledgements to the old Makara collective, the Asian Canadian Writers Workshop, the people at Cordova House, and John Haugen of the Lytton Indian Band.

Thanks, Jim, for the title.

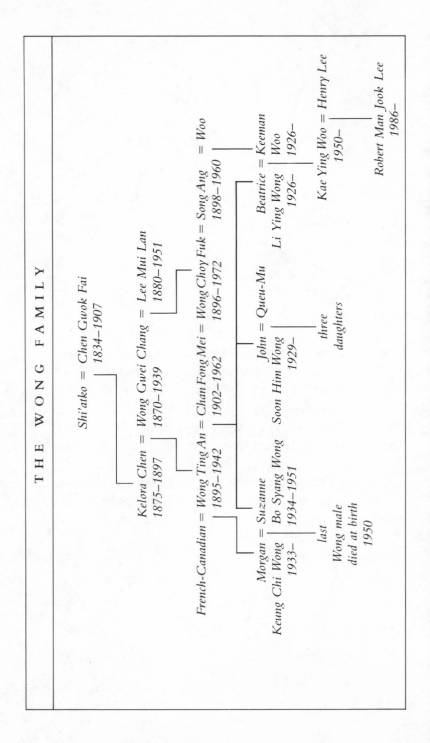

THE WONG FAMILY

Shi'atko = Chen Gwok Fai
              1834–1907

Kelora Chen = Wong Gwei Chang = Lee Mui Lan
1875–1897   1870–1939   1880–1951

French-Canadian = Wong Ting An = Chan Fong Mei = Wong Choy Fuk = Song Ang   = Woo
                  1895–1942   1902–1962   1896–1972   1898–1960

Morgan = Suzanne
Keung Chi Wong   Bo Syang Wong   Soon Him Wong   John = Queu-Mu   Li Ying Wong   Beatrice = Keeman
1933–   1934–1951   1929–   1926–   1926–   Woo
                                                                                                1926–

last
Wong male
died at birth
1950

                                    three
                                    daughters

                                                    Kae Ying Woo = Henry Lee
                                                    1950–

                                                    Robert Man Jook Lee
                                                    1986–

Contents

DISAPPEARING MOON CAFE

残月楼

PROLOGUE

Search for Bones

WONG GWEI CHANG
1892

He remembered that by then he was worn out from fighting the wind. He had to stop and rest in a shaded spot, so he found a smooth, flat stone to sit on, beside a stream that meandered off around a sharp bend. He was bone-tired from all this walking, watching the land dry out and the trees thin out. He wasn't thirsty; he was hungry, the last of his provisions gone days ago. So very hungry, so very tired of quenching his thirst on cold mountain water, sweet as it was.

He wanted to complain out loud, "Why send men out to starve to death?" But the wind snatched the words out of his mouth, and even he couldn't tell if he had spoken them or not. He looked up at the unsettled sky and realized that if a freak storm should happen, he would be finished. He slapped his knees and shook his head. Ill-equipped, ill-informed, he was doomed from the start.

Ha! he thought. A bone-searching expedition! We'll find bones all right, gleaming white, powdery in the hot sun, except they'll be our own. His feet ached relentlessly, throbbing cold from wading through ditches and icy creeks. Already, holes in the thinned soles of his borrowed boots.

"I suppose I should be damned grateful I am still alive to feel the ache!" he cursed out loud. Then there was the loneliness. He didn't

1

want to think about the loneliness; it was the most dangerous struggle.

He didn't know why he'd been chosen. Perhaps because he was young and big, and had muscular shoulders. Maybe because his hair was thick and smooth, and not just black but blue-black. He had two whorls on the crown of his head—the sign of a nonconformist. He also had very big hands. Most likely the old men had liked his face and its look of kind innocence.

They said, "This youth has a tender face, but he has the look of an old soul."

"An old soul?" he asked when they leaned close, looking for promises.

"Yes," they replied, "you have been reincarnated many times. You have lived many lives fruitfully and have a deeper understanding of many things." They told him that he must believe.

"Believe what!" he demanded.

"In your mission."

"My mission is to search out the bones of those who have died on the iron road, so they can be sent back home . . . by you, the Benevolent Associations."

"No!" the old eyes commanded brilliantly. "It is more than that. To believe is to make it live! You must make your mission live, or else you will not succeed."

Thus, they sent him into a trance. Around him, the mountain barricaded with trees reaching into the eternal mist, and the rain pressed down from the heavens. He felt totally hemmed in. His eyes untrained to see beyond the wall of wilderness, his heart unsuited to this deep, penetrating solitude. Hunger had already made him hallucinate, afraid of the rustling leaves and whistling animals.

So he thought she had to be a spirit when he met her. In this dreamlike state, he thought maybe he had died and she was another spirit here to guide him over to the other side.

"Look, a chinaman!" She crept up behind him and spoke in his language. He whirled around and his knees buckled under, the last of his strength not enough to contain his furious trembling. Meanwhile, she darted back into the safety of the underbrush and hid. He couldn't see her, but he could hear her laughing at him; the sounds gurgled like an infant's blown back and forth by the wind. The whole landscape winking and flashing at him.

"You mock me, yet you don't dare show yourself to me," he challenged, peering into a shimmering sea of leaves. "Come out now!" he barked with bravado.

"Ah, so he speaks chinese," the voice observed. Finally, a brown face peeped out of the stems and brambles. She was an indian girl, dressed in coarse brown clothing that made her invisible in the forest. Her mouth did not smile, but her eyes were friendly—a deer's soft gaze. He was astonished when she stepped out onto the tall grass.

"You speak chinese," he said, indignant, unwilling to believe what he saw before him.

"My father is a chinaman, like you. His eyes are slits like yours. He speaks like you." She spoke deliberately and demonstrated by pulling back the skin beside her dark, round eyes. He saw that she was wearing a crude cape made of a worn animal skin. A long blanket served as a skirt and covered her bare feet. A small basket hung across her chest and made her look stooped over. Yet she moved gracefully, swaying from side to side, small intense movements like a little brown bird. He stared like a crazy man, because he thought she would disappear if he didn't concentrate on her being.

"But you're a wild injun." He spilled out the insults in front of her, but they were meaningless to her. In chinese, the words mocked, slanglike, "yin-chin."

"You look hungry, chinaman." She tipped her head to one side as she looked him up and down. From her clothing, she drew out coiled strips of some kind of substance and held these out to him. "My father tells me chinamen are always hungry."

"I am not hungry," he shot back. He could tell she was teasing him, and he was offended that she knew more than he did. She could tell he was hungry, that he had no more power left, that in this wilderness he was lost.

"Ahh, he has no manners," she exclaimed. He could only blink, astonished by this elegant rebuke from a "siwashee," a girl, younger than he. It made him feel uncivilized, uncouth; the very qualities he had assigned so thoughtlessly to her, he realized, she was watching for in him.

It was then he recognized familiar features on her dark face. A melon-seed face, most admired in a beautiful woman. Her hairline high, inkstrokes by an artist's brush down both sides of her face. Cheeks caressed.

Ah, he thought, why be afraid of her! What was she but another human being? Why should she mean him harm? He stepped up to take whatever it was from her hand, but as he reached out, she sprang back, dropping the strange food behind her like one of those shy creatures who sense no great danger but move prudently out of range just in case. Again, he was surprised to see that she was wary of him. It emphasized the distance between them, as if she was not a human being as he was, or . . . as if he was not a human being as she was.

The food was seaweed, both crunchy and rubbery soft. As he chewed hungrily, she watched him and he watched her. After a while, she hoisted a heavily laden basket of freshly dug-up roots and bulbs up onto her back. She secured it with a wide band across her forehead. Her hand carried a slim stick, one end of which was dirtied, perhaps from digging the roots, and the other end of which was carved, perhaps bone. This she waved at him and called out, "Come and sit!" nonchalantly as if the invitation was for any time, as if in a day or two he would not be dead of exposure. "My father enjoys the company of his own kind. And he will be glad to help you find your way."

"Yes," he answered, his mouth full of gracefulness, "perhaps I should have a word with your father."

Then, as if the barren wasteland around him had magically opened and allowed him admittance, he followed her through dense thickets, up hills and down through ravines, a respectable distance between them. He marvelled at her bare feet, which padded softly along the forest floor without injury. Many times he sank to his knees, soaked in sweat, so tired he could hardly hold up his head. He was fearful that she would abandon him, but she paced her steps according to his strength and smiled encouragingly.

4

They followed the big river until they finally arrived at her home, which stood high up on the cliff side of a mountain overlooking the water. By then darkness had fallen and the wind was blowing fiercer than ever, the first raindrops of a storm about to descend.

He knew it was on a cliff because he could see the wide expanse of stars beyond the immediate trees, and he could hear rushing water far below them. She ran into the little cabin first, then a man and a woman came out and stood beside the door. They peered excitedly into the night, looking for their visitor.

"Come in!" said the man.

It was so dark, he couldn't see their faces. He just got the idea that they were older by their voices and the placid way they both moved.

"My name is Chen Gwok Fai. Come in and rest, sir! What is your precious surname, sir?"

"Wong," he said, "Wong Gwei Chang."

Chen put his hands on Gwei Chang's shoulders and led him into the tiny cabin. Beside a small fire in the fireplace, Gwei Chang saw the girl kneeling, her hands in front of her, reaching for warmth. He noted the intelligence in her face, ignited by the firelight; hers was a beautiful face full of vision. He didn't remember anything else, because he fell unconscious right on the spot, and he slept for a long, long time. By the time he awakened, he had stayed for three years.

GWEI CHANG

1939

He was an old man now. And he played with his memories all day long. Or they played with him. He felt he must tell of a most peculiar dream he'd had around that period of his life when he went looking for the bones of dead chinamen strewn along the Canadian Pacific Railway, their ghosts sitting on the ties, some standing with one foot on the gleaming metal ribbon, waiting, grumbling. They were still waiting as much as half a century after the ribbon-cutting ceremony by the whites at the end of the line, forgotten as chinamen generally are.

In his dream, he was strolling down a street in a wealthy residential area of Victoria. He knew it was a street where rich people lived, because it was lined by fine old trees at neat intervals in front of each sprawling lawn. And he was troubled because he was about to turn down a job as a servant in one of these grand houses in order to go on a dangerous, almost senseless expedition. Not only was it going to be gruelling hard work, but the pay was a bad joke. Of course he knew that the rewards for the performance of such work would come later, but his family in China needed to eat now.

As he walked, he noticed some crested myna birds flitting back and forth, looking for nesting sites in the trees. They had a shrill, rasplike cry, which got on his nerves. In order to make himself feel better, he began to search the ground, hoping to spot a glimmer of gold in the dirt, convinced that the Gold Mountains weren't a myth at all. He got so crazed by this idea that he couldn't stop gawking at the sidewalk; then in a mad rush, he got down on his hands and knees, his hands groping and sifting the ground. He didn't care that he demeaned himself nosing through the dirt like a dog. Worse still, he panicked and started rummaging through the garbage cans. Whenever he glanced back, he noticed that the mynas were following him and were getting bigger, their black plumage and crests more and more distinct. But he was so intent on what he needed to do that he took little heed of them.

Suddenly, a huge shadow fell over him, and he heard the flapping of giant wings directly over his head. Unable to fight off his instincts, he crouched and his hands flew up to ward off attack, but he was too late. A bloodcurdling scream shattered his ears, and a windstorm caught him about the head and beat him to his knees. The rest was a blur, but he did manage a glimpse of the menace; huge wings of a black raven swooping down upon him. When its talons ripped into his flesh, he felt neither pain nor fear, just the sensation of being lifted into a flying dream.

KELORA CHEN

1892

Gwei Chang remembered being half-unconscious, with Old Man Chen telling him that it was the isolation that tore out a man's good senses. Then Chen told him that he had been delirious for days. "The white men have a name for it. Cabin fever," Chen laughed, "cabin fever, he, he, he!" and made a grand gesture towards his surroundings. He was without a doubt a most peculiar man.

"I got this cabin from a white man," Chen grinned foolishly. "I climbed up here and found a white man dying of a festering gunshot wound, with his head in an indian woman's lap right here," he pointed to the bed Gwei Chang was lying on. "So, as he died, I just stayed and took over where he left off, you see. I took care of his woman like a wife and his cabin like a home. She had a daughter. Kelora—indian name. I taught her to speak chinese. She's old enough to have a husband now," Chen smiled down at Gwei Chang.

Gwei Chang didn't know whether he could believe Chen. Chen told him lots of strange, elusive stories, but who knows which ones were true and which ones were fragments of his own fantasy? As far as Gwei Chang could make out, Chen had worked on the railroad. He also seemed to have participated in the gold rush over thirty years ago. He also might have come because of the tong wars in San Francisco. For sure, life was hard for a chinaman, and Chen would have had to give up something in order to survive.

Nevertheless, he obviously had led a very enchanted life by the time Gwei Chang happened along. Even though Old Man Chen wasn't a very good provider for himself, he survived very well, because Kelora was more than a good provider—she was also a healer and a retriever of lost souls. Her family on her mother's side was very wealthy, old and well-respected, so their people always made sure that little Kelora was given any little extra that they could spare, as well as her father, of course. They called him "Father of Little Kelora."

So, when Kelora went to her aunties and uncles and told them that her father had chosen a young man for her to marry, they must have known it was just a formality. Still, they all found excuses to drop by her home to take a look at the man "whom Kelora's father had chosen for her." Summertime was a busy time of year, but for Kelora's family of the Shi'atko clan in "the village at the mouth of the two rivers," finding a husband for their sister's daughter was important too. Kelora always had been a bit of a worry for them because, although well loved, she had no rank. But, on the other hand, they knew a girl with Kelora's abilities really chose her own husband. Nothing wrong with that! Not everybody was sure about another chinaman, but Kelora seemed to prefer it, and that was enough for them.

Of course, Gwei Chang was quite unaware of all this. At the time, he thought that Kelora's relatives and people normally dropped by often and visited a lot. For instance, the old woman he had seen the first night was not her mother, who had died over seven years ago, but an old aunt who was visiting.

Another time Gwei Chang awoke, he asked for hot water. Kelora brought him a crude swamp tea which cooled him too fast and started him sweating profusely. Her numerous aunts and female cousins stood about, watching without really looking, as if they were trying to get a sense of him. But after a long sleep, waking was difficult and confusing, made even more abstract by a beautiful woman. Turning his back on all of them, he was about to settle into some more sleep when Kelora suggested he go and bathe in the river. Exposing his already weakened body to such inclement elements was a foreign and foolhardy idea, he thought, but there was a challenge in her voice that quickly restored him.

Along the rock face of the cliff was a natural ridge that led down to the riverside. It was not a difficult descent, but the terrain was unfamiliar and Gwei Chang was still wobbly. He felt slow and awkward beside the children and old women who ran ahead of him.

However, he impulsively plunged into the roiling waters, as there was no other way to do it. Energy such as he had never experienced vaulted through his body, and a cold, raw reward of strength filled every muscle. He flung out his arms and churned through the muddied green water for as long as his lungs could hold out. The river's forces, tortuous with fast-flowing currents, pulled him in all directions at once, but he had no sense of danger and did not struggle.

When he bounced back up to the surface, Kelora was kneeling by the river's edge. She was naked except for her long hair draped wet against her. Naturally, Gwei Chang was curious, so he swam a little closer to the shore. Her old aunts, perched on soapstone boulders around her, seemed to approve of what she was doing; shading their faces against the glare of water and sun, they peered at him as if there was a connection between what she was doing and him. She picked up a small snake and dropped it in front of her. It fell onto the fleshiness of her thighs, twisted itself into the water, and slithered off.

Gwei Chang was shy of Kelora at first, clumsily dodging her stares whenever he could. There was something very untamed about her. Her casual nakedness used to devour him. When she realized this, she toyed with him for her own amusement. The summer got very hot. His first instinct was to run, but always with a backwards glance that grew longer and longer until it made him swell; his fear of her made him wince with love.

Chen's cabin was situated on a very strategic spot. The same ridge which served as a convenient ramp up to his house spooned out into a sizable terrace on which his little log abode stood. It made a cozy sight—his little home and vegetable garden snuggled into the edge of a pine forest that crept in from the windward side of the mountain. And it made a welcome respite for the indians who travelled up and down this busy avenue of commerce— "grease trail" they called it, naming it after the much sought-after fish oil they ate. When they came by they always left a little token for their stay, because they recognized Kelora and her father to be the keepers of this picnic site. The exchange was fluid though, flowed both ways, depending on the seasons of nature. Often enough Kelora and her father would share their food with a boatload of impoverished guests. Either way, it made a good life for them.

One day, Gwei Chang stood on the very edge of the bluff to admire the far-reaching beauty of this tiny spot on earth. The view was breathtaking, like a windy crevice against heaven. It made him dizzy with joy, his toes curled over rock as he pressed his body up against the wind. As the chinese say, "mountain and water": the delirious heights and bottomless depths flung him out into the clarity of the sky.

"A view like a soaring eagle's." Kelora had followed him, and Gwei Chang could feel her soothing powers reach out for him. He looked at her as she stepped up to the ridge, and she looked at him, and they both smiled down at the world, because they knew then and there that they would fly together.

THE BONES

Gwei Chang remembered that, one evening, after a meal of rice, fresh salmon and unfamiliar mushrooms, Old Chen said, "I've been waiting for someone like you to come along for many years—so many years that I even forgot I was waiting." He always looked at Gwei Chang as though he was going to burst into laughter at any time. He said that he knew of many burial sites and had heard of many people who knew of many more, though the bones must be dust by now.

"But the Benevolent Associations have already sent many on the same mission," Gwei Chang replied.

"Yes, but they have not thought to come up here to ask chinaman Chen, have they?"

"Well, it is a little out of the way!" Gwei Chang felt obliged to say, glancing at Kelora whose eyes looked remote and made him want to follow. Already, he was forgetting that there was a whole other world with its own determined way of life out there, somewhere, and that he was from there.

"What are your plans, boy?" There was no edge to Chen's question, merely a sense of duty that had to be recalled.

Gwei Chang turned to face him squarely. "I'm not sure, Uncle." He shrugged his shoulders. Of course, he thought he was just being modest. He had maps, with sections of the railroad numbered. He pointed out the gravesites, haphazardly described at the end of each section. He'd been told that there would be markers, or cairns, or something. How hard could it be . . .

"Hah! You're a dunce!" Chen's expletive clipped him on the chin. "Come with me! Bring your so-called maps!"

"Now? It's black out there."

"Light, dark, what difference does it make," Chen's voice boomed, "when we've got brothers to send home." Since Kelora didn't even blink an eye, Gwei Chang could only imagine that this kind of gesture was not at all out of the ordinary, so he followed Chen out into the moonlit forest.

After a two-hour trek, mostly along the train tracks made silver now and then by an isolated moonbeam, Chen led Gwei Chang to the first of many leftover work camp gangs. This one, an independent group of gold dredgers, dour and suspicious, was camped out on the edge of a clearing beside a stream. That late at night, there were no words wasted. The only remark was from a watchman, that Old Man Chen had come. Gwei Chang was thrown a rag to sleep under, and he wandered about until he found some rotten barrels that would support a plank of sorts, and a sluice box. That was his bed for several nights.

In the morning, Gwei Chang shared their cold rice while they scrutinized his maps and criticized his information. Then he was given a shovel. They talked while they worked. That's how Gwei Chang found out a few things. He found out that old overseas chinese never wasted anything—not their time, not their leisure. They worked unceasingly, as if they would fall apart if they ever stopped. They also sat up all night, gossiping and swearing and laughing. They were strange men, maybe because of the shadow of loneliness and isolation that hovered over them. In their midst, Chen seemed less peculiar to Gwei Chang. In fact, Chen was well liked and a regular visitor. Because Gwei Chang came with Chen, he was immediately a friend. When Chen told them what Gwei Chang was doing, he was taken seriously at once.

News of Gwei Chang and his work went ahead of him. Eventually, he could stroll into any bull gang or small Chinatown, onto any farm or campsite, and they would have been expecting him, ready to share food and whatever else he needed. Over and over again, he watched groups shed their surliness at his approach and spread in front of him all that they had from their pitiful little hovels.

At first, he didn't value their reverence for him. Thinking back, he knew how unthinking he had been then, grabbing opportunities for fun—sitting up all night, gossiping, selfishly filling his pockets with goods and information to make his work easier. He saw the loneliness in the brothers, toiling, poor—left behind to rot because the CPR had reneged on its contract to pay the chinese railway workers' passage home. But he felt only a little disdain for them. He was fresh off the boat from China. When they hankered for news from their villages, he thought he was doing them a real big favour by telling them stories. He was too young, and he didn't understand.

Not until he touched the bones. When he finally did, he was awed by them. At first, he actually dreaded the macabre work. What were a few dried bones to him, except disgusting? But the spirits in the mountains were strong and persuasive. The bones gathered themselves into the human shapes of young men, each dashing and bold. They followed him about wherever he roamed, whispered to him, until he knew each one to be a hero, with yearnings from the same secret places in his own heart.

How could he not be touched by the spirit of these wilderness uncles who had trekked on an incredible journey and pitted their lives against mountain rocks and human cruelty? In the perfect silence of a hot afternoon, he used to stop here and there to run his hands along the sheer rock face of a mountain, the surface still biting hot from a dynamite blast. He imagined the mountain shuddering, roaring out in pain, demanding human sacrifice for this profanity. And the real culprits held out blood-splattered chinamen in front of them like a protective talisman.

By then, he understood. By then, in the utter peace of the forests, he had met them all—uncles who had climbed mountain heights then fallen from them, uncles who had drowned in deep surging waters, uncles who had clawed to their deaths in the dirt of caved-in mines. By then, he wasn't afraid and they weren't alien any more. Like them, he would piece himself together again from scattered, shattered bone and then endure.

The next time Gwei Chang walked into a work camp, he was ready to share with them instead of taking from them. He took on their surliness and learned to talk tough and blunt, a chiselled edge to his words to express the backbreaking task of survival that all of them shared day after day. They talked like comrades-in-arms after the battle, still grateful to feel the ache of so many work-worn years, to fill their lungs with mountain mist, to see their shadows walk ahead of them, homesick.

When Kelora took him into the forests of "the hidden place," another world opened up. She had a way of murmuring as they walked. Gwei Chang remembered chinese women doing the very same.

"We go into the forest," she might say. "It's old. Look at how big the trees are." He watched her as she smiled up at the canopy of wind-swept boughs against a glorious sky. Her braids fell away from her ears, exposing an earlobe that looked inviting, as if it would taste sweet.

"It is hot outside, but in here, it is always cool and wet," she said. When he tore his eyes away from her, he looked up, and wished she could have shot him like an arrow, straight up into the endless blue.

"Look, a yellow cedar tree! If I need to gather cedar, then I have to say a few words to the tree, to thank the tree for giving part of itself up to me. I take only a small part too, but not today. Look, the path is worn and smooth. Many women have come here to gather what they need. When we walk in the forest, we say 'we walk with our grandmothers.' She wore a cotton shift, faded gingham against her deep brown skin. Her baskets, mats and hat hung by a thong behind her left shoulder.

"Look at that swampy place!" Kelora tugged on his arm, and Gwei Chang beamed down on her. "See there! We call those rushes 'the geese eat it' plant. The women say to boil it for medicine when some old men can't urinate." This reduced them to giggles. She gave him a playful push that landed him in a garden of ferns. And he lunged at her, but she took off like a little bird.

Kelora and Gwei Chang wandered high and low in the summers, like deer foraging through new pastures, like children. Summertime gathering was women's work, and Kelora would have to go and gather her berries, dawn until dusk sometimes. And Gwei Chang would have to go and find his bones. Yet they found many ways to flow together, like wind brushing against leaves. Like lake and lakeshore, a slow meandering dance of lovers.

He would help her pound her berries, and she would help him scrape bones and carefully stack them into neat bundles. She wasn't afraid and seemed to understand the rituals that had to be performed around them. More amazing, she had a peculiar intuition for locating gravesites whose markers had long ago deteriorated. More than once, she wandered ahead of him; by the time Gwei Chang caught up, she would be pointing at the site where he was to dig. These occasions made his skin crawl. She laughed at him, tittering behind a cupped hand.

When he asked her how she knew, she said, "Chinaman, first listen to yourself sing! Every soul has its own voice."

Chinamen are a superstitious bunch. Gwei Chang got to wondering what she heard. Before he became a human being himself, he mistook her meaning. Kelora was a strange one, with her own private language—neither chinese nor indian, but from deep within the wildness of her soul. Fascinated, he began to press his ear against the ground too. He followed her everywhere, even as she went about her woman's work. She taught him to love the same mother earth and to see her sloping curves in the mountains.

He forgot that he had once thought of them as barriers. He learned how to cling onto her against a raging river, or bury into her away from the pelting rain. Or he could be somewhere, anywhere, cold and bone-tired, but he would stare at the consummate beauty of a bare branch trembling in the breeze. He would watch red buds bloom into freshly peeled blossoms. Clouds tinted pink-gold, slanting over the mirror of an alpine lake; this beautiful mother filled his heart and soul.

Old Chen came at Gwei Chang with two questions at the same time. He asked, "How are you going to transport those bones down to the coast?"

He also asked, "Do you have anything you can give me as a gift? If you don't have anything, then I'll give you something to give back to me."

Gwei Chang played dumb. "Huh?"

"It's the custom," Chen said, "to give a gift when you take a wife. Even nowadays." Kelora's maternal aunt shuffled in and out of the cabin, excitedly shouting at the young boys who had followed her up the bluff, carrying fifty-pound bags of flour in their arms.

"I have a gold watch," Gwei Chang replied without hesitation, "and a bowie knife I bought off a drunk demon in Spuzzum. Oh yes, those farmers gave me six Hudson's Bay Company blankets in exchange for a few days' work—used but not worn out."

Chen looked relieved. Gwei Chang didn't let on that he had been preparing all along. By then, he was well aware of what caught Kelora's eyes and what didn't.

"Not bad," Chen said, "not bad at all for a boy who was starving, eating 'chinook' wind just a while back! Go with Kelora and give them all to her people. Politely! You and me, of course, we can forego the usual ceremony. They're just to keep the women happy anyway."

The other question was not so easily answered. Gwei Chang knew it would provoke some controversy because he had already tried it on some elders in the Chinatown at North Bend. He figured Chen must have surely heard about his idea by now. He could well imagine the indignant sputters Chen would have had to face.

"You know what that crazy Wong boy was thinking about? Him and that hothead, Lee Chong. Did they get that stupid idea from you? People have been saying that that crazy old Chen had a hand in it. Who else!"

Gwei Chang had a wonderful idea! Lee Chong thought it was a good idea too. Kelora said it was worth a try. When you're young and stupidly proud, everything is worth a try. Lee Chong was a small, wiry fellow—face like a rat in those days. He had quit his laundry job in a huff, and when Gwei Chang met up with him, he was on his way back to Victoria. Lee Chong came up to Gwei Chang and asked if he would give him a job.

"Yeah," Gwei Chang said, "I need someone to take the bones all the way back down to Victoria." Lee Chong looked enthusiastic, which was a relief to him. It wasn't easy trying to find someone who didn't mind hauling a load of skeletons back down the old Cariboo Road, through hostile territory ridden with whites, and camping out alone with ghosts in the mountains, in the dark.

Gwei Chang asked if Lee Chong had a horse and wagon. "Nope," he said, "don't you?"

Lee Chong and Gwei Chang hit it off right away. It was the height of summer then, and Lee Chong didn't have much trouble finding odd jobs here and there, picking fruit, hand to mouth, so to speak, while he waited around for Gwei Chang to make up his mind. Lee Chong wasn't in any hurry. By then, Gwei Chang had been very successful at his bone-searching expedition and thought much of himself.

The Benevolent Associations hadn't given Gwei Chang any specific instructions on how to get the bones to Victoria. The assumption had been that the first bone searchers would find their own way, with the minimum of expense and manpower. All the monies for their transport had been donated, and there were so many bones left still. This was in 1892, the beginning of the retrieval of bones, which lasted well into the 1930s.

Gwei Chang had travelled up and down the Fraser Canyon and

watched many an indian canoe skimming down the white rapids, the travellers whooping and hollering, their hair plastered straight back behind their heads. He thought it an exhilarating way to travel! Those raging waters mesmerized him. They didn't seem like dangerous obstacles. Then, one day, he saw white men, on axe-hewn rafts, come dancing around the bend, men and boxes securely tied down with a strong network of ropes. That decided him. What could be easier?

"Look," he said to Lee Chong, "I don't have a wagon, but I've got something better, faster. More challenging."

Lee Chong and Gwei Chang started to build their craft. They asked around to find out how. They traded with indians for hand-woven cedar ropes, and the indians told them which trees were the most buoyant; the hardwood for sternposts; tough flexibility for poles and hand-hewn rudders.

The other chinamen fumed, "If you capsize and spill your cracked brains, that's O.K. by us, but if you lose any bones, you're condemning human spirits to ten thousand years of aimless wandering."

Lee Chong and Gwei Chang saw things differently. They told each other, "Old women, every one of them! Got no gall! We just want to give the spirits of those mountain heroes one last thrilling ride." Lee Chong and Gwei Chang figured the spirits would laugh at peril. After all, they had died for adventure and daring. Why should they object now?

When they finished lashing their craft together, Lee Chong and Gwei Chang figured it could fall down hundreds of feet of a waterfall without splintering. They were ready to bet their lives on it, but were the dead ones prepared to risk their souls on another long shot?

Well, in order to avoid the wrong people answering that question, early at dawn the next morning, with cedar boxes full of bones lashed down in the centre of the raft, Lee Chong and Gwei Chang pushed off. Once out of Chen's protective cul-de-sac, the eddies of the big river grabbed the craft and threw them along the most dizzying, joyful ride of their lives.

The sun shone through the fine mist spray which lifted out of the river and doused them with fancy. They just let the river take them. Sometimes the river was calm and giving; sometimes it knocked their senses askew. The world encircling them was raw and beautiful. The life that blew into them was inspiring and intoxicating. They careened along, hemmed in by the steep rise of gorges and canyon cliffs. Sometimes the river was fretful, contorting back on itself, treacherous. Other times, the river sprawled and meandered through pastures and rich flatlands; they glided along its shimmering reflections. The pair felt like they had ridden the river dragon, and it had lifted their souls skyward. At the end of their journey, they walked away transformed, feeling a little closer to immortality.

Gwei Chang parted ways with the bones at the bone-house in Victoria and with Lee Chong on Tang People's Street, and began his trek back home to Kelora.

1

Waiting for Enlightenment

KAE YING WOO
1986

I'm so very disappointed. I've been brought up to believe in kinship, or those with whom we share. I thought that by applying attention to all the important events such as the births and the deaths, the intricate complexities of a family with chinese roots could be massaged into a suant, digestible unit. Like a herbal pill— I thought I could swallow it and my mind would become enlightened.

All my life, I have been faithfully told, and I have also respectfully remembered. My maternal grandmother, for whom the chinese term is Poh Poh, had one son and two daughters. Her son, my uncle, whom I must address as A Queu, married a girl from Jung Saan district, whom I must call A Queu-Mu, to indicate that she is my auntie by marriage. She had three walloping huge baby girls. Poh Poh's eldest daughter, my mother, had me—her only child and a scrawny one at that. Poh Poh's younger daughter, my blood aunt, died of pneumonia as a young woman, when I was still a baby. She didn't ever marry or multiply.

My paternal grandmother, or Ngen Ngen, had three children— only my father survived. Both Ngen Ngen and my paternal grandfather, or Lo Yeh, came from destitute backgrounds, torn from starving families too feeble to stay together—but since they had lost contact with those left for dead in China over a half century ago, there isn't much for me to remember about that side of the family. My mother's side is more vibrant, to my way of thinking. My mother sponsored Poh Poh's sister's oldest son, or Ai Bew Sook (which doesn't have an equivalent in english) and his family over in 1959, when Canada's immigration policies finally softened with prosperity, and we've maintained conscientious ties ever since. Especially after Poh Poh died in 1962, of cancer. Her husband, my maternal grandfather, or Gong Gong, puts me in a bit of a dilemma, because the family tree gets tricky here. Let's just say for now that Gong Gong died in 1972, maybe 1942.

So, having swallowed the pill, here I am, still waiting. For enlightenment. Disappointed, yet eternally optimistic!

Oh, and I've been told that it is important to keep a family strong and together, especially in this day and age, so I've come to expect the ceremonies and assemblies that come with families. At funerals, full-month parties, graduations, it was easy to see an inevitable logic underlining life, a crisp beginning and a well-penned conclusion, nice and neat, and as reassuring as receiving a certificate for good attendance or a gold star at the top of the page. Although chinese parents tend not to acknowledge rewards.

"So what!" they said after glancing at my report card beaming with A's. Instead, I was told that excellence was the natural and orderly progression of . . . of things, I guess! Why do I feel they have secrets?

Even grown women get conned into going further. I was. Weddings are celebratory.

"So why don't we get pregnant, dear?"

"O.K., honey!"

I get tricked because I want to be so damned perfect all the time. Now I've found that nobody has told me the whole messy truth about anything!

My mother says, benevolently, "Drink this ginger water. It chases the wind away. You have a lot of wind in your system after birthing a baby."

"Maah," I ask with my whining voice, "why didn't you tell me it was going to be so hard?"

"No good to dwell on these things," the other one answers. "You'll get better! Drink!"

In all my thirty-six years as a young, healthy, able body, I've never been so degraded; never known so much raw pain; never faced such demented panic! In my dreams, a fat, slippery baby suddenly appeared between my legs. The gore was red catsup. I remained calm and dignified, and appeared brave.

Actually, I should feel more shame for having made such an awful scene at my so-called delivery. I admit that I lost control. Well, panicked, in fact, screeching and quivering in front of strangers! How many times in our lives do we lose control like that? I never did until then, and I really felt like I was going to die! A close scrape with death always makes us want to rethink our lives or, to be more candid, rewrite it wherever possible.

But first I had to get therapeutically angry at the two-ply, sterile masks. Mad at the world for unfairly dividing itself into hormonal camps—those who curse (my obstetrician) and those who burst, then are stitched and stuffed with bloodied gauze!

A pretty blonde nurse in a pink uniform arrives by my bedside.

"When can I have another injection?" I ask.

"Anytime," she replies cheerfully, "you want it."

"Now!" I indicate.

"Being a nurse is good," says one mother in chinese, smiling and nodding just as cheerfully back at the nurse, trying to change the subject. "Nice and clean. Wear pink dresses. Play with babies all day." Yet when the pink nurse turns away, the other examines every inch of her back as if she were very alien.

After the injection, the world recedes to a comfortable distance again. The baby, riding in what appears to be a clear plastic bubble on top of a cart, is rolled in for a feed by another nurse, this one older with a ruddy face, singing (to the tune of "A Huntin' We Will Go!"):

> To mommy we will roll,
> To mommy we will roll.
> Hi ho the cheer . . . i . . . ooo
> To mommy we will go!"

I thank her politely.

"This one's got a big head," she adds. Yes, I know; I smile wanly like a newly delivered mother.

My mom, who must be feeling like a venerable grandmother, scoops him up, and with intense concentration unwraps him. She starts to count fingers and toes. She unravels his tightly clenched fists and reads his wizened little face. She pinches his earlobes and prods his entire skull. Peering at private parts, she is thorough; even the underarms have to be examined. Afterwards, she sits down on her chair again, looking as if she wishes with all her heart she could unzip him to continue with her search inside.

"What are you looking for, Mah?" I ask, although I figure I already know.

"Nothing." She suddenly stiffens in a way that is very familiar to me. And she knows! That small gesture's hidden meaning is not lost on me. We have communicated too much and too hard for me not to know, although on the day of the birth of my son, we are all jumpy, like fish out of water. Details could be misinterpreted.

"Ah hah!" I feel like cackling. "Charlie Chan! Cat-and-mouse and mothers!" Great melodrama, a stiffened mother, a stoned daughter and a sleeping newborn grandson together in a boxlike hospital room. Life is an afternoon TV screen. Perhaps if we were caucasian and a little more straightforward with each other, my next line might be, "But mother dear, somehow I can't help feeling that there is something amiss." Instead, I watch without looking. My eyes are half-closed, and I finish my ginger water. In a few moments, it will come—the . . .

"Sigh," sighs my mother. Then another sigh—heavier, sad and troubled! "I see now the baby is fine. The doctor also said the baby is just fine. Ahh . . . I've waited a long time to make sure . . . for your sake, daughter."

Ahh, for my sake! I was wise to stay mute, staring at an exploding fuschia plant barely contained in its delicately woven basket, suspended from the curtain rail. It is a gift from one of my mother's cousins, whom I must call A Ai Bui Jie every time we come face to face. I wonder if she shouldn't have sent me an oak tree instead—old and hard and stubborn, with leaves like ideas that hang on withering, fighting the seasons.

"You don't know, A Kae," whispers my mother, "but there has been much trouble in our family. It's best that what I tell you does not go beyond these four walls."

Thus, the story—the well-kept secret that I had actually unearthed years ago—finally begins to end for me with the birth of my son, Robert Man Jook Lee, on April 29, 1986. It took quite the sentimental occasion for my mother to finally loosen a little of her iron grip on her emotions in order to reveal a little of her past that she thought so shameful—the same past that has shaped so much of my own life, with evil tentacles that could have even wormed into the innocent, tender parts of my baby. No, no, it will not be so unless I make it so. And I will leave it boxed in our past—mine and my mother's, the four walls that we share! At least what they say about childbirth is true—that it's always worth it no matter how hard it was.

The story began, I guess, with my great-grandmother, Lee Mui Lan, sometime in June 1924, as she stood behind the cash register at the front of the even-now famous Disappearing Moon Cafe, 50 East Pender Street, Vancouver, British Columbia.

L E E   M U I   L A N

1 9 2 4

Mui Lan stood very still, severely dressed in a black robe and matching trousers, a concentrated frown straining her hard-boiled face. She was forty-four years old, yet despite her smooth, egg-shaped face, she appeared older. Faced with Mui Lan, people always presented a brave show of politeness and respect, but they tended to avoid her, perhaps because after some contact with her, no matter how minimal, they were always left with a faint, dry dusting of dissatisfaction blown over their faces and shoulders.

If this seemed contrary to her thirteen-year-old role as proprietress of the busiest, largest restaurant in Chinatown, and as the wife of the most admired and likable businessman in Chinatown, well then, life must be full of vexations. But people had a simpler reason for not liking her. Perhaps it was because she had done very well for an ignorant village woman, and under the same circumstances in which a lot of people had not done very well at all. So it must have chafed them to see the chronic pain on her face, as if to suggest that she suffered more than they did. After all, they'd all known the same bare-boned poverty.

"Eh, Mui Lan-ah . . ." a coarse voice leapt into the midmorning calm of the restaurant, "reaping in the dough, and you still look greedy!" Two laundresses came in by the kitchen door at the back, a young one and an old one—mother-in-law and daughter-in-law. They carried heavy laundry bundles in their arms, and each had a sleeping baby strapped to her back. Big, healthy babies, with their adorable round heads dangling and lolling, their fine wispy hair fluttering with every breeze and movement. Babies were such a rare sight in the new world that Mui Lan immediately perked up in their presence.

"Go die, you stinky bitch!" Mui Lan countered good-naturedly at the older. She dived under the glass display case, in search of candies to poke into the ungrasping hands of the infants.

"We're almost broke! These old, overseas chinese are so tight-fisted they can't even afford a cup of hot water, never mind a restaurant meal," she continued at the top of her lungs, oblivious to the sprinkling of patrons a few feet away. And they seemingly oblivious to her.

"Ahh, this restaurant business!" she sighed dramatically after she resurfaced, checking the tight bun at the nape of her neck with a rigid flick of her arms. "Can't even make money if we sold twenty banquet tables every night! That's the honest-to-goodness truth! Drink a cup of tea, Auntie!"

"Hey, you know . . . in devil talk," the craftier, bolder, older one grinned slyly, " 'ca-fei' means coffee place. That means a small place. Why don't you name your restaurant 'Chicken Chow Mein Palace'? That means a big, fancy place. Devils like to eat like that."

"Ahh go die!" Mui Lan retorted loudly. "Who cares how those

devils talk! You see them poking their big noses in Tang People's Street more and more these days. Who's going to sit around waiting for business from them! Those little cow-sitters . . . keeping O.K.?"

"Useless as ever." The baby-bearers threw their noses over their shoulders for a second. "Eat, sleep, excrete. Then eat more, and excrete more. Who needs them!" they added modestly, disparaging their offspring for the sake of politeness.

"You have prosperity!" Mui Lan answered patly, her eyes glued to the soft-snoring infants with the same intense cupidity that always cut conversations short.

"You will too, Auntie, soon."

"Yes, very soon!" the youthful one echoed as they backed off.

Not until the two women had left did Mui Lan's brow furrow deep. With a drawn-out sigh, she deflated until her head drooped onto her chest again. After five years, three months and eighteen days, you'd think the old bag would tire of the same remark. It irked Mui Lan to think that that one—so poor that she and her daughter-in-law scrubbed pounds of table linen for a few cents a day—should have grandsons popping out every year. She herself was rich enough to buy a building for a half-dozen grandsons, yet she was still waiting after five years, three months, and soon nineteen days.

And although Mui Lan was not aware of it, their closeness also annoyed her. She even envied them for their prosaic work because it was something that the two women had in common and did together. A singularity of purpose; the babies would also grow up close to each other. Together, the two women gave an impression of strength, as if they knew something that she didn't.

"Bah, who needs them!" she muttered to herself, not realizing that she referred to a faraway home in her heart that had disintegrated over the years—her old home in the village, made up almost entirely of women except for the children and a few old men. At the time, Mui Lan's position in the village was a high status one. Her husband's overseas prosperity gave her a lot of clout in her community, and she enjoyed that. She missed the daily sweep of woman-talk from morning till night, about who received a letter and who didn't get money; whose husband was coming home and whose son was being sent for. All of them desperately weaving tenuous, invisible threads over the ocean, to cling cobweblike to their men and sons in the Gold Mountains.

Mui Lan remembered once visiting a household—all women—where there was a mother whose son had committed suicide rather than suffer the loneliness high up on some desolate mountain in Wyoming. Wasn't her son's agony the same pain suffered by all their absent men? So the village women stayed up with her to wail through the night. For Mui Lan, it felt good to wail together, to be filled with something, even if it was just a wariness of other people's grief.

One day, Mui Lan received the first indications that she and her boy were being sent for, and she became the brightest centre of attention. A new bride all over again! It was like being chosen by God himself. Her neighbours gazing at her as if she glowed; furthermore, she began to believe it herself. In this welter of woman-sounds, Mui Lan was at her happiest. Propelled by women who could only dream of such a reunion with their men, she landed in the Gold Mountains, full of warmth and hope. Little did she realize that people's most fervent hope can turn into their worst nightmare.

And Mui Lan's nightmare was loneliness. She arrived and found only silence. A stone silence that tripped her up when she tried to reach out. Gold Mountain men were like stone. She looked around for women to tell her what was happening, but there were none. By herself, she lacked the means to know what to do next. Without her society of women, Mui Lan lost substance. Over the years, she became bodiless, or was it soulless, and the only way she could come back was by being noisy and demanding—because if nothing else, she was still the boss's wife, wasn't she?

Nowadays, people were just plain malicious! Gossip! Chinatown was always full of gossip. Her own restaurant reeked of it. Too many idle loafers! She of all people should know. They were always there, all too anxious to size her up. She felt pinned to the wall, like the unpaid bills. Frustrated, Mui Lan sighed, not too noticeably, yet the few scattered men sitting at the shiny counter in front of her stopped to stare, their smouldering cigarettes poised in mid-air. They made her feel like squirming, but that would have been very poor behaviour for a woman. She touched her bun again, as if needing reassurance that the knotted silver hairpin holding it in place was still there.

"Back home in the village," she suddenly heard herself lash out at more than one tired ear, "there were at least customs and traditions which held people in check. There was an established way of life, and one hardly ever heard of a girl going astray, or a boy who didn't at least know his duty. But here, in this wilderness, even the tang people lose all sense of right from wrong!"

What did it matter whether they listened or understood? She owned the restaurant! She glowered at the patrons who didn't so much as grunt a response, so used were they to her quarrelsome ways. Mui Lan knew that she wasn't the easiest person to get along with. Managing a large restaurant such as Disappearing Moon called for a hard nose and a sharp tongue. In fact, she'd be the first to admit that she'd been losing patience too much lately, with customers and workers alike, but if she didn't keep an eye out, they'd rob the "pea-pods along with the peas," so to speak.

Her husband certainly couldn't be relied on. Left to his own devices, Wong Gwei Chang would let his business be eroded in no time into bankruptcy by petty thievery and laziness. Mui Lan often wondered how he'd got along before she came. He was too easygoing.

"Leave it alone!" he'd say when a few bags of rice went missing.

"Never mind!" when waiter number five's gambling buddies ate a free meal.

They stood together as husband and wife, but they weren't close. Too many years apart after a brief marriage ceremony in the village between two shy, shuffling strangers who saw more of their new shoes than each other's faces. After six months, the Gold Mountain guest was gone, and she was pregnant. The next time she saw him, they were both too old to start again.

Secretly, she had hoped for not exactly more love as the years passed but for perhaps more of a mutual understanding. However, nothing turned out as she had hoped. Frankly, even after twenty-eight years of a marriage as hollow as hers, Mui Lan felt she should know a man better than she did him. However, no fancy red wedding bow, no matter how long the ribbon, could stretch over both decades and oceans. She was simply the mother of Gwei Chang's only son. Stamped on her entry papers: "A merchant's wife." A wife in name only, she relied heavily on him for her identity in this land, even though the hard distance remained on her husband's face. And this she could only bear in silence.

She had Choy Fuk though, and she kept herself busy, adjusting her boy, then sixteen years old, to a new life in this strange outpost community. Before long, she found other interests. She found she was very good at a lot of things, especially good at making money.

At night, after she finally turned off the restaurant's lights and locked its doors, and even the late-night laggers had reluctantly left to crawl into their dismal bunkbeds, she'd finalize the daily accounts with the old man. She insisted that he be there, to witness. He'd sit across the table from her, waiting, smoking a cigar butt with his eyes half-closed. Mui Lan enjoyed adding up the day's take, energetically organizing the money into neat rubber-bound bundles. She considered it the most important task of the day. Sometimes, not very often, there would be the odd, slow day and then she wouldn't be able to resist the temptation to wonder what her husband dreamt about in that semidarkness just beyond the range of the dangling light bulb. She knew it wasn't money.

If Mui Lan had any message of domestic importance to convey to her husband, she'd choose this moment of quiet privacy to speak to him. A few nights ago, she had suddenly snapped the last rubber band with a loud crack as if to signal the old man to pay attention. Then she had addressed Gwei Chang in a very businesslike manner.

"Husband-ah, we need to have a few words," she began.

Conversations between the two were both brief and few, so if he was surprised, he didn't show it. The chair beneath him groaned a little, and he took his cigar out of his mouth. He snorted a weak reply, rather perfunctorily, Mui Lan imagined. She immediately began to feel a little annoyed, although she did not dare show it.

She settled her stonelike stare onto his dark silhouette and decided that she would not speak until he at least presented his face to the light.

When he did lean forward, he asked, "Everything at home all right?" He looked at her with a steadfast gaze. At fifty-four years old, Gwei Chang was still a handsome man, the edges of his face smooth and rounded with an easy sense of age and power.

"Fine, fine," she answered tersely. She found she had to look away. "No, it's the same concern I've had about Choy Fuk and Fong Mei for a long time now."

"Ahh . . ." Gwei Chang receded into the darkness. This time, she left him there, and went on.

"You and I are getting on in years," she said. "The longer we wait, the more I worry. Those two married over five years, and still no baby—not even a girl! There's something dreadfully wrong."

"You've done all you could. What else is there? The rest is up to the young people," his voice sagging under the weight of all the number of times he'd had to hear about this pesky subject.

"Bah, that's crazy!" she retorted furiously. "If we left these important matters to young people, there wouldn't be any results for ten thousand years. The Wong name would be dust. Is that what you want?"

The old man sucked on his cigar butt—short, disconcerting puffs. But he let her go on. Who could do otherwise when Mui Lan spoke so convincingly of the possibility of ten thousand years of desolate wandering for his untended soul? Of course, she was in the right. He'd been feeling far too happy and prosperous these days. A grasping woman, Mui Lan had a way of gripping the life out of happiness. He was always careful not to show her his. But Gwei Chang should have been expecting that her flailing temper would again splay open the flesh of their daughter-in-law, Fong Mei.

"And are we to lose face on account of one no-good female-bag?" Mui Lan's lower lip jutted across the table, with chin pointed at her shadowy foe. "And how am I to find peace in that stinky she-dog, barren as a dried twig! We spent a fortune to bring her over here! Who'd have thought we'd have such luck! I looked so thoroughly into her family background! Her own sister already had three sons and another on the way. Now, I ask you, where are we to find another woman in this backwash bush? How will we get another through immigration with those devil authorities treading on the tang people's heads all the time?"

Gwei Chang stopped puffing and began to eye her very suspiciously.

"What are you up to?" he abruptly cut in, with a menacing tone of voice. Mui Lan could not smother the icy scowl in her eyes so she kept them downcast.

"Well . . ." she began to feel the ground crumble beneath her, "if she can't do justice to our family name, then another woman will . . ."

"There'll be no more of that kind of talk!" Gwei Chang declared, smacking the back of one hand against the palm of the other for emphasis. "Our son's wife has already been chosen! That was your woman's business! Babies, grandsons—those are your woman's business too! I try not to interfere with what is woman's business, but I won't stand by to watch this one. We're not in the village any more! Those old-fashioned ideas don't work here. Take a look around you! All these Gold Mountain men who don't even have one woman. And now, Choy Fuk can't get by without two!"

"How do I face people if I let her put on such airs?" There was a slight sneer to his voice. Angered, he brushed her aside by pretending she wasn't even there. His words were no longer addressed to her.

"After thirteen years in this land, she still doesn't understand the people here." Then he paused to let her think about that one. "Bringing in another wife for him is impossible anyway. There's a new Chinese Exclusion Act. What does she think all that fuss is about? The government is saying no more chinese immigrants! In fact, they're looking to shovel us all out." Suddenly, he was calm again. That he had total authority would never be an issue for the patriarch, but he still added meanly, "Open your eyes, old woman. If you've made a mistake, don't embarrass me by flaunt-

ing it! 'The marriage was predestined, no objection can prevail,' "
he closed with an ancient quote.

That night, Mui Lan had to turn away to conceal her bitterness. Stupid old man, she thought venomously, cares more for what coolie labourers think than for his own family's good fortune! If it hadn't been for me, where would he be?

My dumb great-granny! I don't know why she wasn't asking more relevant questions, like where does one go for comfort and relief from such a barren life? But there probably were no halfway houses for women, no places to hide out from a rocky marriage. Ejected from a cloister of women into the stony society of Gold Mountain men must have been a bit like being smashed against a brick wall. She wouldn't have known what had shattered her. It wasn't just that my great-grandmother was pathetic—she became a tyrant. Having never been in control of her own life, she suddenly found herself in charge of many people's lives. Frustrated and isolated from the secluded life she understood, Mui Lan had to swallow bitterness, so she made her suffering felt far and wide. I should understand that impulse to splatter pain as far away from oneself as possible; and she didn't much care whom it soiled either.

Besides, her motives were ordinary enough. She wanted a grandson to fulfill the most fundamental purpose to her life. A baby with a brow as clear and as promising as his future. A little boy who came from her son, who came from her husband, who also came lineally from that golden chain of male to male. The daughters-in-law who bore them were unidentified receptacles. From her husband's side, Mui Lan would certainly claim a share of that eternal life which came with each new generation of babies. What could be more natural, more ecologically pure?

I should re-examine my own motives. Why do I need to make this ancestress the tip of the funnelling storm, the pinnacle that anchored chaos and destruction close to earth? Why do I need to indict her? Why not my grandmother, say? Both are dead. Actually, both are to blame (if you like that kind of thing), but since I've landed up paying dearly for their deeds, and I know of others who've paid with their lives, isn't it my privilege to assign blame, preferably to the one I understand the least, the one farthest away from me and from those I love?

WONG CHOY FUK
1924

When Mui Lan heard, "A Maah," she was probably comforted enough anyway. Her son, Choy Fuk, now twenty-eight years old, walked through the same doors by which the laundresses had left a few minutes ago. He spied his mother perched on a tall stool behind the till at the front of the cafe, looking much like a ruffled hen, dressed in black wool, bright beads for eyes on a powdery white face. Behind her, the sun shone brilliantly through the window with its painted sign, onto the huge pots of prickly cactus plants displayed on the window shelf.

Disappearing Moon was divided into two front sections, with the kitchen and the storeroom at the back. The dining room was the largest in Chinatown, perhaps the most beautiful in all of Vancouver, with its teak carvings on the pillars and gateways. The rich dark-blood of the rosewood furniture was enhanced by the tangled emerald-green of the ivy foliage. Cultivated jade trees, with leaves like precious stones, overflowed the dragon pots. On the walls, long silk scrolls of calligraphy sang out to those patrons who could read them. It was a nostalgic replica of an old-fashioned chinese teahouse, which accounted for its popularity not only amongst its homesick chinese clientele but also outsiders who came looking for oriental exotica.

However, Choy Fuk liked the more modern counter-and-booth section better. He loved the highly polished chrome and brightly lit glass, the checkerboard tiles on the floor, the marble countertop. And except for the customers, his mother, and perhaps the cacti, there was nothing chinese about it.

Immediately he headed over to the glassed-in icebox for a helping of sweet milk pudding. Unlike his father, whom life in the west had hardened and tanned, Choy Fuk was small of bone and pasty of face. They had the same easygoing personality, although his stemmed more from a lack of need and soon shifted into laziness, whereas his father's had been tempered by hardship into a tolerant and relaxed way.

Luckily for Choy Fuk, laziness was good for business. His shortcuts saved money. Besides, he could always rely on his best buddy, Ting An, to bail him out whenever necessary, especially where his old man was concerned. Mostly, Choy Fuk and his father got along because Gwei Chang never paid very much attention to his son.

As his mother had said often enough, sixteen was not a good age to disrupt a young man's life. Had he come here at a younger age, Choy Fuk would have grown to love his father and would have emulated his ways more. Or, at a later age, a lot of his teen-aged tomfoolery would have passed like a light tropical shower, drying up quickly in the more restricted life of the village.

As it was, from the time Choy Fuk stepped off the boat, he felt indifferent to his impenetrable father, who spent his time huddled around the back dining-room tables in a tight clique of old men muttering softly about hard times and the old days. Choy Fuk made lots of friends as well, but his gambling joint buddies were brash and crude, and much less cliquish. The more swearing and cussing, the more disgusting their drunken behaviour, the more Choy Fuk enjoyed his friends' foul ways. And he himself was amazingly quick to shed his bumpkin ways in favour of a more cocky western style, complete with sennit straw hats, narrow-shouldered jackets and starched high-collared shirts. These, he felt, were more appropriate for his position as the heir of a well-to-do businessman.

Mui Lan had once hoped that bringing over a wife for Choy Fuk would make him lose interest in his trashy friends. Then what would he have in common with those hooligans? But that hadn't worked out. She blamed Fong Mei for this, of course. The girl wasn't devoted enough to her son, even though Choy Fuk seemed quite fond of her—but how could he, the dear boy, be expected to keep track of the real reason for her keep!

"Ahh, you're back, son!" she greeted him enthusiastically.

"Hai-le, Maah," he answered her with a milk-filled mouth.

"Did you deal with that no good iceman?"

"He say no candoo, Maah!'

"Paahh!" she spat viciously. "That dead white devil! Cheating us all these years! Selling us tang people the leftover ice for full price. I'm sick of it!"

Sometimes, for Choy Fuk, a simple talk with Mui Lan could turn into a very eerie experience. She was his mother all right, but he could never be sure where exactly he stood with her. Inwardly, he trembled like a leaf in her presence. Like any other village type, she could shriek, cackle and swear with the best of them. In their neighbourly gossip from house to house, across the alleys, over blackberry bushes, up to third-floor windows, they didn't care how salty their language or who overheard them. Yet, when Mui Lan turned truly angry, her whole demeanour changed. Her face froze like white porcelain. Her voice lowered until it was almost inaudible, and she spoke in a slow deliberate monotone, with terrifying conviction.

"If that sonovabitchee," she continued, "doesn't want our business, then he doesn't want any of Chinatown's business. Yuen Fong, Yip Hay—all those stores. You go to all those places! Go to Japantown even! You and me . . . we'll figure out a way to bypass that 'no candoo' and get more for our money even. There's that little italian iceman. He can supply all of us if you make a special deal. You go talk english to him!"

As she spoke, Choy Fuk watched her very warily. Her eyes darted from here to there, and he knew they weren't seeing too clearly.

"Aww Maah, why don't you send Ting An?" He deliberately broke the spell. From far away in the kitchen he heard the sound of glass shattering. Sure enough, cursing and loud arguing ensued between the cooks, blaming each other for causing such a bad omen, and it still morning.

Mui Lan leaned anxiously over him as he resumed his spooning. "Why do you talk like that? Are you farting through your mouth?

Ting An is not the boss! You should be! We've spent a lot of money to send you to learn good english . . ."

"A Ting is native-born. He knows how to deal better with ghosts." Choy Fuk began to wipe his mouth, but his mother automatically grabbed a damp counter-cloth and started dabbing at the pudding that had strayed down the front of his starched shirt.

"No matter," she snorted in disdain. "This business is your business, not Ting An's. He's just another worker . . . Choy Fuk-ah," his mother's voice shrank to a murmur, her hand still clutching his shirt, "you must learn to be your father's right-hand man. A Ting is just a nameless nobody who's been trying to get in good with your father. I know, I've been watching him all these years."

"Well, what does it matter who goes! He'll probably get a better deal."

"Don't talk like that!" His mother scowled at him as if he were a cute two-year-old who had just learned to swear. "If you did it, we could tell your father that this business deal was all your idea. Wouldn't you become the apple of his eye! You know, I don't have anything against A Ting, really. He's a good enough worker for what we pay him. But people are bound to compare you two, being close in age, more or less. Naturally, Gwei Chang too. You being his only son, of course he's interested in knowing how you do! But you know you can do better than Ting An if you spend less time with those rough-housers and more time with your own father. You'd think that those no-good chums of yours are family, and your own father an outsider. You don't know but those snakes will lead you down a black road, and it'll be too late by the time you find out. You listen to your mother talking!" She paused and glanced back along the counter to see if any ears were perked in their direction.

"Hai-le . . . O.K. Maah!"

"And don't drink too much. Drinking is no good. And no smoking that shit—that goes without saying!"

"Hai-le, Maah." Choy Fuk pushed himself away from the counter.

"Everything O.K. between you and A Fong Mei?"

"Fine. Fine. No problems."

"I don't know how much longer I can wait for some good news." The woman was relentless.

"I better be getting back to work now." He started inching away with his hands stuffed in his pant pockets.

"Come closer here!" His mother swept her hands inward. As though he didn't have a will of his own, Choy Fuk climbed back onto the stool in front of her.

"Low-low sek-sek, just between you and me, son," she began all over again, "you've been married over five years now. That's too long not to see good results. Something has to be done again!"

"Please don't trouble yourself, Maah!" Choy Fuk felt his feet go cold.

"If I don't trouble myself, who's going to trouble themselves, you dead boy!" she sputtered with indignation. "If I don't do anything, nothing'll be done!"

"There's really nothing you can do, Maah!"

"I can stand up for the good name of our family. Let me tell you, people are already talking . . ." she imparted in a harsh whisper. "People over here delight in vicious two-faced gossip. They're jealous of those who are more successful than they are. You don't think I know what they say when they guzzle vinegar . . . 'What good is all that Wong money when their family name can't even be assured?' " she mimicked hatefully.

"In the village," her voice rang crisp and clear, "the customs were clear. Life was brutal. A coldhearted mother-in-law would have thrown her out the door a long time ago."

Completely taken aback, Choy Fuk's hand flew to his cheek as though he had been slapped.

"Maah, that's . . ." he gasped, "that's just old-fashioned talk!"

"A Fuk-ah," Mui Lan tapped his hands down, "I realize that we live in more lenient times. That is why I myself am willing to be flexible in dealing with this problem. I'm just trying to save her face, after all . . ."

"What are you up to, Maah?" Fuk looked somewhat unconvinced.

"I was just thinking . . ." she began, but glancing up, she spotted her daughter-in-law, Fong Mei, approaching.

The sudden way the conversation came to a halt convinced Fong Mei that her mother-in-law and husband had been talking about her.

"Dead ghosts!" The curse flashed angrily through her thoughts, but she squashed it just as quickly and seasoned her mouth with a guilty little smile instead. She forced herself to walk right up to them.

"A Maah, A Goh," she greeted both of them sweetly, addressing her husband as "Big Brother." But her husband ignored her and kept staring at his mother. Mui Lan masked her face and pretended to polish the till. She grunted back, but Fong couldn't tell if it was actually an acknowledgement or if she was merely clearing her throat. She didn't mind much because this was the way elders often greeted those who were younger, especially daughters-in-law. But surely Choy Fuk, her own husband, didn't have to turn around and ask so coldly, "Don't you have work to do in the storeroom?" He made her heart ache like ice in her breast.

My grandmother was a renowned beauty in Chinatown. I guess Wong money could buy the very best. I do know of her indirectly through my mother, who used to hug me all the tighter whenever she talked stories about her own mother to me. Everything about her seemed so good and beautiful, like a fairy goodmother. When I was young, I used to get her mixed up with my mother all the time.

"Tell me about the little girls' house you lived in, in China, Mummy!" The two lives flowed together, one into the other, so perfectly.

I knew my grandmother only briefly, when I was very young and she was very old; a woman who was not really there, sitting primly on her crocheted cushion, in a wheelchair, on the lawn of a respectable old folks home. She bent down and told me very solemnly that she was the only chinese there.

This I do imagine. She was once a woman with finely tuned instincts, like cat's ears pointed in what I still believe were the right directions. She also had her own pure motives; at least mother-in-law and daughter-in-law shared that. In fact, I like to think of her in these terms: every rule has its own exception, right? Well, if Mui Lan was the overbearing rule, then Fong Mei would be her pretty exception.

Someone once wrote in my grade eight yearbook,

> Your future can be read
> like newly driven snow.
> Be very careful how you tread,
> 'cause every step will show!

However, if integrity is what really counts in the end, Fong Mei got lost in the snowstorm.

HERMIA CHOW
1971

During my first year at the Peking Language Institute, I had a roommate, an overseas chinese from Switzerland named Hermia Chow. Today she is Dr. H. Y. L. Chow, M.D., Ph.D., F.R.C.P. (London). I still chuckle at the memory of our schooldays, when she used to sneak rich and sticky erotic chinese classics into our drab women's dormitory. We used to hurriedly gulp down a belt of that earth-shattering Napoleon brandy, which she hid in her shampoo bottle and of course tasted soapy. Or we'd sneak up to the roof of the building to suck down a doobie of the imported thai that she carried around in her plastic pencil case. Then we'd push our army-issue bunkbeds together, jump in, and pull our thick quilts over our heads. There, like a heaving pile of dirty laundry, we'd snicker and crow with laughter, muffling our throats raw and hoarse, cramps in our overstretched faces. Giddy, amatory girls reading priceless, ancient sheaves of consummate poetry.

"Kae, you're an *artiste*. You think like an *artiste* totally. Why are you barking at the wrong flea?" Hermia once pointed out to me when I told her that I would finish my economics degree. I was terribly young and brittle then. If there was anything at all to criticize, I was mostly the kind of person who would have hopped on like a flea. But I would have forgiven Hermia anything. I wasn't the only one.

"Don't be *triste* with me!" she'd say and be exonerated totally. When I first met her, I used to think that no one dared not to forgive Herm her trespasses because she was the daughter of a notoriously ruthless and powerful Hong Kong gangster. He was obviously very virile, too, because she used to say she had no idea how many half-brothers or sisters she had or would have. In fact, in order to see him, she had to make an appointment, then fly in from Geneva. "Daddy," she had once said to him, "I'm afraid I've totalled my Porsche. Please, may I have another?" I marvelled at her situation.

As soon as I came to know her better, I realized that people responded positively to Hermia because she was simply being herself: charming, magnetic, an ingénue—artfully artless.

After all, I figured, when somebody beautiful (and she had to be beautiful) spills her soul out of her sleeves the very first time you shake hands with her, you should make an effort to tread about softly at least for a while, or for as long as you can. Hermia gave you so much power over her, like a bare and naked newborn. I was much older before I realized that that was exactly her power.

I used to marvel at how carefree she was and wondered how anyone chinese could be that lighthearted. As for myself, how intoxicating to be given such total authority over another human being! I couldn't have abused it! Could I?

"Kae, I see it in your eyes," she said to me another time, "that drive to love and create. Why do you want to deny? Women's strength is in the bonds they form with each other. Say that you'll love me forever! The bond between true sisters can't be broken by time or distance apart! Say that, Kae . . . tell me!"

I don't remember what I answered. I don't know why I couldn't answer her simply. Why do women always want to dig beneath the surface, looking for the dirt and the smut? Are we not happy enough? Are we looking for more loyalty? More purity? Is that why I went to China? There, the traditional values had been turned inside-out in search of radical truths. And we believed that things were supposed to get better despite the mistakes of past generations.

"Come, Comrade Kae," Hermia once said, when she showed me where she got her exquisite books. "I want you to meet an old slave of my grandfather's." She enjoyed teasing my brittle idealism.

She took me for a frosty stroll in a bustling inner city park. We walked, linking arms and snuggling tightly against each other as chinese girls who are friends do. We looked like stuffed blue cotton teddy bears, stopping near the edge of a pond to enjoy the wintry vista of a moon bridge perfectly mirrored in the frozen water. Beside us, an equally well-padded, old chinese peasant type squatted on a chilly stone bench and stared at us the way all the old chinese sit and stare at passers-by. With a graceful tilt of her knees and a delicate tug on my arms, Hermia suddenly swooped up the man's discarded newspaper. He lit a cigarette.

Back in our rooms, she unfolded the *People's Daily* to reveal another yellowing, rice-papery pamphlet; a part of an elaborate tome, tied with bright satin strings; a remnant of Hermia's immensely cultured heritage, not that long ago abandoned. It had survived the Great Cultural Revolution to be smuggled out of China, and would probably end up in the hands of an elitist New York connoisseur who would continue to hide it away and protect it, as it had been hidden away and cherished like an illicit mistress for over two hundred years.

Hermia grinned at me, one of those high-flown smiles of hers that made me feel like peeling her off our crumbling ceiling, and said, "Epatante . . . n'est-ce pas, chérie?"

I, on the other hand, didn't have anything as elegant to show Hermia, but after the summer vacation of 1972, I had the letters from my grandmother, (Wong) Chan Fong Mei, to her sister, my great aunt, (Mok) Chan Fong Bo. I had visited the latter, still alive and very mindful at seventy-two, in the southern cantonese village of O Saan, in Hoy Saan district, where she had pulled them out of a pungent mothball-smelling cardboard "MacGregor's Men's

Plaid Socks" box. One of my family's old stores used to carry MacGregor's plaid socks.

In her carefully constructed schoolgirl calligraphy, my grandmother poured out all of her feelings but only some of her secrets to her older, married sister. At the time, Fong Mei was not quite seventeen, and her sister barely nineteen. They were very close to each other. I used to hear much about the huge fortune Poh Poh spent travelling back to see her, and the big risks she took, first with canadian immigration, then with chinese communists, trying to get her sister out. Then one died and the other got too old, didn't want to leave the village.

When I deciphered the letters with the help of Hermia's advanced chinese, they made me wish many times over that I too had a sister as my grandmother did. My eyes flickered over Hermia's bent neck as she examined the old letters. I wondered what it was like to be the misplaced bastard daughter of a gangster and his moll—no matter how moneyed. I would be afraid of an identity like that. Why was she in China? Not to learn the language surely. I imagined she was guilty of something, but what? Less than righteous family connections?

What a coward I was! I was afraid of risks, and I had to cling to the ground, pebbly and jagged. I wallowed in petty detail and ignored the essence. Legitimate, traditional and conventional were the adjectives to wear in those days, especially when I suspected my own identity might be as defective. Worse still, I thought that they were the ones illegitimatizing Hermia; not I.

LETTERS

1919

In her earliest letter, dated March 27, 1919, Fong Mei wrote:

"To beloved and honoured Elder Sister; I hope this missive finds all in your family to be in good health and prosperous. I hope your little sons are growing big and strong, showing adequate signs of talent and capability. May I also inquire after the health of Father and Mother? As well, I hope that the early planting season has gone well for you, and good weather will soon yield a good crop. Everyone's health here is fine.

"There is so much to tell you, but as they say, 'When there are too many bright flowers, the eye knows not where to look.' My new life here in the Gold Mountains has been very exciting. My new parents are even more prosperous than we could have imagined. And my husband Choy Fuk has been so extremely kind and gentle. Everything here is so 'ultramodern.' You don't know what that means, but everyone here likes that ghost word. It means the best and the newest. Nye Nye and Lo Yeh have a refrigerator to cool their food. I hear say that it cost $47.95, canadian currency. That's more than enough to buy rice for your family for several years in China. It may sound incredible to you, but people are like that here.

"As you see in this photograph that I have sent to you, Lo Yeh and Nye Nye's house is very large and stately, made of wood. It has three storeys and a large porch in front and back. It also has an indoor toilet. There's so much land here, without any use for it; however, at the back of the house, there are some fruit trees. Before I came, only three people lived in that whole house. This is what Gold Mountain houses look like. White people live next door to Lo Yeh's house, and our house is even bigger than theirs.

"Can you see my Lo Yeh sitting on the bamboo chair on the porch? People's ways here are so casual. He's a good man though. His eyes are never homeward, but he is a soft-spoken man to me. I hardly dare look at him, but I know he is never cross with me. And I know the old lady has no power over him.

"That is my husband, Choy Fuk. As you can see, he is very nice looking, tall and big. He was trying to make me hold hands with him, according to ultramodern western tradition, but I just couldn't hold still long enough for his good friend, Elder Brother Ting An, who works for Lo Yeh as well, to make this photograph. We tang people are not flamboyant like that. I'm just not used to these new ways.

"I know as surely as if I were sitting right next to you on your bed, that you'll say I've lost a bit of weight when you examine me more carefully in this photograph. I often think I know exactly what you would say, and even how you would say it. In fact, you're all I dream about day and night, Elder Sister, and how I wish I could be home again with you! Yes, I have been a little ill. All I needed was rest to recover from the dizziness and vomiting of the long ocean voyage, but from the moment I set foot onto this strange land, I've needed the strength and endurance of ten men.

"First of all, I along with my travelling companions were detained in prison for days. We were interrogated by white-devil immigration officers. I was terrorized. They looked so hateful and cunning. And everyone warned me of their devious trickery. I answered them very carefully, so I wouldn't be ensnared into their traps, but I was ten-parts nervous. Who knew whether they would be satisfied with my answers to their absurd, senseless questions?

"At night, I was too afraid to sleep in their 'pigpens.' I was told horrible stories about other hapless women, who were actually dragged off during the night; and when they were returned, they had become like petrified stone with bruises, their clothes torn, Elder Sister! This is true! Many kind aunties who had been there longer than me verified this story, and others too. They warned me to be especially careful because I was young and alone and so pretty, they said. They hid me at night. After the ghosts put out the lights, different aunties would switch bunks with me, so that any evildoer would find that he'd dragged off a wrinkled, toothless granny for his lecherous troubles. I thought they were so brave to risk themselves for me—a stranger not even from the same village, after all. Yet, here in this hostile environment, we are all like family. Too bad they were headed towards other places like Victoria; one to a farm by Lillooet. We giggled a lot. Some of us used to sit up all night, talking about our homes and our families. Then we'd become all teary and homesick.

"I was reminded of our happy, happy days as youngsters in the 'little girls' house.' Do you remember, Big Sister, all those good times? In Cousin Chan's abandoned house right in the middle of our neighbourhood, a dozen or so girls living together, cooking together, working the fields, laughing and gossiping the entire day. Lucky for us, it was such a large house. The elders used to say, 'So many girls in this generation! Some will surely need to be married far away from home.'

"Well, dear sister, I guess I'm the first to be married far from home. And everyone thought I was so lucky. I was the first to leave the 'pigpen' too, perhaps due to the Wong family's money under the table. Now, come to think of it, I didn't know when I had it good. You used to be so proud of my betrothal to a rich Gum Saan Hock, you got me excited too. Yet, what did I know of the world beyond the village? Our clansmen were the only people I knew. Now, to have travelled so far!

"Remember, Big Sister, our schooldays, and our teacher, Master Chui, who took us to that western moving picture show in Toy Saan City! We were so thrilled we couldn't sleep all night long. Here in the Gold Mountains, we go often to the picture shows which let chinese in, but no matter how hard I try, I just can't recapture that same wonderful feeling as before. Our life together in our beloved village was like that. Everything came straight from the heart. But now it's gone, no more than an astonishing dream to me. I can't believe that I left barely two months ago.

(The letter, carefully preserved all the years, is unmistakably tear-stained.)

"Now, I wouldn't be able to claw my way home as a beggar. I'm lost among strangers, with 'no road and no destination.' There's no one to turn to, and I think of home constantly. I've forgotten why I ever wanted to come to this forsaken place . . .

"There, I've cried my unhappiness out. I'll continue with this letter and follow the advice of this poem:

> I will swallow my tears,
> and pretend to be happy.
> Deceit. Deceit. Deceit.

"The marriage ceremony was western style, and so incredibly opulent. The gold I received weighed so heavily on my chest that I could barely catch my breath. And so many guests—forty tables if I remember right. People told me it was one of the largest ever on Tang People's Street. So many people staring and staring at me.

They watched me and talked about me. 'Look,' they'd say loud enough for me to hear, 'look at the beautiful bride!'

"Everyone was in fact being formal and polite. Remember at home the grownups used to really tease the bride, embarrassing her with lewd comments until she broke down in tears? Girls can't bear to hear such talk, yet it's more bearable when it's just our own close kin, don't you think? Here, everyone was full of compliments, but this made me even more uncomfortable, as though I was being scrutinized all the more severely. At first, I couldn't understand why I could hardly bear to be standing before these strangely aloof people. Each moment seemed endless. I thought it was the white bridal gown, with its flimsy veil. I couldn't hide my face, so now I know the embarrassment in being a 'barefaced bride.' In that way, the old-fashioned red silk veil had more compassion for us. I tried to be modern. I smiled and I tried to be brave, until I slowly realized that except for the pitiful handful of women who attended me, all the rest of the guests were men.

"I tried so hard, but my dearest love, it was the most terrifying night in my entire life. Tell me, Sister, why did I have to marry at all? What is a husband to me? Why did I have to come to this place full of risks and dangers? Oh, why couldn't I have stayed with you forever? Have pity on me, dearest! I am so miserable that as soon as I'm alone in the toilet chamber, my tears flow endlessly. My new family must wonder why I spend so much time in there. But you see, even at night and in my sleep, I must be on my guard. There's a strange man in my bed now . . ." (*The letter dissolved.*)

My great auntie became extremely concerned. She wrote back immediately, on the twenty-first day of the third month of the lunar calendar, in the ninth year of the Republic.

"A woman," she wrote, "whether married in the next village five li away, or across the ocean ten thousand li away, is just as foreign to her maiden family. This is the way of women. She doesn't retain ties to her childhood past. Your own mother would be shamed and laughed at if she lifted a finger to care for her own daughter's children. People would say, 'What, feeding the children of strangers!' Our lives belong to strangers. Eventually, we must all learn to accept our fates. For instance, you and I who are loving sisters, must accept that we may never meet face to face in this life again. Women who don't, their souls will be pulled apart; they will meet their end at the bottom of a well, mark my words!

"Little Sister, you are still young and unaware. And I must confess I have been guilty of harbouring rather than hardening you. You being so pretty, and favoured even beside your brothers. I too couldn't bear to be separated when I was wed, so I brought you along with me. Eventually, however, our venerable parents had to arrange your marriage too, which they did with concern and affection for you in their hearts. Don't bring shame onto them!

"Remember, a good wife must be chillingly correct. You must dress modestly. Even the way you walk must be subdued. Keep your eyes to yourself! It is entirely up to you to beat down even the faintest suspicions of scandal. Also, a good wife is useful. You are both young and strong. Work at your husband's side! Cater to your new parents, Nye Nye and Lo Yeh! When you have sons, cherish them! Your hard work will convince others of your righteousness as a woman. If, however, you're a no-good wife, even the ancestors will curse you! And future generations will abandon you!

"This letter also brings salutations to your honorable Lo Yeh and Nye Nye. There isn't a sufficient way to express our parents' immense gratitude for the gifts and generous allotments paid by your new father. Please convey this to your Lo Yeh. Of course, our parents hosted a huge feast right here in the village in honour of your new family. With eighty tables of guests, this one matched the wedding feast of Auntie Hwa, forty years ago. They say that she married an american Gold Mountain sojourner, who came back to sire a son. Unlike you though, she never saw or heard from her husband ever again after he left.

"Also, tell your Lo Yeh that with the money, our parents purchased one hundred barrels of store-bought brides' cakes, twenty roasted pigs, sixty catties of liquor—all parcelled out in the good wax-brown paper to friends and even the least related of our clan. You should have seen the house, full of visitors and festivity! Laughter every night for a week! All the customs and traditions fulfilled even in these hard times; no propriety omitted, giving our parents great face!

"Perhaps you can keep this to yourself as you see fit, Little Sister, but Eldest Brother finally bought that plot of land too. You remember, the one on the northeast corner behind his house which Father and he have been eyeing for years.

"So, while our little community was still humming from the celebrations, more gifts from A Lo Yeh. There hasn't been a neighbour within ten li who hasn't stopped by and commented on your Yeh's generosity. They're full of big-shot words about how well-respected and well-received you were by this rich family. Father is just full of himself these days.

"Among the gifts, we received the western-style album of wedding photographs. I still trudge the distance from my house to A Mah's house just to gaze at those photographs. My old man slapped me and scolded me for going out to visit too much. He said I was neglecting my work, but I don't care. With little Poy on my back and A Buck in my arms, I go. Those pictures are fabulous visions, like magazine pictures of film stars or emperors. I can't bring myself to think it's you—my very own sister, beautiful as a fairy, in a long flowing gown and veil.

"Like you, my tears flow endlessly from missing you, my little sister. You were my heart and liver! Yet I see very clearly the advancements bought with this marriage, not only for you but for our parents as well. So, isn't the pain of separation a very small price to pay after all?

"From the photographs, I say that those are real pearls embroidered all over your bodice. Your father-in-law is obviously not a man to scrimp on expenses. But someone said that they can make imitation pearls nowadays, especially for westerners' dresses. Others said that those were just buttons specially made to look like pearls in photographs. What do these ignorant village females know? Why don't you tell us?

"In fact, you hardly told us anything about your wedding. In the photographs, the banquet hall seemed to be filled with huge sculpted garlands and bouquets of flowers for as far as we can see. Were they very fragrant? Canada must be a land of flowers, although the men deny it. I don't think men notice things like flowers. What did your guests eat? Was a photograph specialist hired to follow the wedding party and take pictures wherever you went? In a garden! This is unheard of! Your new family must be so rich and so broad-minded too!

"Little Sister Mei Mei, you are so lucky to have entered lofty doors! How hard can it be to perform your duties as daughter-in-law, when your new family welcomes you with such fanfare? Every new bride feels awkward and alien. However, this will pass. Enjoy your first year of being a new bride. It'll be over sooner than you think! When the first-born comes, you'll be too busy to even eat. Then, you won't even give your big sister another thought, will you? If it is a boy, your status in this great family will be assured. Then, how you'll laugh at yourself for behaving peevishly. Listen to your elder sister teach!"

FONG MEI
1924

Fong Mei withdrew as quickly as she could from the front booth section, knowing that her only defence against her mother-in-law and husband was to be silent and invisible. Although Mui Lan would certainly never embroil her in a family quarrel in front of customers, Fong Mei was too afraid of her explosive temperament to stay one second longer.

Fong Mei retreated to her desk at the back of the storeroom. There, she picked up her fountain pen, fully intending to resume her desk work as if the unpleasant incident at the front of the restaurant had never happened, as if she had never left this desk, thirsty for a simple drink of boiled water. She took a long, hard suck of air deep into her lungs and poised the pen, but the raging demon within let fly before she realized that she had lost control. Hurtled against the white pages, black ink from the stubby pen exploded over her neat ledger accounts and trickled into the centre-fold binding of the book, where it threatened many painstaking hours of columnaded figuring. However, Fong Mei didn't seem to notice the hazard. She was too busy considering her own botched-up life.

"Will there ever be an end to my humiliation?" she lamented to herself, her head suddenly too heavy a burden to hold up. She started to push away the abacus, which would have held up her head's descent towards the table. But her fingers were smeared with ink, so she was forced to sit upright in spite of her dejection.

"I can't face any more. She wants me dead so badly, I may as well go and drown myself then!" Fong Mei stared at her hands in horror as if they were dripping with fresh blood.

"That old she-dog won't stop until she sees me bloated with sewer water! No one would miss a slave anyway! Go ahead, do it!" she muttered to herself, wanting to summon change and at the same time fearing it. Her hands poised feebly, in a rather touching gesture, as if to ward off some dread.

It was very true that Fong Mei's situation seemed hopeless. And against such a mother-in-law, she hadn't any defence at all. In fact, although she didn't realize it, Fong Mei had not stopped being terrified since the night of her wedding banquet. There's a proven logic to marrying them off at a very early age; seventeen-year-old girls are like mush. Impress upon them their worthlessness, and what was once firm, young backbone will shrivel with eternal shame! They will become genuinely stupid, unable to take a step forward, or backward, or sideways, for fear of treading on the very feet that trammel them relentlessly.

What with Mui Lan so very busy baby-bashing, Fong Mei totally forgot that having a baby had once been her own childish dream. There had been a time when unguarded thoughts of babies brought playful smiles about her mouth. A perfect baby had been her one desire—something for which one's body had to be bartered away in marriage. But recently, the idea of a baby swelling her stomach had seemed grotesque, a symbol of her enslavement. She had nightmares of a baby with Mui Lan's face leeched onto her breasts, draining her dry.

"Why not?" came another soft hiss. "I'm just a dead girl-bag anyway, useless to everyone. Let them stomp on me! Dead ghosts!"

Without other young women to compare herself to, Fong Mei couldn't have realized how feisty her words proved her to be. A less stalwart woman would have knuckled under long ago. In spite of the smothering self-pity, she was young. And even after five years of exile and drudgery, she was still only twenty-two and resilient. Nor could she have known that her time would soon be up, that she was on the verge of breaking out.

As she pondered her prison term, Fong Mei's face hung in the air like a sad wooden mask suspended on a hook. A hand suddenly loomed in front of her and hit the ledger book on the desk with a resounding slap. Fong Mei sprang from her chair, her face tingling hot as if she had been the one smitten.

"Little Auntie Fong," drawled a familiar voice, "are you so clouded up that you can't see what a fine mess you have made here?"

She barely glanced at the cheerful face hovering above her as she resettled back onto her seat. The keen hands mopping up the ink with a rag hardly placated her growing anger at this heavy-handed intrusion.

"Here, A Ting, you take this and clean it up! Somewhere else!" She scooped book, rag and pen off the table top, and shoved them at him roughly. She was not in the mood for Ting An's roguish ways. And she was sick of him popping up at her at anytime, anywhere. Who did he think he was? Just because he had worked for her father-in-law so long, he seemed to think that he was part of the family.

"Hey, hey, watch the white uniform!" he warned. "Ink won't come off, you know. And I'm waiter today, for the lunchtime rush."

"Don't bother me!" she pouted, turning away and trying to hide behind her thick, shoulder-length hair.

"There, there, you can't fool Big Brother Ting. I know something's up . . ." the young man crooned, ducking this way and that, trying to poke his big nose in front of her face. "Let me guess, a smart fellow like me can tell chop chop! It . . . it couldn't be that nasty Nye Nye again, could it . . . with the big, long whip? You look whipped, he, he, he!"

50

"Don't you have work to do somewhere else?" The same remark that earlier had wounded her like a blade. She waited for
Ting An to be stopped dead in his tracks, just as she had been. But
why should he be as sensitive as she? He wasn't the one who'd had
his skin rubbed thin and raw year after year until he felt himself
screaming a stuck-pig scream!

"Looks like I have my work cut out for me right here," he answered, undaunted by her black mood, "teaching you how not to
treat the accounts book." He paused, waiting for a response. "And
here I thought you were smart." When it still didn't come, he continued to chatter idly, filling up air. "After all, if the boss lady Nye
Nye should happen to see this, you're not going to earn any more
blessings from her today, are you?"

"Wait a minute here, Big Brother Ting! What makes you think
that Nye Nye is bothering me? Who's been filling your ears with
stories?" Fong Mei demanded, staring piercingly hard at him.

Hah, he thought, her response was even better than he had
hoped. He looked at her, liking the full attention he was getting
from her large, startling light-brown eyes, her face so earnest and
full of candour. He liked the way she didn't wind her hair tightly
into those strange, thick sausages that dangled and bounced so
comically. Instead, she kept it sleek and straight, and blunt.
Teasingly, he slowly stretched his face into a patronizing grin,
noting with deep affection her two bird-winged eyebrows creep
ever closer to each other in consternation.

"Well," Ting An sounded pretty cocksure of himself, "you tell
me, Auntie, what troubles could a young bride have in the world,
except for mother-in-law troubles. Not that a vulgar bachelor like
me, who has never set foot anywhere near the Middle Kingdom,
would know much about these matters, but I certainly know your
Nye Nye, and I don't blame you for shrivelling every time you set
eyes on her. She scares me too . . ."

"Don't call me a bride, you turtle!" Fong Mei blew up unexpectedly. "I've been married five long years. And if you can't answer me honestly, then get out of here! I don't want to look at
your face!"

Her face crumpled, this time with genuine suffering. Tears

glazed her eyes. Wah! Ting An was completely taken aback. Her situation must be even worse than he had suspected. This was obviously not a time for pestering. As she wept, he hung his head in shame and tried to sneak his hands into some pockets, except in the waiter's chinese-style uniform he got lost.

"I can't face you, Auntie Fong," he said solemnly. "I see now that you're upset. Has there been trouble? Your elder sister, everyone at home O.K.?"

Silence. Yet he persevered, coaxing gently, "And don't bother to tell me to go die! I'll not be put off so easily. Hey . . . I'm very sorry I upset you so much! We're still good friends, right?"

Fong Mei relented a little. Glancing up at him, she barely answered, "Yes, we're still friends."

She thought, he makes me laugh—the only times I ever laugh any more. Then, it occurred to her that he was in fact her only friend too, and he a man at that. Men and women can't be friends, she thought, recalling an edict of the Great Philosopher: "The hands of men and women must never touch!"

"Aie, it's not you, Elder Brother. It's my fault. I'm not feeling . . . I don't even know what's bothering me. Too much yang—I mean yin . . . maybe!" Suddenly, she felt so self-conscious that she flushed with embarrassment. She gave a nervous little giggle and tried to cover up. "Silly of me . . ."

Ting An was puzzled. In all the years that he'd known her, she had always been a plain-dealing person, perhaps a bit too animated for all of the time, but what did he know of women. For instance, after a year or so of being an "idle bride," she had wanted to learn bookkeeping, and she had asked very straightforwardly, "Big Brother, would you be kind enough to teach this stupid Auntie some simple bookkeeping so she can make herself useful?"

She had never giggled or acted rabbity until now. She was a resolute kind of person, eager to learn, and never forgot what she had been taught. She would ask to learn english like this: "How do you tell the delivery ghosts to not knock over the garbage cans at the back when they park too close to the back door?" Always businesslike and specific. And she had an ostentatious way of being secretive. Once she told Ting An, "Of course I'm not sick! I just need to rest. Please don't make a fuss! Nye Nye certainly doesn't need to know. I'm sure I'll feel better this afternoon, but perhaps you could do me the favour of quietly helping me out for a few days."

Even after he had worked with her for a long time, he never broke through her composure. Every day she was the same easy person to get along with, with the same unruffled face, although a bit too unfailingly courteous and poised, considering the kind of life she must have under Mui Lan. Ting An just attributed that to the chineseness in her which he found rather appealing. Well-bred chinese women were like that, he decided. Always thinking of others ahead of themselves. They'd sooner die than embarrass anybody else with their own personal problems—terribly imposing to let on they felt like slitting their wrists in a minute or so.

He had watched her play the role of the perfect daughter-in-law all along, always eager to please, to work tirelessly, never bitter, so it was easy for him to see her gradually abandon the once very bright, very genuine zeal for her new married life. A bit more every year, until nothing was left in her eyes but solitude. All the rest a shell—a thin, delicate porcelain shell. So translucent he could see right through, and he always wondered why nobody else ever could.

To an outsider perhaps, she was still a young and happy girl. Who remembered that it was already over five years since they'd drunk at her wedding banquet? Everyone still called her the newly arrived auntie, not out of politeness but more out of absent-mindedness. Women would be more exacting, but these old chinamen—who among them ever recalled that back in the village, a woman married five years would have a tiny baby in front, one on her back and a big one clinging to her pantlegs? If she had children here, a woman like Fong Mei would have a firm stake in this land. Besides, women like to have babies, dress them up, show them off, that sort of thing.

Fortunately, Ting An wasn't what you might call an outsider. The source of her troubles was obvious to him. She was squashed under her mother-in-law's big thumb. And that old bag would have a sadistic knack for making life miserable for a daughter-in-law. If only Fong Mei had one baby, her problems would be over; she'd be able to tell Mui Lan off. That's the way with mothers-in-law and daughters-in-law. What could Mui Lan do then—throw her own grandson out? Dead, stinky bitch! Let her try!

Ting An was still there, planted squarely in front of Fong Mei. She knew she'd been too rough on him; she stole a glance at him. People used to say that he was half-indian—his mother a savage. Before, Fong Mei used to search his face for traces of this, but she only saw a chiselled face, gracefully masculine, like a chinese from the north.

It wasn't his fault that he had walked in at an inopportune moment. Any other time, they would have chatted amiably about this and that. Never for any length of time—that would have raised eyebrows! The door to the kitchen, where others could plainly see them, would always be wide open. Often another worker would be in the vicinity and be easily led into their lighthearted conversation. He always had a juicy bit of gossip to entertain her with, or he'd tease her about commonplace things. Being local-born, he was peculiar, to her way of looking at things, and his friendliness used to make her nervous at first, but he certainly wasn't as brash as white ghosts. Anyway, she should have been more appreciative of his efforts to cheer her up even if they were a bit clumsy and rough. Still, this was the first time she had actually broken down in front of him, or anybody for that matter. She chewed her lips bravely, hands pulling nervously on a belaboured handkerchief. He was still waiting intently for an explanation. But she didn't have a safe one.

She glanced shyly at him and made a painful attempt. "I know a man will just laugh, but it's frightening being a bride . . . I mean wife. We just get thrown into the clutches of strangers. I didn't know what to do, except what I was told. Well, now it seems that isn't . . . enough," her voice emptying. "Oh, how could you understand! I'm so stupid," she finally muttered.

"Auntie Fong, I wouldn't laugh. Why should I? Remember, I am an orphan myself!" Ting An didn't like the way his voice squeaked with too much responsiveness. It occurred to him that for all of the talking they'd done, they'd never really talked at all.

He began again, his voice tamed. "A Fong, my mother died when I was a baby. I never even knew my father. Then, after my grandfather died, I was twelve years old, penniless, and I had no one . . . except for your Lo Yeh. Gwei Chang took me in as a worker and gave me a bed. He treated me real good, but sometimes it's been lonely. I'm not that sure of things, myself . . ." He had never spoken so candidly, never exposed himself. He was a bit dumbfounded, but what followed was a silence which seemed to purr with warmth, a long forgotten warmth that renewed his senses.

When he looked at her, he found that she was stretching out her fingers to him, and they almost touched his arm. But then, she drew back immediately. And when she looked up at him, she saw that he had seen. She flinched with embarrassment. Her eyes trailed off, but the shy smile never left her lips. For a brief moment, both of them seemed to be entranced by their closeness. Without having to look, she noticed the resolute firmness about his mouth and jaw. Her own husband's jaw was always slightly slack, his mien almost shiftless. Ting An leaned forward, and his slender hand reached out to brush a stray hair aside.

She had to shrink from his touch. It was her duty. With her voice strung tight, she appealed to him not to, by saying, "Now, I feel even more stupid!" Adding an artificial laugh. "I mean compared to you, what do I have to complain about? Being separated from my family at seventeen years old? A grown woman already. But how heart-wrenching for you, Elder Brother"

"No, not really." He smiled down at her. Yes, he would let go for now. "Sudden separation is always worse, especially for some people." And he would continue to play his part. "As for me, you're wasting your pity on me. I'm a bull-demon, don't you know!" He thumped on his puffed-up chest. "Lived with rough labourers all my life. They used to feed me rancid goat's milk from old liquor bottles. Never knew a woman's touch! Never missed it . . ." Yet, to himself, he thought: until now.

"Still, how wicked of me to complain!" Fong Mei demurred flawlessly. She wished she could tell him how much she appreciated his friendship and understanding. But she, like him, as if paralyzed from a spider's vicious bite, couldn't move from her side of what suddenly yawned into a huge chasm.

Soon he pulled himself away from her desk, leaving her to herself in the dusty back recesses of the storeroom where the discarded things of the Wong family business were shelved.

II

Ties Overseas—A Ticket In

MUI LAN

1924

Tyrannized by her own helplessness, Fong Mei cowered on the floor in front of her mother-in-law and wept piteously. Mui Lan sat at the secretary in her bedroom and stared at her daughter-in-law, a sneer frozen on her mouth, her plump, slippered feet tucked so neatly under her chair that she gave the appearance of being a cruel court eunuch in an opera. On the dainty desk top, strategically placed, a marriage certificate, a neat stack of immigration papers and miscellaneous receipts. On the four-poster bed, a camphor chest inlaid with mother-of-pearl, full of Fong Mei's wedding gold and jewelry, rested its case. Strategically gone, both the Wong elder and son, to their respective vocations, thus qualifying Mui Lan for omnipotence at home.

A gentle breeze blew through the tulle curtains at the window. Outside, a thick, hazy summer's midmorning, the air unctuous with the cloying scent of overripe fruit. Raspberries oozing sweet juices rotted and dropped from their limp canes, smashing in the dust like the bloodied carnage of a badly executed slaughter.

"Her male offspring guarantees the daughter-in-law's position in the family. You are barren and thus may not be accredited with one!" Mui Lan brought the matter of concern home with a single daggerous plunge! After this, she would no longer have to address the petrified younger woman. As far as Mui Lan was concerned, Fong Mei was a dead person.

"Damned, stinky bag!" she spoke into the air. "We received her into our home in the most flamboyant style. With the costs of hiring the go-betweens and the negotiators; with the costs of her passage and the bribes, never mind the gifts; and of course the cost of the wedding itself—never mind the risks we took with our Wong name and livelihood in a government investigation to secure HER immigration status . . ." Her face contorting violently, she screeched out, "Your mother's stinking . . . no one, absolutely no one would dispute me if I claimed publicly to have borne you in your flowery sedan chair across the ocean on my own back!"

Mui Lan had escalated to such a brain-bursting pitch so quickly that she had to pause to regather her corporeal forces. It had become stifling hot in the upstairs room. Taking great gulps of air, she started again.

"For five years, five long years, we've housed, fed and clothed her. And for what end? So that she could disgrace our ancestors' good name and bring bad luck onto this family, and ultimately risk our future descendants? Where am I to find peace in such a situation? Who do I go to for justice? Damned stinky she-bag!"

Having no face left at all, having lost her standing as a human being, Fong Mei's colour drained away, her neck limp and weak as if broken. She had been expecting a scolding for a long time, but this tirade of raging obscenities left her flaccid with fear. Snot drivelled out of her nose; tears trickled after each blink. Sobs, chokes and mucous muffled into her sleeves. Mui Lan's eyes fixed on her, black as hell, as if yearning to rub her off the face of this earth.

Ha! Mui Lan thought to herself, looking over the results of her exertions, satisfied with the slumped remains of her daughter-in-law before her. That despicable pig-bitch wouldn't dare wrangle with her. Her standing as a human being was all but lost. She might as well die!

Actually, in the beginning, Mui Lan had been afraid that Fong Mei would balk at her. One could never be sure of this younger generation of wild chickens who dared to presume that they had rights. Her daughter-in-law was no simpleton. She could have learnt very quickly to turn against the old ways when they didn't suit her any more. Who knew what she might attempt, from beguiling her husband to turn against his own mother to shamelessly running away to the Jesus-ghosts who would no doubt harbour her?

Mui Lan glanced down at her hands and the small key held in her own unconscious grip. She had stolen the little brass key from her husband's ring of keys while he slept. If the old man were to catch even a whiff of her plans, he would veto them with one big puff of his smelly cigar. Then, where would she be? Still, Mui Lan was willing to risk her old man's ire to play the trump card that she now pushed towards Fong Mei.

"Here, look!" Mui Lan said decisively. "Here are your entry papers, marriage certificate and wedding gold. According to our tang people's customs and laws, they are all meaningless now. Even this marriage contract! Useless too. Take them! Take them and go! Roll your useless female eggs a long way from here!"

Fong Mei gave an agonized shriek and sprang to her knees. "No, no, Nye Nye!" she begged and kowtowed. "Have mercy! Have mercy! Where am I to go?"

"Go back home to your own family! You have more than enough gold here to pawn for a passage." Mui Lan sneered, knowing full well that a spurned daughter-in-law would rather commit suicide than go back to her parents' home, for all the ten generations of everlasting shame that she would cost her family, in fact her whole village.

"No!" Fong Mei gasped as if strangling, and broke down into uncontrolled heaving and sobbing again.

"I don't care where you drag your dead body. You definitely have no right to stay in the way of my son's son. Who's going to speak up on your side? Resist, and other people will hold up your stinky thing for ridicule. Ha! They'll all say Lee Mui Lan has right on her side," she sniffed like a fretful badger, this way and that.

"If we were in the village, not even your father would dare say a thing. Who else would have the patience and virtue to keep a big-eating cow, a downright fraud, in her home for so long." Still shaking with pent-up anger, Mui Lan stopped again, her breathing fast and strained.

After a long sigh for dramatic effect, she fussed: "Haven't I done everything possible?" And her voice cracked with emotion as if she were the one hard done by. "Spared no expense to ensure you 'get happiness' and bear a boy—even a girl—to my son? You've eaten our best food, had all the required medicines. I've sent gifts, and money to have incense burnt at the temples at home, to have amulets made. I've even risked our reputation to send you to that dead, immoral, white doctor-specialist. All without results. You have no future. You're no good!"

I have her now, thought Mui Lan, and waited until the torrential sobs subsided. Confident that her daughter-in-law's life was now entirely in her hands—to have and to hold, to squeeze or to let live—Mui Lan began gently. "Listen, Fong Mei! I'm not so hard-mouthed as to want to disgrace your parents. What is there in it for me? But our customs are clear and practical too. If the first wife cannot bear a son, then she stands aside for another. That way, the family is assured of a yellow, 'lucky' road. Otherwise, who will there be left to honour even you, to sweep your grave? Now if we were in China, A Fuk would simply bring home a concubine. And when she bore a son, he would call you 'first mother.' You know these traditions. It's not as though we are out to strike you in the face!"

By now, Fong Mei was all but cried out. She still knelt on the floor, covered in a cold sweat, as if drained from some kind of wasted exertion. The funny thing was she didn't know why she should be exhausted. Her life was like that of a work beast. When old and used up, it is bovine and calm, placid about its fate, and does not expect mercies. She had accepted this long ago, and now she tried to fix this image in her mind, if for no other reason than it would give her dignity. But tears quickly oozed beyond control, and fear made her grovel before she could stop herself. Suddenly, she realized that there was rage as well. So, it was rage, pushing her body beyond its limits! Rage that made her body shudder with icy fear.

Mui Lan thought Fong Mei was nodding in agreement, so she

went on. "As daughter-in-law, though obviously not flawless, your behaviour is above reproach. A Fuk is fond of you, is he not? As am I and Lo Yeh! The past five years, you have learnt and worked a good deal." Mui Lan's words skidded together, and Fong Mei recognized their insincerity immediately. "But no matter how much you do, you have done nothing until you have given a son to us."

This idea of a baby was a trance-inducing chant that had long ago lost its meaning. Fong Mei was being punished, not for something she had done but for some apparent blank part of her.

"However," Mui Lan continued, "no one can accuse the Wong family of having 'a wolf's heart and a dog's lung.' Here, we are living on the frontier with barbarians. We stick together. Who wants to turn you out?" Adding slyly, "It's more a matter of whether you want to stick with us."

"Living in a land with foreign devils makes it very difficult for tang people. How can we bring another woman into the country without exposing ourselves to another, even more treacherous government investigation? Then, by their laws, concubines are illegal. So A Fuk would need to divorce you first." Mui Lan stole a sly glance at Fong Mei, who stiffened on cue. "And we tang people don't like to subject ourselves to their courts. It would be like placing ourselves in the paws of a tiger."

Each detail flawlessly revealed; every angle precisely designed for Fong Mei's unconditional surrender. Strangely enough, Mui Lan felt a twinge of guilt. She suddenly became aware of the glass wind-chimes that hung on the porch downstairs. Was it an isolated gust of wind, or did she just now hear the thin, incessant tinkling drift in through the window? It made her slightly uneasy.

"Here in this wilderness," she said, more loudly than she'd intended, "there are no chinese women who are suitable for marriage into a respectable home. What few there are, are no good; but perhaps with the right connections and a sizable sum of money, we can pay off a clean enough woman to have a child for us! In secret of course, if you want! Then, after she brings him forth, the baby is yours. And no one but the four of us will be the wiser."

Yes, her plan did sound very simple after all. Mui Lan looked almost elated after she heard her own words. After all she wasn't the sort who enjoyed this kind of sneaking about. If only she had stayed in the village, none of this would have been necessary. It would have been a simple matter to have Choy Fuk take a wife more of her own choosing. Then, how blissful things would have been!

Dote on her grandsons! Wait for letters and money from an 'old rooster' who might never have come back into her life! Sit around the threshold, splitting melon seeds with her front teeth, chattering with the neighbours to her heart's content. Delighted with herself, Mui Lan began to ramble on, forgetting the presence of her daughter-in-law who observed her very carefully.

"I know a woman's heart! What woman would deny that yearning for a baby son, or even a baby girl to begin with. First-born daughters bring good luck, he, he, he! Do you think that I haven't shared the emptiness which you must have suffered, being childless these long years? Well, now you have the opportunity. All you need to do is give up your old man for a few days, and soon you'll have a son—and with him, security, prestige, honour, and the glowing warmth of a family to look after your old age. What could be easier? And where's the harm in that?" she asked innocently.

Mui Lan wasn't really expecting an answer. And of course there wasn't one.

K A E
1986

I myself was not present, but I've often wondered. What if, maybe just for a second or two during this lengthy monologue, my grandmother's young eyes—albeit puffy, bloodshot and glassy—had raised up to her mother-in-law as if to make bold? What if they had betrayed her innermost thoughts for that instant?

"You ancient she-dog," she might have cursed, very quietly of course, "look at yourself! Frothing at the mouth one moment, grinning dementedly at your own dreams at another! Would you take in another woman's offspring? You old bitch, would you give over your man to some diseased slut?"

Obviously, if such a flash of defiance had happened, my great-grandmother's steely stare would have crushed it in a second. More shrill curses would have rained upon my grandmother's bent back.

"And don't believe for a moment, you foul female stench, with your modern-day thinking about rights and freedom-ah, that you're too good for this bargain. What are you but just a woman!"

But my great-grandmother was a woman too. What did she mean by that? Was she referring to the substance we as women have to barter away in order to live? In order to live with men? In the male order? Then, what was I referring to? How we turn on ourselves, squabbling desperately among ourselves about our common debasement? Branding self-hatred across our foreheads—I wonder how deeply it seared into Fong Mei's flesh. And how willingly we fuel the white fire with which to scar other women. What choices did she have? Like so many hordes of women, didn't my grandmother consent to give away her own destiny? Who but women would do that?

A whole lifetime later, lying prone on a postpartum bed to rest my "female-bag," I still wonder about . . . everything, I guess. My mother has gone, and I am alone. I wonder too, about the volatile lunacy that wasn't my great-grandmother's alone, but lurks in our peasant backgrounds, in our rustic language. This craziness that drove many beyond the brink towards self-destruction. Agonizing passion worth more than life itself, then dragging still more along that black road of anguish and guilt after the suicide.

An ache from the depths of my womb pulses through my body as I think back. Sadness washes over me from a deep, dark, secret pool. Staring at the ceiling—such an untouched white—I suddenly remember Morgan.

MORGAN KEUNG CHI WONG
1967

"Do I have a choice?"

I had asked Morgan that over the telephone. Nineteen years ago, I had just arrived home, dripping wet from school, when the phone rang. I was exhausted. I was piqued. My ski jacket hung heavy like lead weights, and my toes were frozen from my long trek through the snow and sludge. Having recently broken up with my steady, Terry Paling, I had lost my cosy ride home every day as well. And at that age, I was always starving, so I was not in a receptive mood.

"Of course not!" he replied curtly. I could hear him crunching potato chips over the receiver. Morgan was actually my uncle, even though I wasn't supposed to know that. The understanding between my parents and me was that Morgan was the notorious skirt-chasing black sheep of another branch of the family. And I was to under no circumstances have any contact with him. That was why he was calling at that particular time of the day. He knew no one would be home except me.

To me, Morgan was quite simply a haunted man. I was seventeen at the time, and of course frightfully sentimental. Now, there is no doubt in my mind that it was Morgan who made normal guys like Terry Paling pale in comparison.

"Gee . . . Well, I don't know, Morg . . ." I tried to squirm out of this commitment as nicely as a nice girl could in those days, "I mean, I don't feel like going out in weather like this just to spend another evening watching you sleuth in the university librarinth, you know!"

How could I have possibly said what I really thought? "Morgan, at twenty-nine years old, you're too old to be a perpetual student, and I don't care how graduate! And besides, I just don't feel like push-starting that stupid ancient Morgan you drive when it conks out in the god-damned snow . . ." a strong emphasis on "you know what I mean?" Cute! A Morgan driving a Morgan—both wounded, helpless dinosaurs.

I went. My white patent go-go boots hopelessly inadequate

against the elements. Miniskirted, with a rabbit-fur minicoat, my ass practically quivering right off the icy leather bucket seats. The Morgan had no heat. Sneaking sidelong glances at the munificently dashing man driving me to distraction. I just couldn't believe that he was my uncle. I couldn't believe his whole sordid story.

"Well, you yourself said that my great-grandfather was supposed to have a reputation for fair dealing," I argued in the library. "How could all this deviousness go on right under the big boss's nose?"

"Aahh yess! Great-grandfather . . ." Morgan replied, as if my great-grandfather was his great-grandfather. "The benevolent patriarch of Disappearing Moon. All Chinatown turns to him in times of trouble," he murmured, seemingly to himself, while cranking the roller handle of the microfilm viewing machine. Shadows of old newspapers flew by. The air in the underground library was unbearably dry and hot, permeated with the smell of crumbling literary effort.

He finally answered, "Well, Great-grandfather is as famous as your great-grandmother is infamous. Even after she had gotten the word loud and clear from above, she still went ahead with her secret plot. I mean she really thought she could pull it off."

"Oh, I still can't believe that! There must have been easier ways to come by a baby," I maintained. "Lots of those rich, old Chinatown guys had several wives. You know the Kees and the Chens. They had lots of local-born daughters too. If you ask me, she could have easily gotten rid of my Poh Poh, and good riddance! Even if she didn't, in those days Gong Gong would still have been free to marry any one of them."

"Yeah, well, the old broad was definitely a bit of a cheapskate. Still, the family was nowhere near as rich as the Kee family. Great-grandfather was too public-minded. And what rich little local-born girl would want to be a number-two wife, when she could have had her pick of horny bachelors? Six males to each little girl in those days!" he whistled meaningfully at the impossible odds. "I hear your Gong Gong was no prize either."

Uh oh, another little dig, a less than kindly shove perhaps, and I pretended I was too polite to notice. Of course, I didn't trust

Morgan. Him and his sly little pen scratches on paper! Was his story the same as my story? Or should I have said, is history the same as mystery? If I had had any savoir faire at all, I would have headed for the hills, saved my skin, but this kind of scenario is exactly what keeps me glued to my seat, even today.

Too bad for my family that money couldn't buy long life (prosperity couldn't buy posterity either); too bad for me, I could have simply asked. Instead of dead, silent ancestors who kept me hanging by a million possible threads, someone would have told me—I'm sure. Instead of Morgan busy fraying the tapestry, I could have claimed my righteous inheritance to a pure bloodline. I wouldn't have fallen in love/hate with his/my truth and wasted all these years trying to answer him.

"O.K. Now listen!" Morgan cut in. "You want to know what I found out? It's 1924 . . . in the heat of summer, the news rips through Chinatown like wild fire! A white woman is murdered! The prime suspect is a chinese houseboy named Wong Foon Sing! Chopsticks drop and clatter in surprise! Clumps of rice stick in throats . . ."

"Morgue, what are you sputtering about?" I couldn't bear to hear any more. I cringed and glanced nervously around the stacks, hoping no one had heard his embarrassing comments. Chineseness made me uncomfortable then.

"Listen!" he repeated. "This Janet Smith murder case kicked up a lot of fuss in Vancouver. Don't you want to know more about it?"

"What for?" I was beginning to wonder if this vacuous pursuit of still-life wasn't unbalancing his mind.

"Summer! 1924 . . . remember why your great-granny had a free hand at plastering your grandma's face against the floor whenever she felt like it? . . . Come in Manila!" Morgan had such an irritating way about him, as though on some subconscious level he was out to punish me. What had I ever done to him? Still, I crumbled like a cupcake in his hands, because I let him go on.

"The old patriarch was too busy becoming a big-shot, muscling in on all the action to worry about daughters-in-law. Hey, when old guys in Chinatown tap you on the shoulder, and say, 'I once shook your great-grandfather's hand. He was a good man,' it's precisely because of those bizarre times. Let me tell you, the whole town went nuts! The Chinese Exclusion Act—the Day of Humiliation—and then this killing."

I smiled ever so sweetly and chose not to tell him that I didn't ever go down to Chinatown except for the very occasional family banquet. And I certainly wouldn't ever let any dirty old man touch me! Those little old men were everywhere in Chinatown, leaning in doorways, sitting at bus stops, squatting on sidewalks. The very thought gave me the creeps.

I looked over at Morgan to see if he had any inkling of me, but he was already in midair, springing into a high-pitched performance. The bitterness of it surprised me.

"People became openly obsessed with splattered brain matter. At dinner tables, they might as well have been eating coagulating blood pudding. Newspapers egged them on at breakfast. More lovesick but banal diary tidbits for tea, dear?"

He flung his arms about and squeaked out a female stereotype, "Inflammatory rumours all over this hot little town! How did our dear little Janet meet her demise? B.C. Telephone operators wore their dear little fingers to the bone, incessantly plugging in first the fantastic, then the freakish, finally the fanatical. They began to swoon on courthouse steps."

Then his voice turned sinister. "The crowds began to get restless and ugly. All over the land, men on soapboxes cried out, 'It is our God-given duty to protect our poor, white, working-class maidenhood from those filthy minded, slant-eyed vermin, even if we have to string a few of 'em up by their ten-inch finger-nails . . .' "

"Morgan," I gasped again, my ears burning red-hot. Until then, I had been laughing nervously. I mean what else could I do? He was mad! "Pipe down, will you!" I begged.

He had been scribbling furiously as he talked. He suddenly looked at me and grinned blithely. "How do you know," he asked, "which of the two were going to get strung up? The poor white maidens? Or the slant-eyed vermin?"

Morgan calmed down, but he continued to lecture at me, as

though there was an entire classroom full of adoring students (female, I would imagine) behind me. In fact, I had to keep looking over my shoulders to make sure there wasn't.

"You know, there was once a law prohibiting chinese men from working too closely with white women, and vice versa, I suppose. But it backfired in the end because, given a choice, employers tended to hire the cheaper, more-for-their-money chinamen; and as a result, white women got protected right out of a job. By and large, this masterful bit of law-making was successfully ignored until some of the more upstanding white citizens tried to pursue it again, over Janet Smith's corpse. This time, as you know, it was our very own great-grandfather, Wong Gwei Chang, who had a big hand in stepping in and stopping it."

"It was a historical landmark in British Columbia's usual pattern of interracial relations," said Morgan. "Chinatown fought back the rising tide of virulent hatred headed their way, and for a change, they won!"

"The 'murder' itself was a simple, though unsolved 'hole in the head' story, but it told a lot about Vancouver then. The intrigues and plots, the coverups and scandal, which flourished as a result of a young white female body, clearly revealed the seething hysteria that, up until then, had successfully remained the suppressed sexual undertones of Vancouver's church-goers. The story had something for every kind of righteousness. For those who hated chinese and thought they were depraved and drug-infested. And for those who hated the rich and thought they were depraved and drug-infested."

"And Chinatown in 1924," Morgan continued, "seventeen years after the race riots of 1907, had become quite the thriving, respectable little establishment. The streets were clean. Mostly paved. They even had street lamps. It was a self-contained community of men: sold its own suspenders, had everything from its own water pipes to its own power elite. There were a few things in short supply once in a while, like when registration cards for chinese were suddenly deemed necessary. So tempers were short, for instance. And only one thing missing—women!"

"Oh," I sighed, "is that all?"

"Yeah," he piped in, "who needs 'em!"

I had been listening, draped over the desk, my chin cupped in my hands, idolizing his face, breathing in his after-shave lotion. It certainly wasn't what Morgan said which interested me. After all, this private inquest could have only impressed him, since he actually lived in the very basement where this murder had taken place. A bright Sani-Queen washer and dryer now blocked the exact spot where illustrious legs once littered the floor. Morgan grew up there, and after his mother remarried, she left him the fading glory of this notorious Shaughnessy address, 1414 Osler Avenue. Ubiquitous irony? Well then, life must be full of vexations! But again, I bet there was a simpler explanation for this too.

Like, I'm willing to bet that Morgan's father, Wong Ting An, who was a pure businessman at heart, really did pick up the house for a song, regardless of its history, when real estate was real depressed towards the end of the Depression. Now, whether he got sentimental about the good old days, who can say?

Yet Morg has always maintained that his dad acquired it from a german family with four children, who couldn't get rid of it fast enough, even to a chinaman, because it was haunted by a willowy, tuneful scottish nightingale.

I had to ask, "Why didn't she haunt you guys, Morgue?"

"Why?" he echoed, and I waited. By the tilt of his head, I could almost see him pluck a suitable explanation right out of the air. "Because . . . ah, because she and the chinese houseboy were actually friends. And we're chinese too, you see."

"Your mother's not. She's french-canadian."

"You know, Ying, for a supposedly intelligent girl, your thinking is awfully one-dimensional. No matter where you turn, we're all related in the end."

Morgan implied that since he had both proximal and apparitional insights into this murder, he was going to make "a killing" by naming the person who had committed the most spectacular, unsolved scandal-page murder in Vancouver. Fascinated, I rested my chin on my interlaced fingers and coyly sighed again. He said it was a risky business though. If word got out, there were still plenty of people who'd take drastic measures to keep their grisly secrets.

I wonder if Morgan ever realized that he didn't need to embellish his task with romance to keep me at his side, evening after evening, in that library. It occurred to me perhaps he needed these flights of fancy to keep himself there. But as for myself, I only needed to stand close to a heroic man, with an upturned collar and a burning cigarette, who'd smile down on me tenderly. After all, it's written: "When placed face to face with one's superior, one's ego can do nothing but declare love!"

JANET SMITH
1924

When the scottish nursemaid died in a most unnatural way, and the only other person who would admit to being with her in the stately manor was a chinese named Wong Foon Sing, patriarch Wong Gwei Chang and his cigar-puffing clique in Chinatown immediately saw the writing on the wall. They were only too aware of the obscene implications of this situation. Those whites who hated yellow people never needed an excuse to spit on chinese. So the idea of a young, lone, yellow-skinned male standing over the inert body of a white-skinned female would send them into a bloodthirsty frenzy. The first instincts of the chinese told them to board up their businesses and barricade Pender Street, with enough rice and salted fish stockpiled to outlast a siege.

"Victims," said Morgan, "always being the first to consent to being victimized."

Late that August night, nervously huddled at the back of Disappearing Moon, the old men's memories kept flickering back to the white mobs of 1907. Back to the rioting with clubs, the rocks hurled through the air, the sound of splintering glass. If that happened again, they'd have much more to lose. Many of them had already passed many-times-ten years over here. No more could they say, "I've seen too much of their white hate," pack up, sell out and move back like so many others before them. More and more, memories of the old villages had faded into a vague distance, too far to retrace now. And their roots had sunk deeper in this land, so deep that to pull up stakes would mean death.

Old Chu, once a miner, hunched in the corner, wheezing like a wounded bear. After a slurp from his coffee cup, he suddenly yelped, "We tang people will fight. We won't be pushed around this time. The best defence is to show our strength now. They wouldn't dare come to bother us. Damn their mother's cunt!" However, even this effort seemed too much for the old gent. He fell back coughing, his face a cooked-shrimp pink!

Wong Gwei Chang puffed on his havana like an irrepressible volcano, his eyes guardedly neutral. His starched collar stood valiantly at attention against his massive, perspiring neck.

"Umph," the patriarch cleared his throat, "we don't need to be so hasty. Panicking at the mere mention of rumours. Let's not overreact, at least until we find out the real story!"

The heavy veil of cigar and cigarette smoke swirled around the back booth in silence for another few minutes. Everyone looked worried and grey.

Then, Mr. Niu, the editor of the local *Great Han* newspaper, offered up some more information. He said, "There've already been some reports of . . . of discord . . ." The men shrivelled noticeably. They all leaned over towards Mr. Niu, who was slight of build; a studious man with glasses and a nervous squint. He piped out, ". . . from a japanese fruit and vegetable pedlar. I understand his story to be as follows. One morning, his truck breaks down on the south end of the Connaught bridge. So he climbs out to fix it, thereby slowing down the traffic. As he is kneeling beside his truck, this huge white woman in a green dress with big flowers suddenly jumps out of a car. She starts beating him with her heavy purse even before he can get up. She yells out something like, 'Yeurr stunkee, yeller, slimee snake! Marrk me werrds, yee willna' gitawa witit!' The driver of the car, perhaps her husband, just sits behind the wheel and watches. Then she jumps back in, and they drive off, just like that."

The patriarch asked, "The japanese fellow hurt?"

"Oh no, just shaken—I suppose!" Mr. Niu peeked around the crowded booth, looking for an appreciative response from his peers.

"Wow your mother's cunt!" they muttered and spat.

"Savages! Waiting for an excuse to cut hunks of flesh off us!" they cursed and hawked up. The little mounds of ashes, cigar butts and burnt-out matches grew and grew. The spittoon slowly brimmed.

"Uh umph, there's more!" offered up Mr. Niu again. The cigarettes drooped.

"A white friend of Ting An's has in fact confirmed some wild rumours that the murdered girl's body will be exhumed." This time the cigarettes dropped.

"But they just buried her. You mean, Uncle Niu, they're going to dig up their dead before its time?" asked one.

"But they don't like that. They consider it desecrating their own graves!" exclaimed another.

"Well, you see," replied Mr. Niu, "they'll probably autopsy it again."

"Au-top-see? What's that?"

"They chop it up to examine it so they can find out how she was killed."

"Examine it, diddle your mother's stinking vagina!" they exclaimed in disbelief. "And after they made so much fuss about our exhumations of bones. Remember, Uncles? We were 'ghouls' this, and 'heathens' that in Victoria that year!" The old men's speech chafed with indignation. "As though our chinese customs were the ones that were barbaric, when all we wanted was to make sure that the ancestors got back home."

"Hah. Mutilating their own dead will only bring the wrath of their own Jesus-ghost down onto their heads," someone commented.

Again, Niu interrupted. "And there's supposed to be pressure for a second inquest. Lots of powerful whites out for blood from . . . from . . . well, from us, I guess!"

This bit of news was too frightening; there was total silence around the table.

Wong Gwei Chang quietly stepped in. "Has the felon's rope caught up with the Wong boy?" he asked.

"No, not yet," answered Mr. Niu, "but it won't be long."

"Then there's no time to waste. Elder Uncles, if you will give me permission, we must conduct our own investigation into this matter." He spoke matter of factly, leaving no room for doubt.

Immediately, the community leaders burst into a flurry of activity around the table.

"Is that wise, Uncle Wong?" demanded one participant. "How could we have any contact with this thing without casting suspicion on all of Chinatown? You know yourself, they're only looking for the slightest excuse to bring disaster down onto all our heads."

"No, Gwei Chang is right," countered another, "we must get to the bottom of this gruesome matter."

"Yes, when we tang people have to wrangle with such people, we cannot leave anything to trust!"

The final decision that the accused man's uncle, who was also a domestic, should be summoned in all haste, was an easy one to make, since patriarch Wong was also the head of the Wong Clan Association. He told the association's secretary, Wong Loong, to send word out to the white suburbs that the uncle responsible for the young upstart was required to make a statement on his behalf to the Chinese Benevolent Association.

Before the end of the week, both Wong Foon Sing and his uncle, Wong Sai Jack, were perched on the edges of two of the dragon-chairs that lined the entire wall of the second-floor meeting hall in the newly built Chinese Benevolent Association building. They didn't sit together, but three chairs apart. Under the high ceiling, both their faces shone like pale, moist moons in the gloomy hall. Around them, the heavy chinese furniture formally and coldly arranged; tall, rigid scrolls of calligraphy barked out messages of loyalty, filial duty, benevolence and righteousness.

The elder Wong kept shifting in his chair, nervously fingering his hat. But the younger Foon Sing, twenty-six years old, appeared very calm, almost elegant and scholarly. His face smooth and supple as he awaited his fate. Only a string of perspiration beads across his upper lip betrayed any inner distress.

Suddenly, a heavy heap of old-men footsteps thundered on the bottom stairs. The two guests listened intently as they knew it had to be patriarch Wong Gwei Chang and his followers climbing the wooden steps, shaking up the dust. They heard when he paused at the stairwell of the cheater floor, so-called because from outside appearances, this floor was hidden to evade taxes. This extra floor housed or rather rough-housed a perpetual party of gamblers and socializers. No one could ascend to or descend from the pious sanctity of the meeting hall upstairs without the notice of all the unofficial caretakers of this floor. Today, it was especially crowded, noisy with shouting and swearing and the clatter of mah-jong. The air filled with excitement, as if they all shared in the pursuit of a great sport.

When the two disgraced ones had climbed past earlier, the tables had hushed—all the men seemingly intent on their cards, tiles and dominoes. Uncle and nephew did not dare stop at this doorway, but they sensed that their every footstep was being carefully studied until they settled into their lonely posts of abeyance upstairs.

Then the clamour had resumed, until Gwei Chang arrived outside the gamblers' door. He made a magnificent entrance, raising a cigar-yielding hand like a returning hero, to the sound of males greeting males. Chairs pushed back as they rose in respect. Then the room hushed.

"Elder Uncle Wong. Off work today, are you?" The real caretaker of the building was of course the first to the door, the first to address him, talking just like a little dog grateful for a job during times like these.

"A Lo Soong ah . . . hai . . . ah . . . ah," he greeted one, then nodded at everyone else. "Wow your mother! Hot, eh! Tiger heat, this!" To emphasize his point, he dragged out a crumpled white handkerchief and mopped his brow. Gwei Chang looked uncomfortable, although all the men who clung onto his every word hardly noticed. He was conscious of his bright white starched shirt shining like a single light bulb in a dingy tenement. His new suspenders and tie stood out from the mended and fraying cotton garb that humbly surrounded him.

These men seemed to want him to say something, but beneath it all, Gwei Chang was a modest man. He was sometimes awkward with his role as so-called patriarch, given to him when he became one of the privileged few who could hire his fellow chinese. Also, he was the generous type, who paid as much wages as he could and gave out as much food and shelter as he could. His business thrived, and he was able to hire more and more. As a result, in chinatown, Gwei Chang was both well-respected as a fair and honest boss to toil under, and very much admired for being a ten-parts smart and reliable businessman.

Gwei Chang fidgeted some more, nodding and stammering agreeably, then he turned and continued up the long, narrow stairs, his entourage much expanded.

Upstairs, Wong Foon Sing's uncle automatically rose out of his chair, ready to face his inquisitors. Wong Foon Sing followed suit as if in a dream.

"That sonovabitch Wong Foon Sing isn't going to tell us a thing! We've been up here frying him for four hours. He hasn't let us in on a thing!" Lee Chong, the treasurer of the Lee Association, bawled loudly, his spittle flying at Foon Sing, whose appearance had drastically deteriorated since he had first walked through the doors of the association building. Men hovered around him, some sitting on the couches, some leaning against the walls. The front doors and windows leading out to the balcony were tightly shut despite the soaring temperature.

The young man shrugged his shoulders; perspiration drizzled down his face and along his black hairline. He tried to wipe some of it out of his eyes with his sleeve. Somehow, the boy's seemingly nonchalant shrug infuriated the official sent from the Lee clan all the more. Lee Chong suddenly wound up and slapped maliciously at the side of the boy's head.

Foon Sing covered his ears and fell to the floor, crying in desperation, "I don't know . . . I mean, I don't remember . . . I don't know anything." He crawled slowly back onto the chair again.

"You dead snake! You don't even know right from wrong. You're just a troublemaker! What can you be thinking of? Buying women's intimate underwear for a white girl for a present! And then she gets a bullet hole in her stupid head! What do you think people will think of that? A no-good chinaboy sniffing after white women's asses." After sneering to his heart's content at Foon Sing, Lee turned and snorted at the others, "A rotten fish matched with a stinky shrimp!"

"Who'd ever think that he'd be that stupid?" someone commented from the side of the room.

"He's like a caught pig. They'll hang him for sure!" said Chuck Him, the butcher, another spiteful bald-head with a deadly mouth. He raised his voice shrilly, to imitate a woman: "Buy me this, chinaman! Give me that!" Then, his voice fell like a cleaver, "And he falls for it!"

"Maybe . . ." another voice slithered out from the farthest corner of the room, Duck Toy, a baker who owned the Jing Ming Bakery Shop. "Maybe Cousin Foon Sing is actually being a smart boy. He looks like a beautiful boy. Women like beautiful boys. Maybe there's a lot more going on that he's not telling us about, eh? Eh, A Wong boy, what do you say?" As he urged, his captive listened with a air of dumb helplessness.

"You must have had a pretty cozy situation up there in a big empty house. Working all day long, so close to a nice young girl, eh? Maybe it was too much of a good thing for a pumpkin-head like you to bear."

All of Wong's interrogators pressed forward, fixing their eyes on him, anxiously waiting for some telltale twitches or skulking around the mouth. "Tell us, Cousin! Was it enough to drive a man crazy? Crazy enough to want to . . ."

"Enough!" a clear powerful voice suddenly commanded, "I'm sick of this kind of talk! Makes me want to vomit!"

Wong Gwei Chang hadn't moved from his vantage point directly behind Foon Sing, yet he held the roomful of irritable men spellbound. They muffled their growls, retracted their claws, and crouched back into their corners.

From where he sat, the patriarch couldn't see the young man's face at all. Not that he was particularly interested in what he had to say any more. But the interview had taken a nasty turn; it left a vile taste in the back of his mouth. There was a fierce mood of choked violence in the room, full of rancour and hatred which made him sick. He wanted to hawk up and spit out the sour. He looked around the dim room, knowing that the men were staring and waiting. They were afraid, and rightfully so. If there was misconduct on the part of the Wong boy, then the whole community faced repercussions. Still, he hesitated, wondering if the situation was as simple as trying to make a young man tell the truth. A menace loomed bigger out there—he wasn't sure what it was, but it felt even bigger than the pent-up fury of the men in this room.

There was a time when Gwei Chang would have felt the same as the other men, when he would have wanted to reach out to tear out a handful of hair too, where he could. He too was once a hungry worker who sold his body for wages, who swallowed the bitterness of being cheated every day. These overseas chinese were like derelicts, neither here nor there, not tolerated anywhere; an outlaw band of men united by common bonds of helpless rage. Fuming and foaming, talking just as malevolently, wanting to inflame as if that could appease their own pain! Aah, but he was an old man now—very old in spirit, if not in years. And he had learned that anger only splatters pain, like hot oil onto shrinking skin. Nothing assuages pain, except maybe time. Even then, pain only tempers into a hard, glinty edge which cuts without warning. He had been cut enough times, so he knew.

"Fuck! What's the good in such lewd, dirty-minded talk?" he barked loudly. "Take a good look at yourselves! You're all like mangy dogs sniffing after the stink of a dirty she-bag! So cut out the high notes and listen to what I have to say! We're here to conduct business!" Patriarch Wong stood up and glowered around the room, ready to flush out any would-be dissenters lurking in his presence. There were none.

With a stout cigar clipped under his forefinger, he stuck both his thumbs into the leather loops of his suspenders and leaned slightly towards Foon Sing. But with the same subtle motion, he seemed to recoil as if he didn't want anything to do with him.

"Aah!" he sighed heavily on the clichés. "It's true, you who are young in years simply don't have the sense to know the colour of fire!"

The room was hot, and sweat dripped down his face as fast as his handkerchief could mop. Gwei Chang longed for a breath of fresh air, but he couldn't see an end to this difficult situation.

"Throw open those doors!" he ordered. The fresh, cool air, which immediately flooded in and basked the room with its soothing sweetness, surprised him. He breathed in deeply; the silken breeze touched his face and neck, and slipped in under his soaked shirt. For a precious instant, he remembered another smooth caress. One he once cherished. For a brief moment, he remembered a time when he had soared beyond all human reach. But the feeling passed as it always did, and he was again left behind, always disappointed, always dazed. He couldn't bring himself to face what his life had come to. A locked roomful of anxious men.

Pushed by his need to be outside of this, he stepped right up to the window's edge. There, as if searching, he stared up at the cloudless, brilliant sky, feeling an old tug on his heavy spirit. Away in the distance, he followed the movements of what might have been a pair of hawks or eagles circling in the sky. Maybe they were just crows, but he suddenly remembered a love poem:

When a pair of magpies fly together
They do not envy the pair of phoenixes.

Gwei Chang turned listlessly back to the matter at hand, but he hardly knew where to begin. Eyeing the boy with cold anger, he decided that he had no choice except to condemn him first.

"Very well, you claim to be innocent. That may or may not be true," he said, "but this we already know. We know that you know a lot more than you're telling us. O.K. If you don't want to tell, then you're on your own! I guess you're a real tough guy, aren't you? You don't want the help of the associations? Then you're alone! You know as well as anybody what kind of treatment you can expect from those whites. But maybe, just maybe, you've forgotten about what we do to traitors who make trouble for us . . ."

Wong Foon Sing muttered, "What can Tang People's Street do for me? You don't have any say in police matters."

"You dead boy-bitch!" Lee Chong muscled in with a loud screech. "You can't even guess how much we know, never mind how much we can manoeuvre in tricky situations like this. We know your bossman Bay-Kah is a drug trafficker. How clean is your reputation? We know you've been chasing after a no-good she-ghost . . ."

"Lo Lee, shut up!" Mr. Niu yelled in a panicky voice.

Gwei Chang shook his head. That many-mouthed Lee Chong had really bungled things now, revealing details that should have been kept secret until the appointed moment. But this meeting had been out of control since the beginning. He should have ensured that only a few trustworthy elders would interview the Wong boy and his uncle, and barred entry to these useless loafers with big ears who hung around to spread gossip later.

And how could he blame Lee Chong? He was an old confidant, a loyal if simple-minded sort who had sweated blood in a laundry for years before he hit on his San Francisco Noodle Company. After all, he'd just got hot under the collar and blown off his mouth. Lee Chong, like many others, couldn't understand the complexities of this matter. He assumed that all chinese were his compatriots, and that it was all right to mouth off since everyone within hearing range was chinese.

Wong Gwei Chang knew differently. He realized that the old ways in Chinatown were fast disappearing. He played a so-called prominent role in the associations now, because the old-timers had agreed to give him big face. In the old days, they'd had to band together to survive. Share a little more during good times, share a little less during bad. Years ago, the game had been deadlier; protection was sought. Everybody needed to play by the rules, abide by a leader. But Chinatown had grown. He had no real say in this motley social order anymore. More and more, the patriarch came face to face with young, hostile loners like Wong Foon Sing, who'd just as soon tell you to go die! Fart in your face! They had no respect. Why should they follow you? As soon as they got off the boat, they were all out for a good time and easy money. Like wild beasts, they'd eat their own kind for it too. However, if they found themselves in trouble, they'd surely come back then, trailing police-devils behind to ransack Chinatown. They didn't care that the devils would gladly wipe out the whole fellowship for the folly of one individual.

Gwei Chang decided to try a different tactic. The boy he must deal with in private, later. First, he had to clear the room tactfully, without rousing the citizens' ire and suspicions. The gossip would expand and shrink all over Chinatown, as if it had a life of its own. In an hour, everyone would have their own version of what had transpired in this room.

"A white woman has been killed! And you don't know anything, and you don't care!" he pretended to speak directly to the culprit. "And we're not supposed to care either! But who gets blamed by those white hoodlums? You alone? All of us! You tell me, boy! Why should we suffer for what you have done?" he asked. But he could tell by Foon Sing's apathetic slouch that the boy would remain unreachable. Gwei Chang paused, then he shrugged his shoulders like a seasoned politician.

"Uncles," he spoke eloquently, "how can I face you if I let this mangy dog bring retribution down on Tang People's Street! Already, the situation is a very tense one, and we must work hard to avert a crisis. However, one and all, please rest assured that the damage he has done . . ." he paused again to give his words more clout, "will be cleaned up without a trace! That this falls directly under the jurisdiction of this association is without question."

There followed a murmur of consensus from around the room.

"Uncles, I don't need to remind you that the reputation of one man can reflect upon our whole community. So, it is up to this association to keep this dead boy's stinky reputation at all costs. He's a dissenter . . ." he paused to spit a scowl of such repugnance at his subject that the spirit of the men in the room again brightened.

"We won't tolerate dissenters," Gwei Chang barked, "and he's going to keep his mouth shut against the authorities if we have to stuff it with his own hot dog."

The room roared.

"And when we're finished with him, he'll understand that we mean business. In the end, this Wong boy will understand that his suffering is not only for his own good but the good of all of Chinatown."

With this, the patriarch turned to stare out the window at the blue sky, his mandate as clear as the heavens themselves.

Wong Loong, the secretary, stepped in immediately, his manner ingratiating.

"Uncles," he said, "your attention to this matter is very much appreciated. I know the association has taken up too much of your time already. Many of you have other business to attend to, so we will not impose on you any more. Ah . . . of course, I'm sure I can count on your discretion once you leave. We officers, however, still have much to teach our insignificant little brother. And we will teach him, he, he, right, he, he, even if it takes a few days."

When Gwei Chang spoke, no explanations were necessary. He didn't have to take his eyes down from the peaceful clarity of the heavens as he listened to the men reluctantly shuffling down the stairs without a word of protest. Those who dared stay certainly knew that they could.

"Someone should stand guard! Make sure no one is loitering about," a voice said. "It is essential that this kind of tricky business doesn't go beyond these four walls."

After the room was emptied, the doors shut tight, Wong Gwei Chang stepped back to his chair and sat down behind the houseboy in question. There, he wouldn't have to look at his face.

K A E
1967

Morgan and I didn't study particularly late that night. Perhaps the thickening snow flurries outside made us a bit restless. It was such unusual weather for Vancouver. I finished my two physics labs, which potentially freed me up for the upcoming weekend. Morgan finished another five pages of frenzied scribbling. I looked up from my slide ruler to find him staring intently at me. I smiled nervously back, but he just maintained his grave face, staring at me as if I were a ghost.

"So Morgan," I asked in a teasing tone, "do you want to take me for a pizza . . . so you can explain to me why you're staring at me so strangely?"

It took all my courage to look straight into his eyes. Even then, I had to do it in a smart-alecky way. I was too young to be sensitive to it then, but I have since realized that the pain in his face was extremely daunting. His eyes, brown with a bilious green hint, were always bleak.

"If you want one, I'll take you," he replied softly, his eyes never leaving my face. "And I study you because your face is so 'ching,' or clear. You look so serene. It's . . . very nice!"

His compliment made me feel helpless.

"Morgan . . ." my smile faded, and I looked at him very seriously, searching for some kind of crack in his armour. He made it so difficult to get close to him; and I was so inexperienced. Impulsively, I got up and walked around the study table to where he sat. Once behind him, I bent down and put both my arms around his neck.

"What is it that troubles you so much?" I asked, pressing my cheek against his sweet-smelling, brylcreemed hair. Actually, I wasn't expecting an answer; I was too excited about my daring and our new-found intimacy. For Morgan, the masculine thing to do was not to admit to personal woe, and of course he did not answer. Yet some of his tension did leave him; he stroked my arms gently, and his head drooped against my cheek.

"Well, tell me!" I persisted with a whisper.

He just took one of my arms, led me around, and pulled me down onto his lap. The next few minutes passed like an eternity, because within those few minutes Morgan captivated me probably forever. And all he did was hold me around the waist, squeezing with just enough pressure to be purposeful, and look at me. His face seemed to unfold, and I have never seen such a beautiful look on a man's face. Slowly, he drew my hands up to his face and pressed his lips into the palms.

This gesture startled me. I don't know why I had to break the spell. Most likely my own shabby imagination, because I suddenly felt uncomfortable. I sensed an omission. There I was, perched like a bird on this seductively handsome man's lap, feeling his long, hard muscles on the back of my thighs. He knew he was thrilling to me, and I knew I was alluring to him. I should have let myself be seduced, although I know now it wouldn't have happened like that.

"You're driving me crazy," I protested weakly. I tilted his chin up and forced him to look me in the eyes. "You know you're driving me crazy! You kind of lead me on up to a point, then you play games with me. Why did you tell me you're my uncle?"

I watched him grimace as he pulled away from me.

"Don't you believe me, Kae? Didn't you verify it with your parents?"

"No I didn't!" I pouted and lied. That wasn't exactly the answer I wanted to hear, and I was beginning to get more than a little bit alarmed. I certainly had mentioned Morgan to my parents. I was very close to them, being their only child, and they were great armchair liberals. (Although my mother had more traditional pretensions then, but I'm sure that was more a side effect from raising a teen-aged daughter.) Yet, their pained expressions when I casually mentioned meeting a certain Morgan Keung Chi Wong at the Champagne's last Christmas party. My father glanced over to my mother, who looked as if she needed to choke. Well, so what was I to think? All along, I'd had Morgan pegged as a big phony, either with his hand out or just fooling around by claiming to be my uncle. But this response, totally out of character for my parents, surprised me. I watched them as they recovered as fast as they could.

When my mother finally managed to look piercingly at my dad, he took a deep breath and said as nonchalantly as he could muster, "Strange that you should remark upon him. He's so much older than you. Almost thirty-something, I think."

"Twenty-nine!" I stated confidently. My dad actually sagged, and my mom looked almost panic-stricken. So, they did know of him. And in a big way! I was going to find out all I could about this dreamboat.

My dad said, "He's not twen . . ." but he caught himself. I gave him my intensely interested look, and his eyes involuntarily flickered over to my mom again. She, however, had nothing to offer him.

"I guess . . ." my adorable father, never stuck for words before, struggled now ". . . he's kind of a distant relative . . . you know, in a village sense. Same village, same surname. We consider him a relation."

He was a terrible liar. For one thing, my father seemed to have forgotten that Morgan was eurasian, which totally occupied my mind. After all, I had understood that kind of thing just wasn't done in nice families.

"We're not in close contact now," he continued bravely. "He's actually got a terrible name about town! Ruined more than one girl's reputation. And a good candidate for youngsters like you to stay away from. You certainly understand what I mean."

That not only signalled the end of the conversation but also the kind of protected girlhood I had. Sex was something that had to remain purely intellectual—understood. And my parents were awfully good at the academics of things. Anyway, they did manage to convey some vague idea that "ruining a girl's reputation" was possibly the worst stigma one could imagine. It meant getting a girl pregnant out of wedlock, and all sorts of grimly aborted possibilities.

Still on Morgan's lap, I wondered if this was the fate he meant for me. If it was, he was going about it all wrong. It was hard to

imagine a seasoned womanizer who couldn't come up with a better line than "I'm your uncle. Did you know that?" when all he
meant was that his forefathers came from the same village in
China.

"No, Kae," his voice eased in as if he knew what I was thinking.
"I mean that your grandmother had a lover—my father. Your
mother and I are half-brother and sister," Morgan revealed almost
apologetically.

"What a filthy, bloody lie!" I bounded off his knee, hissing like
an enraged goose. I pulled at my skirt, which had ridden up my
thighs beyond any semblance of reserve and good faith. Tears
blinded me. I groped my way back to my books and started stuff-
ing them into my bag. I couldn't think any more. At the time I was
not conscious of why I needed to flip off the handle in such an ex-
cessive manner. Suddenly, I felt so ashamed for lusting after this
incredible creep, this blasphemer who was assaulting the integrity,
the sacred legitimacy,' of my family origins. The honour of ancestors and descendants was at stake! And the more money, the
more righteous!

Stomping out of the library, splashing slush and snow all over
the insides of my ill-clad legs; the melting freeze dribbling down
my nylons into my white patent boots. I was furious that I could
be taken in by someone as vile as this lying pig-cheat! Beside the
fountain choked back by ice, I realized Morgan had run after me
when a firm hand took my arm and swung me around.

"Kae," he cried, "you can't go home by yourself in this
weather."

I despised that guilty look of concern and worry on his face. I
felt he was mocking me. The tears of hurt pride again dammed up
my vision.

"How dare you . . . presume . . ." I howled against the pelting
snow. Continuing the same momentum that he had used to swing
me around, I deftly wound up my heavy bag full of math and
physics texts, and, with a shriek of rage, butted him full on the
chest with it. I shocked even myself!

My granny on my father's side had always remarked right in
front of me that I had a spiteful temper, and it was lucky for my

parents that they could afford to give me everything I wanted. I could not believe that I would ever want to hurt another human being like that, but realizing that he wasn't even winded, I stumbled off to the nearest bus stop.

Completely absorbed in my thoughts, I was oblivious to the wretched, icy dampness which had seeped into my hair and clothes. Maybe he meant the wrong grandmother, I groped in the dark. Did he say his mother . . . or my father was his half-brother? No, he surely meant Poh Poh, my mother's mother, but that couldn't be. She was rich and staid, and had a husband who outlived her. Then it had to be my father's mother, Ngen Ngen. She had been a waitress for many years, and very poor. Also, Lo Yeh was a gambler. Of course, my mind tinkered away. Ngen Ngen never fought with her husband, no matter how poor they got. That was suddenly very suspicious. Wouldn't any woman hate to be tied to a compulsive gambler who frittered away her children's daily rice without any forethought or afterthought? Ngen Ngen must have been terribly guilt-ridden, even grateful to him, for letting her stay on after her infidelity. Compared to my prim Poh Poh, she was casual, too easy and sloppy, although I just could not picture her with a secret lover no matter how hard I stretched my imagination. Yet, come to think of it, she did have this sleazy way of walking. It must have been worse in her prime—perm-burnt frizzy hair, rouged lips, bedroom eyes glazed over with indolence. A swaybacked shuffle from booth to booth, slowly swinging her voluptuous hips from side to side. It must have driven those Chinatown bachelors wild with lust.

This last idea suddenly made me blush, since not ten minutes ago hadn't I been drooling over that rotten-egg bastard? I gnashed my teeth, thinking about how foolish I was. It was too embarrassing to even think about. I blamed myself entirely. My parents had warned me. So how could I have been so taken in? Exposing my most agonizingly secret desires, only to have him humiliate me!

Suddenly, it occurred to me that I was allowing him to soil my Ngen Ngen's divine memory too. She was a wonderful woman, kind and giving. When I was four years old, I smashed my nose on the sidewalk after being pushed off my tricycle. My granny, yelling at the top of her lungs, her fat hips jiggling, carried me, bleeding profusely, to old Dr. Ng's office two blocks away. I'm sure she would have gladly died of a heart attack in order to protect me—her only child's only child! She loved me that much when she was still alive. So why did I let him instill doubt in me? And what was he up to, saying such awful things to me?

I was so preoccupied with my thoughts that I didn't notice a noisy green Morgan pull up to the bus stop. Before the fact registered in my mind, Morgan jumped out and grabbed me by the arm. He pushed his face up close to mine as if to kiss me, except I twisted away and struggled.

"Come with me!" he hissed, loud enough for the other chilled students waiting for the same bus to hear. "Don't be such a baby! Or how can you stand to hear the whole story?"

"I don't want to hear your stupid story!" I snapped back.

Anyway, we made quite the scene—Morgan and I arguing and yelling at each other. He persisted beyond all reason, and my histrionics must have warmed up an otherwise tedious wait for all the bystanders. Finally, when Morgan threatened to beat to a pulp a stout boy with a white furry razor-cut, who had gallantly tried to come to my rescue, I gave up and got into his car. As he drove, he tried to reason with me, but I was completely deaf to anything he had to say. To me, it was all an incredible snow job.

Still, we were both very lucky to be alive. That stormy night, Morgue drove his car under a '48 Ford pickup which had gone dead at the bottom of the Tenth Avenue hill. All I recall was that I was glowering out my side window at the mist, which I imagined to be a dancing haze of snowflakes against an indigo hue, in order to keep his voice out of my head. Suddenly, the vehicle jerked a little and slipped sideways. I heard Morgan yell something like, "Duck, Sue!" which of course I thoroughly disregarded. Then, about the same time, I heard a muffled metal crunch, and someone tried to yank a handful of hair off my head. My head lopped forward, and my nose hit the dashboard with a sickening thud. I lost consciousness, although I'm sure I regained it soon afterward. When I did, I looked over to Morgan, but the driver's side seemed to be obliterated. Where Morgan should have been was a rusty fender and a bent tailpipe. Naturally, I panicked, screamed at the top of my lungs, and groped underneath for Morgan's body. Instead, I grabbed a handful of shattered glass fragments, which pierced a few minor capillaries. The sighting of my blood further escalated my hysteria, until Morgan's face without a scratch on it finally appeared at my door.

Morgan the man got off a lot better than me. Morgan the car was a total write-off. The whole thing was all very embarrassing: clotted blood all over my white fur, my black hair; snowflakes melting mascara all over my face; my nose tumid like a wet sausage. Carried off on a stretcher by goliath firemen and policemen; ambulance screeching and flashing red all the way to the general hospital—I felt a little obscene.

Crouched at the foot of the emergency room stretcher, I could peek through the partially closed curtains, beyond the nurses' station into the waiting room. My pulse fluttering with dread at the prospect of facing the outrage on my parents' faces. They probably wouldn't overreact; still one never knew, since they'd never been tested to such limits.

I saw my parents rush through the double doors on their frantic way to see me. By their wan expressions, I could tell that my injuries had probably been magnified a hundred times in their minds, my parents being so unbearably protective of me.

Morgan stood up as soon as they came through the waiting room. So they both spotted him at the same instant.

I had told them that I was going out to study again, but I had neglected to mention Morgan Wong. Again. Well, I felt it was a minor detail, but a look of such venom and loathing as I could never have pictured on my sweet gentle father reared on his face. It took my breath away, and I stared as if permanently paralyzed from that one particular split-second when one's body and soul fall apart.

My mother turned her face away abruptly as though she couldn't bear to look at him, clutching at her throat as though she needed to protect it. I couldn't see Morgan's face until my mother tried to sweep past him. When he turned, trying to keep up with her in this strange dance, he looked as if he was in the depths of hell! I realized, then, that this was an encounter between longtime, mortal enemies. Everything that Morgan had tried to tell me so far was true then, and whatever he had to tell me yet was going to be excruciating.

As far away as I was, I distinctly heard Morgan speak to my mother in our own village dialect. He said ominously, "You think just because you have money to buy people, you don't have to face your crimes!"

My father glared at him with snarled lips, his fists clenched. Then my mother blurted something, but bitter tears choked her words back. "Not ours . . ." she said. "You."

Morgan seemed to want to hold her back, despair and rage crawling all over him like a mass of worms. But he turned sharply on his heels and walked away.

I curled myself into a tight ball and pulled the thin white bed sheet over my head. My mind spun out instant replays over and over again. Like swooning on a merry-go-round gone out of control. Without my realizing, tears had already splattered the hard plastic slab they called a pillow.

III

Triangles

FONG MEI

1925

On a warm evening in late March 1925, Fong Mei hurried down the street on her way home. She didn't usually walk home alone in the dark, but today had been such an exhausting day at her father-in-law's new store that she decided not to wait for a ride. The balmy spring weather and the evening walk revived her, and she thought that she should walk home more often now that the days were getting longer and she herself was getting stronger. Actually, there was another more compelling reason as to why she had to get home early. Before running up the front porch, she glanced around the side of the house. There was still a light in the back upstairs bedroom. Tonight, she thought, her husband Choy Fuk would not get away without her seeing him off personally. Both in-laws were still at the Disappearing Moon as they were most nights, so she and her husband would be alone together.

She let herself in very quietly. Once inside the front entranceway, she took her key out of the door lock and purposefully slammed the heavy door hard enough to make the leaded glass windows vibrate. She smiled slyly to herself and waited a second or two longer in the dark. She could well imagine the look of consternation on her husband's face upstairs. No doubt he was getting ready to leave in a hurry, hopefully before she got home. But whenever she could, Fong Mei would not let him off so easily. She clattered up the stairs and stomped down the hallway. A touch too abruptly, she threw open one of the doors. Sure enough, Choy Fuk stood in the narrow toilet chamber, razor in hand, shaving soap all over his face. He looked like a sheep. She stared at him coldly, mutely. She knew he hated this silent stare, and he finished his shave as quickly as he could, nicking his tallowy neck twice. Fong Mei narrowed her eyes at each wince. Why doesn't he slash his useless throat? she thought viciously.

Hastily, he put on his shirt. When he started back to their bedroom, he stepped on his dangling suspenders, dragging his pants down around his knees. Fong Mei followed closely, openly jeering at the ridiculous sight he made. In the bedroom, he finished dressing. Finally, Choy Fuk threw on his jacket, grabbed his hat and stumbled out without a single glance in her direction, not even bothering to tie his shoelaces. She still hounded him as far as the front door though, slamming and locking it after him.

"Go, you turtle," she muttered to herself. "I can't stand the sight of you any more than you can stand me."

As soon as he left, Fong Mei relaxed. These mean little triumphs were getting to be a bit boring since she started them last year in the fall, but now her ego absolutely refused to give them up. Whistling a tune, she readied herself for bed. Tonight, she might have a few minutes to start a letter to her elder sister before she got too sleepy. Before springing into bed, she threw open the window and looked down at the garden in the moonlight. She loved to sniff at the night air. Although not like the warm, moist, subtropical one of her girlhood, the night seemed animated, filled with all sorts of wonderfully intoxicating possibilities.

In bed, she made a cosy nest out of the flouncy pillows and was about to pick up her fountain pen and writing pad, when she felt a strange pang of guilt. She should stop harassing her husband! What was the use of being so vindictive! She certainly wasn't angry at him any more. And his sleeping with the waitress didn't gnaw at her pride as it had before.

She had changed these past six months. Where the loathsome living arrangement that Mui Lan had forced her into had once made her blood boil, it in fact suited her now. Fong Mei no longer felt like she was a part of somebody else's plans.

And quite truthfully, Fong Mei had never borne any malice towards that poor, unfortunate waitress-woman. She was being paid well enough to lay with Mui Lan's son, but as Fong Mei knew by now, she wasn't getting such a wonderful deal. Pitiful thing—just a sore bag who didn't seem to have enough gumption or sagacity to manipulate a better life for herself.

Mind you, it was hard to imagine how wretched the waitress's life was. She seemed so beaten. Fong Mei wondered how she herself would have fared in the face of such raw poverty and abuse. That waitress hadn't even a pretty face to help buy her way. But, if nothing else, the woman had freedom. That thought made Fong Mei tighten her shoulders a little, because, for all of her new plans, her life was still not her own.

Fong Mei had always been a little intimidated by the waitress, who was an older woman, and had never made any friendly gestures to her. Her big, clumsy frame shuffled about, from kitchen to booth, booth to kitchen, seemingly impervious to the sniggers and lewd remarks from the more obnoxious patrons. Whenever the tables were slow, she drudged in the dirtiest parts of the kitchen, elbow deep in lye or grease. If there was a moment of respite at all, she would droop on the lowest corner stool, near the back of the restaurant, always dumb. Even with Mui Lan chattering beside her, she was the same listless kind of person.

To Fong Mei, the waitress belonged to that other class of women—the one without male patronage, barely existing, mute in their misery. It never occured to her to think how she herself was silenced by luxury. Fong Mei was too self-absorbed to be conscious of how her eyes hardened against the waitress's dirty clothes and hair; of how her nose crinkled slightly at the suspicious odours about the woman; of how her long white fingers dropped the weekly pay envelope into the red, chapped hands as if from great heights.

Not long after accepting her mother-in-law's terms, Fong Mei had discovered how much she had been set up. That old bitch Mui Lan had struck a baby deal with the waitress long before approaching Fong Mei. Why Mui Lan had bothered to waste an entire morning debasing Fong Mei and forcing her to her knees was beyond comprehension. She knew that Fong Mei had no choice in the matter. It made Fong Mei feel all the more acutely her predicament, the lie she had to live in order to fill her belly. It made her despise Mui Lan and her son all the more for their cowardly, underhanded ways.

To Mui Lan, the waitress must have been of course the perfect choice; she was "clean enough" and cheap and easily available. More importantly, the woman would keep her mouth shut. Fong Mei found out that she had come over on the same boat with Mui Lan and Choy Fuk, thirteen years ago. And Mui Lan had helped her out a lot. No wonder Mui Lan trusted her so much; she must have thought that the waitress owed her something!

As one of the naked poor hakkas or "guest people" in China, the waitress had been married off at the age of fourteen to a very old, shell-shocked, overseas chinese despot left over from the building of the Canadian Pacific Railway. He used to beat, rape and abuse her atrociously; and she would have died of her violent beatings if it hadn't been for the not infrequent intervention of Lee Mui Lan, who carried considerable social clout and, more importantly, had a piercing tongue.

Mui Lan had taken a liking to this shy, defenceless child, perhaps because she was about the same age as her Choy Fuk. Or perhaps because she was the kind of daughter-in-law Mui Lan would have preferred to have. Soon after the young girl had tried to commit suicide by suspending herself from the rafters in her old man's chicken coop when she was pregnant with her first, Mui Lan stepped in and shamed the old bugger into clemency for the poor girl. The beatings didn't stop for long, though; they went on even beyond the birth of her second boy. He broke her nose and collarbone at least a couple of times.

Mercifully, the ugly old gizzard had died in his tracks of a burst blood vessel in his brain. However, except for the leaky shack and chicken coop on the muddy fringes of False Creek, he left her and her babies destitute. She tried to work the small garden plot herself and practically starved herself and her children to death.

Chinatown, being the tight watchful community it was, soon stepped in with aid. Still, misfortune hounded her. Both boys died within days of each other of Rocky Mountain fever. Too depressed this time even to attempt suicide, she would have simply died of neglect if Mui Lan hadn't come in the nick of time to nag and goad her back to being a human being again.

The woman had come to work for Mui Lan in the kitchen of Disappearing Moon, scraping garbage off the floor. Then she was offered work as a waitress. And she accepted. It meant more money, with tips, although she must have realized that in this sexually suspicious street of village-bred men, a waitress meant no better than a prostitute. A lone woman serving tables of dirty-minded men who righteously looked down upon her was an ironic twist for a descendant of the hakka people who, no matter how poor, never sold their girls into prostitution or slavery. Then, as the years passed, she became known as "the waitress" because there was no other in Chinatown. Many people never even bothered to ask her name.

How, Fong Mei thought magnanimously, could she have borne any hard feelings at all against such a pitiful beast? She sank back against softness. Moonlight filtered through the windows into the dark room, illuminating the porcelain-blue in her complexion. On the pad of onion paper beside her head was written another beginning:

"My beloved elder sister, I am sure that my trials and tribulations are now over. The air around me is sweet and cool, and I can see clearly now."

CHOY FUK

1925

Choy Fuk breathed a big sigh of relief when he stepped out into the spring air and strutted down Georgia Street towards Chinatown.

Ah, women are no good! he thought mournfully to himself. He adjusted his tie, smoothed it down, and tucked the end smartly under the waistband of his trousers. They're always dissatisfied with one thing or another. What is it that they want? He glanced back over his shoulder for no particular reason. The street was clear, lit by the occasional street lamp, hardly a horse or wagon anywhere. A spattering of white picket fences and fancy fretwork here, there. Neat lawns and freshly turned flowerbeds. Daffodils out in full force, glowing yellow embers in the murkiness. A few porch lights illuminated his way in the dark. The warm, rosy glow of lamps in parlour windows reassured Choy Fuk that the world was still safe and hospitable. But when he turned away and started jaywalking across the street, he caught his loose shoelaces in some cedar blocks left exposed where the pavement had worn away. When he tried to pull away, he caught his other heel on a trolley-car rail, skidding and twisting his ankle. "Sonovabitchee!" he swore angrily under his breath.

Choy Fuk felt sure he was headed for trouble. He could easily ignore this problem for a little while longer, but he should at least think it over a little, maybe! So he paused in front of an empty lot full of tangled brambles and bushes to light a cigarette and relieve himself. Sucking the smoke greedily into his lungs, he wondered how many months this had been going on. Wow your mother, it couldn't have been six months already!

Well, then, no wonder he was tired. In fact, more than tired of all the whining, weeping women around him. He was sick to death of his mother nagging him. And he was fed up with his wife—the smouldering hatred in her eyes when she slopped his congee spitefully into his bowl in the mornings. How long could a man live with this one's meddling, with that one's obstinacy? He felt like a squealing pig bound tight in a woven bamboo cage, poked fun at by man-eating ogresses.

Six months ago, Choy Fuk had yelped at his distraught wife, "It's . . . it's not my fault! You yourself agreed to it. What can I do? I don't want to slap you in the face."

"Go die!" his young wife had howled back at him. "You want to go. You can't trick me! You enjoy rolling around in that pig-sty bed of hers."

"Women!" he had sputtered like the fine spray of a sneeze! There was no ready reply to such a vile accusation, he thought. He was a man. And it was not for a man to withhold his vital life-force stream on the spiteful whim of a barren wife. So what if he enjoyed the woman? What could be more natural for a man? Of course, since the opportunities for his pleasure had suddenly flourished, how could he be expected to contain his exhilaration and glee? Who wouldn't sink his teeth into this juicy ham bone? But as the saying went, "When eating beside a woman of mourning, the master dares not eat his fill."

"And what about me?" his wife had sniffled, a swollen, hurt pout about her lips. "How do you think I feel? Twenty-three, and a discarded rag of a woman already. I sit on the edge of our bed and have to watch you prepare to go to her every night now. What is there left for me except an empty bed and . . ." She wanted to say "and an empty crotch," but didn't have the brazenness.

"What, would you have me not go? Both you and I will catch trouble then. Just bear this through for another month or so, and I'll be finished. The old lady'll leave us alone then."

His wife had stared at him. What a stupid man to think that the end of his coupling duties with that woman would mark the end of this whole sordid mess.

Choy Fuk had given her a hesitant, sidelong glance, and said ever so carefully, "Then, you'll have my baby to care for . . ."

Fong Mei had let out a strangulated squawk, which startled him. "You cracked-brain . . . you'll never understand!"

Torrential tears had followed, beating down what little patience Choy Fuk had to begin with. He was the man, and she was his wife. She was supposed to follow his wishes. Why should he waste his time listening to all this soggy female noise? She was supposed to bring forth a son and heir. What else could he do if she was as fruitless as a broken twig?

He remembered staring stupidly at her white arms reaching out to him and thinking that she was ten-parts more beautiful than that "wild chicken." And he was really fond of her.

"Don't go!" she had begged. But he was anxious to go. It was too bad that she could no longer be the recipient of his precious manly juices, but that was just the way things had turned out. He couldn't understand how that mangy waitress of a woman could make his cock soar like she did. And night after night, he never tired of her. She infuriated him with her sagging milk bags and mangled belly button. Yet the sight of her in her shack, lying on that ragged sack cloth bunkbed, seared him with fervid desire. He never dreamed such passion was even possible. Emotions bottled up in his mother's big house burst out of control in the outlying shack. His own wife was but a darling pink child; he felt more of an inclination to pet her. But this one with her hard face and cool indifferent stare made him want to squash, pump and squeeze all night long. She made his toes curl. He fantasized that she was the demon-fox lasciviously draining off his fresh male sperm. And he, her spellbound victim, growing weaker and weaker, losing control of his faculties. Sperm was liquefied brain matter. Once drained away, he would go about Pender Street with a dull, vacuous stare. Hah! His old parents would have to take care of an idiot for the rest of their lives.

Suddenly, a childish voice chanted out of the night:

Chinkee, chinkee chinaman, eats dead rats.

Eats them up like gingersnaps.

A gang of young ruffians popped out of the side of a building and blocked his way. Choy Fuk flicked away his cigarette and loosened his shoulders, ready for a scuffle. There were four or five of them, no older than fourteen years old. Searching their faces for the ringleader, he spotted him—a skinny, tall kid with a horselike nose and dirty blond hair, wearing a tattered, filthy sweater which had shrunk in hot water a long time ago. Without warning, two of them wound up and threw things at him. Choy Fuk ducked one, but a wet paper bag smashed on the boardwalk and skidded between his legs, its contents splattering a foul stench over his pant legs and shiny shoes. He let out a loud growl and lurched at his chosen one. But the dead boy-bitch was too fast. Springing like a cat, he got away easily. Choy Fuk, much too pudgy and clumsy, knew he couldn't hope to catch him, so he lunged for whatever was the closest. He managed to secure a small one who was too inept to run away on cue. Clutching a handful of tangled, furlike hair, Choy Fuk shook and rattled him while those good buddies of his laughed and pointed at them from a safe distance. He also gave the howling little shrimp two sound kicks on his scrawny butt, one with each foot, taking care to wipe off his besmeared shoes at the same time.

As he watched the boy hobble away, tears streaming down his cheeks, scuff marks on the back of his pants, Choy Fuk contemplated the inequity of life. He himself was also a hapless bystander led astray by his own innocence, just like that yellow-haired devil. The boy looked like he was the youngest. And he wasn't the one who had thrown the rotten garbage. He probably didn't even realize what his peers had intended. However, it was precisely this kind of ignorance that turned him into easy prey. People always vented themselves on easy targets.

Choy Fuk knew the punks had gone ahead of him, hiding in wait behind another shadowy tree or fence. They'd hound him to their evil little hearts' desire. A chinese—who couldn't report them to the nearest constable—made fine prey. In fact, if they had harassed him in daylight, a chinese wouldn't even dare lay a finger on their butts for fear of repercussions from other whites, especially the constables.

Choy Fuk peered into the darkness and decided he would not go to Chinatown tonight. His social club would have to wait until he had talked to his waitress, until he had reasserted his manliness.

He took one resolute step after another, until he reached her little farm. By then, the night was coal black, the forest even blacker. Shimmering in the distance, the few lights of shantytown on the far edge of the marsh.

The waitress's tarpaper shack was all dark. He knocked on the door, but no one answered, so he lifted the latch and let himself in. He struck a match to light the kerosene lamp, which he placed near the one and only window. She couldn't be far off. Perhaps she was still working out in the back fields. She was a strangely fearless woman who did not seem to notice night or day. If she had to chop wood or dig up potatoes, she'd do it regardless of dark or damp or snow. But the light in her window would bring her in.

The waitress's little hovel reminded him of the village. The same threadbare paucity. On a plank nailed to the wall, a small crock of pickling vegetables stood, its wooden cover secured by a granite rock. Beside it, a square tin box to hold her raw rice and worn coconut shells for lopsided rice bowls. The front wall was plastered with newspaper, and a thin scant cotton diaper shivered sadly in front of the drafty window. Off to the side of the bed, a monstrous wood stove, way out of proportion to the tiny shack, squatted like a big black bear. Choy Fuk threw a couple of logs into its pot belly and poked around a bit. Through the vents and the slits, the flame flickered in a promising way.

Before long, he heard timid movements along the path behind the house, like an animal treading softly. Then he heard voices, so he opened the door and stepped out onto the porch. The light from inside flooded out to the waitress as she bent over the front steps, scraping mud from her boots with a stick. A gaunt man stood very still beside her, a hoe and shovel slung over his shoulder. He stared dryly back at Choy Fuk, who recognized him from the fantan tables. Last name Woo, an unfriendly sort who gambled a lot and spoke little. Didn't ever work as far as Choy Fuk knew, but then he had never really bothered to find out much about him. Men like him—there were so many.

"Go home," the waitress ordered Woo, without a glance in his direction. The man obediently swung the instruments off his shoulders and leaned them against the steps. Then he disappeared silently into the obscurity of the night.

"Here so early," she said to Choy Fuk. She stepped out of her muddy boots into a pair of homemade cloth slippers which had been left waiting beside a post. Then she took her boots and knocked them a couple of times against the side of the porch to dislodge more mud. She shuffled over to the end of the porch and left them on a wooden crate. After that, she put away the hoe and shovel. They had already been cleaned, perhaps by that fellow. Choy Fuk watched her every move, and when she disappeared into the shack, he followed.

"Have you eaten?" she greeted him, checking the wood stove. She also turned down the lamp to save a bit of fuel. Her diligence was beginning to irritate Choy Fuk.

"I came early to have a word with you," he announced

brusquely. The waitress immediately sat down across the table from him. She became very still. Under the glow of the lamp, she looked serene, even soothing. Her small dark eyes flickered softly over his face, then looked down politely at her hands, still grubby with work.

Choy Fuk's problem was that after six months of spine-tingling sexual intercourse with the waitress, night after exhaustive night, she was still not pregnant. He tapped his fingers on the table top and looked at her.

There she sat, the waitress, radiating sympathy and patience, but definitely not pregnant. He had resolved to ask her about this, since she was getting paid, and handsomely, to be pregnant with his child.

Whether she was or was not with child did not stir any kind of emotion in Choy Fuk. This whole affair was after all his mother's idea. When she had first approached him, he couldn't believe his good fortune—a wife and a whore! However, now that he was fast on his way to becoming the biggest laugh in Chinatown, he couldn't help but get a little clouded over, because it woke him up at night now, dripping with sweat, gasping for breath, groping for deliverance.

Suddenly, in his dreams, he was fifteen again, within a few months of coming to the Gold Mountains. It was a brilliantly jew-elled summer's day, and he stood naked and tremulous on the edge of a cliff, overhanging a swimming hole. From this vertiginous height, Choy Fuk stared into the cool green water. He could see the fishes, eel-like, lazily sifting around the pond. He could see his companions, as fluent in water as long-legged frogs, their white buttocks gleaming wet.

"Jump, Fuk boy! Jump!" they egged him on relentlessly. It was his turn, and he longed to jump, to fly carefree through the sunlit air like the rest of them. Tears blinded him. He heaved for breath. There were white boys who joined in the chant too.

"Tiew-ya! A Fuk-doy a boya! Tiew-ya!" they mimicked parrot-like.

"Fly, you celestial! Fly!" they sang. Choy Fuk simply couldn't do it. There was no confrontation. The boys, both chinese and caucasian, began frolicking with each other in the shining water and quickly forgot about him. But Choy Fuk was still up there, lurking on the brink.

Having lost his intention to be calm and resolute, Choy Fuk set upon dishevelling his waitress's composure instead.

"What was that broken-down dog doing here? Do you sleep with him when I'm not around? How can I expect to trust a slut like you? I drop in unexpectedly to find men hanging about like flies."

The waitress bided her time, concentrating on her work-worn hands.

"Well," he persisted, "what was that beggar doing here? Answer me!"

"Exactly what you saw. He was helping me dig up the back acre," she answered crisply.

"Do you sleep with him?"

"No, I don't sleep with him," she answered neatly.

"Why does he help you with your work then, and why don't you sleep with him?" he demanded peevishly. To Choy Fuk, this particular brand of logic made a lot of sense.

The waitress looked at him full in the face and answered precisely, "He helps me with the turning of the sod because I am his friend. And I don't sleep with him because he is my friend."

Enraged by her impertinence, Choy Fuk sprang out of his chair and poised the back of his hands over her head as if to strike. "You bitch! I should cut you out right now! It's part of the bargain, you know! If I so much as suspect a man within a mile of those female parts of yours, you're out without a penny!"

The woman did not cringe as Choy Fuk had wanted. She slowly moved herself back a little more on her chair, foxlike eyes penetrating his innermost secrets. He deflated and sat back down. What's the use, he thought, this woman doesn't have feelings like other women.

"What . . ." the waitress asked slowly, in as even a voice as she could muster, "did you come to talk to me about?"

Now it was Choy Fuk's turn to occupy himself with his hands— smooth, and white, and thick. A splendid egglike burmese jade ring on his fourth finger. A ring like that could do a lot of damage in a fistfight, bruising tender eye tissue, tearing flesh with a sharp jab. He could almost feel the teeth crumbling under his knuckles, cheekbones collapsing bloodlessly. Thwack!

"My mother's going to cut off the money. We've been at it for six months, and you're still not pregnant. Are you?" His confession tumbled out of his mouth so easily; his anger dissipated as if it had never been real.

"It's too soon to tell this month," the waitress shrugged, to Choy Fuk's dismay.

"Listen, that's not a good enough answer any more. I don't dare tell her that. She's hard enough to bear as it is. She cornered me again today and threatened not to pay you another cent unless she knows there's going to be a pregnancy. Lucky for you, you don't have to work with her any more! She won't have you back, you know. Remember that!" Fuk enjoyed that little bit of extra leverage, pausing to search for a reaction on the waitress's face, but she gave none.

"It hasn't been easy for me, you know," he continued to circle aimlessly. "She hounds me until my head reels round and round."

"So, go back to your wife." With that answer, the waitress got up and headed for the wash basin. She filled it with hot water from a dark urn on the top of the stove. Then she hauled a bucket of cold water up from the floor and poured in some of its contents. By the time she unbuttoned the front of her dress and slipped it off her bony shoulders, Choy Fuk was panic-stricken.

"Just like that? You think it's over just like that!" His arms flailing. "How can I face my mother, huh? How can I dare show my face in Chinatown, huh?"

"You shouldn't have opened your mouth in Chinatown." The waitress dampened a thin rag in the warm water and rubbed it against a rough bar of soap. Then she began to wash herself, starting with the face and neck. He watched as she knocked her breasts about, this way and that. Water dripped down the hollow between her breasts with their huge, almost black nipples. Then the rag explored the armpits. Choy Fuk wet his lips as she swept each damp dark crevice and sweaty fold.

He sighed heavily and complained, "How can I stop those many-mouthed birds from spreading rumours? How can one keep such a secret in such a place?"

"You've made things difficult for me, yourself, and especially your mother. I hope she never finds out why I really left. No matter what, Mui Lan's always been good to me." She spoke so quietly and matter of factly that Choy Fuk felt guiltier than ever.

He knew her words were very true. For a few moments of dirty-minded jocularity with his drinking pals, he had revealed just enough to capture their attention. He had to admit that when he had first started this sticky business of "fishing with his sturdy green-stick," so to speak, he'd got too cocky for his own good.

Having always been the centre of attention, Choy Fuk knew only what it was like to be in an enviable position—to have wife and whore, to be heir to a small fortune, to be blissful. He couldn't have been expected to know what it was like to be one of the envious who-didn't't-have. Those stripped from "mutilated families," whose need for vindication became greater as their dreams of becoming whole again diminished with each passing day.

The waitress lived in too isolated a part of town for their affair to be readily found out. But once Choy Fuk dropped a few too many innuendos, he had set himself up for others to speculate upon. Then, of course, the mystery was easily unravelled; Choy Fuk enjoyed his notoriety too much to stop swaggering. He did not notice the contempt of others swarming over him like mosquitoes. The waitress noticed immediately, and she retreated out of Chinatown, out of their target range, not only for herself but also in the hope of saving Mui Lan from embarrassment.

Burying his fat head in his soft hands, Choy Fuk tried to console himself. "Who cares?" he said shakily. "This matter is already old hat. Besides, it's only my friends who know."

The waitress just lifted a naked leg up onto a wooden crate and tilted her pelvis forward for easier access to the dark-skinned parts between her thighs. The rag began to roam gently in the purple petals of her flowery creases. Choy Fuk stared, entranced by her hand hovering over her warm wetness, water trickling down her white legs. He glanced nervously at her face, but found it impenetrable, afloat in her own thoughts, apparently unaware of him.

"Is it my fault that the old bitch chose another worn-out bag for me?" he growled. He jumped up and pointed an accusing finger at her.

"You . . . if there are rumours about, it's because you've been blowing foul air all over Tang People's Street, haven't you? How do I know that you haven't been smearing my family's good name with every sonovabitch who offers you his hot dog!"

She nonchalantly rinsed out her washcloth and resoaped it.

"You want to get me into trouble, don't you? You want to see me with a shamed face . . . so . . ." he searched excitedly for the words to convey his distress, "so you and your lovers can have a good laugh."

At that, she jutted out her dimpled haunches and slipped her soapy hands down the sepia crack between the two great moons. She moaned.

Choy Fuk lunged at her and grabbed two huge handfuls of flesh, squashing as hard as he dared. He twisted her around, frantically kneading her breasts; the basin of sweet-smelling, frothy water slopped onto his shoes as he tangled his legs around hers and clung hopelessly in a passionate embrace with her.

"Wash my feet!" the waitress said hoarsely.

TING AN

1925

Later that evening, Ting An ducked into the back door of a blood-coloured brick building on the corner of Pender and Columbia. Inside the lobby, he walked past a little box office, unmanned and unlit, towards two great, heavy doors ornately carved with gold-flamed dragons. Exalted beings that they were, they writhed and frolicked silently in a cloud-petalled heaven under his fingers, yet out of his grasp. Ting An pushed one back, and the door opened just enough for him to slide into a darkened theatre. Immediately, the thin wail of a lone chinese fiddle reached out to him. Surrounding him, rows of empty benches lined the large floor, patiently waiting for an audience to fill them with gaiety and laughter. Far away, a small stage gave off the only light; it was empty except for a lion dance headpiece artfully arranged in the centre, mouth open in perpetual surprise.

After Ting An's eyes adjusted to the dimness, he made out a few bobbing black tops of heads inside the orchestra pit underneath the wooden stage. From there, a tired voice directed in a patronizing tone, "A Low Lee-ah, three clangs of the cymbals like this!" Brass cymbals crashed together, followed by high-pitched, off-key falsetto singing. "That way, O.K.?"

Ting An stuffed his hands into his pockets and sidled up to the musicians to greet them. "Still hard at it?" he asked cheerlessly.

They all grunted at him, worn out and edgy.

"Yee Gaw," Ting An singled out the director, "why don't you go a little easier!"

"Pah, go die!" Yee Gaw sniffed irritably "With the first performance tomorrow night, these good-for-nothings still can't get it right! We miss your flute too," he added.

The other musicians were already starting to pack their instruments away. Yee Gaw stretched his back with arms akimbo. He was a tall, thin man with sharp features and pointy elbows.

"No more time, Big Brother!" answered Ting An.

"What's this no-more-time business? A young loafer like you! What's so important that takes up your time now?"

Ting An just smiled a little stupidly and shrugged.

"Too much whoring in those Powell Street whorehouses, you pretty boy!" Yee Gaw added lightly as he put away his clackers. A dark shadow flickered across Ting An's face, but no one noticed since he quickly snuffed it out. He didn't like that kind of talk. He deliberately pushed both his sweaty hands deeper into his pockets and wiped them against his legs.

"Let's walk!" he commanded good-naturedly, to switch the topic of conversation. "I'm thirsty."

He immediately headed for the stage door, anxious to taste the scotch whiskey he knew was waiting for him at the Kuo Seun Social Club. Once there, he'd be able to relax and sink into his thoughts, with his close friends around him laughing and enjoying themselves too much to take notice of him. That was the way he liked it.

"If you want, we go!" His older friend slapped him on the shoulder, urging him towards the front doors instead. "But everyone is at the Lucky Money Home Club tonight. We're going to join them to find out who won the lottery."

Ting An jerked back. He didn't want to do anything out of the ordinary, and he didn't like the patrons of the Lucky Money Home club. He was the type who liked to sit in the same seat, to listen to friends he trusted, and to know that he didn't have to say a thing if he so chose. Most of all, he didn't want to meet up with Choy Fuk.

"What lottery?" His voice annoyed and resistant. He stopped dead in his tracks. The other musicians swept past them.

"Hey, you really haven't been around, have you? Having too good a time 'plucking flowers by the roadside!' Ha! Ha! You pretty boy!" Yee Gaw offered with a wink of his eye. He had a nasty habit of flicking his fingers against Ting An's chest, who was getting extremely angry. He moved away, scowling, until Yee Gaw sensed his displeasure and commenced an explanation.

"This is a very special lottery." Yee Gaw couldn't refrain from giggling. "People have been betting on how long it would take Choy Fuk to fill his waitress's tummy with happiness." His hands mimicked the graceful caressing of a woman's globular belly. He jabbed Ting An in the ribs again, then doubled over in a hysterical fit of laughter. "Now who would have guessed over six months and still no hint of a bulge!"

The man was almost rolling on the sidewalk. Tears squeezed out onto his fine eyelashes, as he tried his hardest to gasp out, "I . . . I just have to know who won!"

Ting An was horrified. He stared open-mouthed.

"What are you sputtering about?" he scoffed. "You're crazy!"

Yee Gaw was about to poke again with his index finger, but Ting An took a step back and made a hesitant half-turn as if to leave. The finger missed its mark.

"You mean . . ." Yee Gaw said, "Don't tell me that you of all people don't even know about Choy Fuk and his waitress."

Since Ting An hated calling attention to himself, especially in relation to this affair, he steered the conversation away again.

"Of course I heard! Aah, go die! Who takes this kind of foul-mouthed talk to be real? This kind of gossip's not for me. You'd think that people had better things to occupy themselves with, especially at times like these."

"Aiya, Lo Wong, get off that high horse of yours! Not everyone has the opportunities for diversion that you seem to have. Even I couldn't resist two bids." As he spoke, Yee Gaw extracted from his sleeve a tiny bit of tissue paper with a red number brushed on it. "Coming or not?" he urged already walking away.

"Pah!" Ting An waved him off with a gesture which clearly suggested how disgusted he was with such activities. Under his breath, he muttered, "That dead boy Choy Fuk has no future."

Things have gotten out of hand, thought Ting An. He had been aware of Choy Fuk bragging about his escapades, and there was nothing he could do to protect Gwei Chang's family except sneer at anyone who dared perpetuate such talk in front of him.

Ting An glowered up the street where Yee Gaw was already beginning to melt into the night. This dead town was full of vicious ghosts. He stood alone on his corner of the street, but up along Pender Street he could see bands of idle men dotting the poorly lit doorways like ink spots, underneath flashing electric signs, wherever there was a bench or window ledge to perch on. At every wooden window, crowded faces looking inward; on the second-floor balconies, more batlike forms dangled off the railings as if the never-ceasing clatter of mah-jong tiles would drive them off the edge. The cackle-talk of their trapped spirits; grim laughter rolling off like distant thunder. Ting An felt a swell of fury rising inside him—a pounding fury trapped within the tough shell of his gut, hardened from a lifetime of soul-wrenching bitterness. The source of this fury remained elusive, but he recognized in it the smouldering ferocity of an animal that had known only boundless freedom before walking into a snare.

His human form told him to reconsider. If this kind of malicious thing was going on, better that he should know all about it. "Big Brother Yee, wait up! I'm coming!"

The other one turned and jerked his head to and fro. His big teeth, a bright white grinning from the darkness, wagged at him like a street walker.

Ting An was not a gambling man. He was not that easy to please. Instead, he was the meticulous type—the type who would chew through iron chains to gain his freedom. The Lucky Money Home Club was larger, rowdier and dirtier than Kuo Seun. Slurped up by its chaos, he felt nullified as he looked down at the men at the dominoes table, tap-dancing with their chips and fingertips, faces powdery dry. They played several games at once, addicts needing the flimsy thrill of a win to unlock their minds, shovelling away their meagre earnings with both hands. Tomorrow morning, their corpses would be found floating in the creek, and no one would blink an eye.

Lotteries, at least four a day. Even the most cloistered of merchants' wives, who never set one lotus foot outside of their husbands' homes, participated whole-heartedly, through runners who were either young boys or old gossipy men. This guessing game on Choy Fuk's male potency had to be more of a private, ongoing joke, but this was the first time Ting An had heard of such unrestrained malevolence.

When they found their table, Yee Gaw immediately yanked Ting An off his wooden feet onto a nearby chair, and asked around, "Where is he?"

"Strangely enough, the man's not here," someone answered sarcastically, setting off a round of ribaldry.

"Give me a drink!" Ting An demanded gruffly. He knew these guys had no heart. They had always hated Choy Fuk because he was not one of them and despised him all the more for trying so hard to be. Even if the poor idiot had been sitting right in the middle of the club, these underhanded pranks would still have continued right under his nose. Ting An began to sweat. Who knows? This could even be happening to him too, right now. He knocked back his liquor in a couple of gulps. Soon his head began to clear a bit.

Whooping and hollering from the next table caught his attention, signalling a potential win. A crowd gathered to watch the finale. He looked over at the unshaven faces focussed exclusively on their chips. There was a blind lunacy in their eyes, like the full moon reflected in a wine bowl. Greasy hair snapped back only when the length of it threatened the vision of both eyes. These gamblers might have been there for days; shirts almost shredding off their backs, flies carelessly left undone after a piss, suspenders dangling. Dirty plates strewn about; they had guzzled their food without missing a turn.

Yee Gaw had long ago slipped out of sight in the clouded room. Someone with a pipe clenched between his teeth asked, "You going to play, A Ting?"

"No money," he answered flatly.

"You, no money! You dead boy, who's going to be taken in by that?" someone else retorted.

"Go die!" another voice. "You're just jealous someone else has a bit of money saved up. You good-for-nothing." The talk rumbled around the table like an empty stomach. Ting An deliberately kept quiet, his lips pressed tight so he wouldn't have to feed it.

"Look at that fat proprietor. You tell me if he's not already eyeing you suspiciously. This isn't a kiddies' club like Kuo Seun, you know. They don't like it when you sit around not playing."

"Give me a bottle then!" Ting An demanded.

Yee Gaw came back with news that no one had guessed the right number of days. "They're all way off," he snickered.

However, in a case like this, the nearest number got the jackpot. No one had come to claim it yet. Everyone agreed that a six-month lottery was long enough for this sort of thing. After that, Choy Fuk was a dead boy.

"Anyway, I didn't win," announced Yee Gaw, chewing up his lottery ticket out of habit.

○

SONG ANG
1925

Choy Fuk woke up in the waitress's little hovel with a start. It was so dark that it took a few seconds for his eyes to find the outline of the window in the pitch black. It couldn't be more than a couple of hours past midnight. The stove was shedding the last bit of warmth that it had left. There'd probably still be enough glowing embers to restart the fire with a handful of kindling, and he would have liked to be warmer, but the waitress was a frugal person and it was her house. He felt her stir. She was a light sleeper, and she always knew when he awoke.

"I'll throw a few more logs on the fire," she said, starting to get up. She knew he had to go.

"No, no, A Song! Stay in bed a while!" He called her by her name, which was Song Ang. "I want to talk to you."

It felt good to talk into the dark, because it was faceless. "You'll have to get pregnant, A Song. If not by me, by somebody else. But you must have a baby." His voice stripped as bare as a beggar.

After a long pause, the waitress said, "I don't know if I can do that to Mui Lan."

"Do it for me then! I'm not asking for her. I'm asking for myself. You know that I need to show them a baby. You know I have no other choice. Please, don't do this to me!" He was desperate.

"I haven't been that bad to you, have I?" he dared to ask, but he didn't dare wait for an answer. "I realize that you haven't been doing this just for the money. I know that you have a good heart. But . . . I can give you more money—much more if you want. Just name it! As a favour for all your patience and . . . what you've had to give up."

An obliterating stillness followed. Who knew if he was getting through to her! She was like a succession of closed doors. But his mention of money seemed to give him more strength.

"Look," he decided to try more directives, "all you need to do is go out and find yourself a fellow. How hard can that be? Who's going to be the wiser? And you'll actually be doing my mother a big favour. You're very devoted to Mui Lan, aren't you? Think about it, the more this goes on, the more obvious it's going to become. And who's that going to hurt? Listen, I want you to give my mother what she asks. And believe me, you will be fulfilling her most fervent wish." The more he spoke, the more he felt like his old self again. He thought he sounded rather convincing. Moreover, he knew her; she wouldn't say no when a friend was in trouble.

"What have I had to give up?" asked the waitress.

"What?" He couldn't understand her question.

"You said, 'What you've had to give up.' "

"Oh, that! Well, you know . . . a lot, I suppose . . ." he was reluctant to say.

"And what have you had to give up?"

"I don't know what you mean," he answered a little too patiently. She didn't try any more.

"Well? What do you say?" he pressed.

TING AN
1925

Still later that morning, Ting An woke up with a burning dryness in his throat. He had to sit up on the edge of his bunk because the sick feeling in his stomach started to rise, threatening to eject. His temple throbbed relentlessly, and he needed to prop up his head with his shaky hands; he felt very sorry for himself. Stupid to drink so much again! Made him want to dig his nails into his eye sockets. Maybe he could rip away the hurt.

Then he heard a small cough. It wasn't much, but at least it was something to focus on, away from his own misery. His sore eyes trailed across the squalid room and settled on the other plank beds. The rumpled one across from his was still occupied. He reached out with his foot and nudged the sleeping body with his big toe.

"Hey, Big Brother . . ." Ting An had no idea who was sleeping next to him. There were four wooden beds built into each corner of the room, and the men who slept on them came and went. He just had the idea that the guy was probably broke. "You wanna earn a couple of bucks today, go to the alley behind Disappearing Moon and ask around!"

Even before the man could identify himself, Ting An had pushed a hat onto his head, his feet into his boots, and was walking out the doorway to start his morning pickup and delivery route.

In the stables on Union Street, Ting An found himself fingering the old bridle for Loongan, or Dragon Eyes. Its leather, salty and brittle, should have been replaced long ago, but the old mare that he'd been harnessing up to the same wagon painted with "Lee, Wong & Yee Produce Co. est'd 1895" for the last twelve years was gentle, plodding along the same routes for so long that he barely used any pressure on the reins any more.

Lee had died suddenly twenty years ago, sitting in this very wagon. The ghost authorities said that his heart had stopped, but Yee maintained that there were lots of foul ways to make a chinaman's heart stop. Unnerved by his partner's death, Yee sold out his share and went back to the Four Counties District where he lived comfortably enough. Only Wong Gwei Chang remained in the Gold Mountains and thrived. The little vegetable pedlar fattened into a restauranteur. Then he bought buildings and rented them out. Recently he'd been developing an import/export business—rice, tea, silk, herbal medicine and the like, to be wholesaled to out-of-town and occidental companies. Gwei Chang was not an exacting businessman; he was just flexible enough to use all of the best resources available to him. Unlike many others, he was not afraid to deal with white-ghost businesses, so the money rolled into his hands rather than someone else's.

"Step right up to them!" he advised Ting An when he was a youngster. "Ask them for an estimate! If you don't like their price, say so! So what if you don't 'speakee Engrishee' so good; our money, their money, 'alla same'!"

Ting An had worked for Wong Gwei Chang for eighteen years,

more or less as his apprentice, although no one had ever specifically referred to him as such. Years ago, he had always been at the
big boss's side and had taken his orders directly from him; but back
then the business had been small, so no one thought much of that.
Now the companies had multiplied, and naturally his position had
been elevated as well. But he was such a modest man that workers
approached him for direction without even realizing that he was in
fact second-in-command. People remarked that he spoke english
like a native speaker; he behaved much like a ghost too, never very
visible. He drove the horse and wagon around town a lot, and he
bought and sold stuff, hauled things from here to there, not much
different from anybody else who worked for Boss Wong. Well, he
also kept some of the books, but how many realized that? He dealt
with most of the business outside of Chinatown too. There were
lots of others who could get by in english, but Ting An got along
really well with the devils. He had a way about him, and he was
the reliable type who didn't shoot off his mouth. People readily accepted that he was a loner, more at home in the stables than with
his own kind. He preferred the grassy smell of horse piss to the
nauseating stench of his own cramped human condition.

Every morning, Loongan's friendly horse sneeze and the same
loving snort greeted him as soon as he stepped over the doorsill.
Patient, adoring eyes watched him as he shovelled a ration of oats
out of a can for her. Hers was an unconditional love forever.

On this particular morning, while Loongan munched, he
stroked her and whispered into her twitching ears as if she were his
only friend, "You saw what happened. You tell me if I'm a rotten
egg." But he knew that he was safe with Loongan. He cleaned out
her stall.

For Wong Ting An, it would have been so easy to steep in the
bitter brew that was his life. Days which were surly; men without
women. When he was a boy in Lytton, his grandfather used to take
him to the work camps, full of chinamen. He remembered a few of
them, lonely for their own children, liked to play with him.
They'd pull him up onto their laps in front of a rough table to
show him charcoal characters scratched on torn newspaper. The

character for "good," they said piously, trying to teach him reverence, was a boy and girl together. Male and female together to express harmony, that all was well. Even at that early age, Ting An disapproved vehemently. He had never known a female in his life, and wasn't he good enough? Why did he need a girl to be good? There wasn't even a female within miles of there. Easily exasperated, the chinamen swept him emphatically off their knees.

All his life, he'd had to tread quietly among them, careful not to be touched by their violence. Despair was so infectious among orphans and orphan-men; he did not want the pain, and they could not afford the wasted kindness on him. Mind you, Ting An had been orphaned for as long as he could remember. He had learned to take comfort from the small things that come from the sensation of solitude. A friendly nudge and the dusty smell of horse hair were enough to make him whole again, at least for the moment. And what else can you expect, thought Ting An, except what you can get from moment to moment.

He manoeuvred the rig out onto the chilly wet streets. Loongan knew the route well, every pothole and cranny. There was nothing for him to do except try to keep warm, try to not think at all.

Ting An hardly knew a closeness to kin. His mother was an indian dead of a fever by the time he was two. There was no father except his chinaman grandfather, who had died in the bush when he was twelve or so. Ting still remembered how shaken he was when the old man really had succumbed. Night after night, his grandfather had lain watching him at his work with adoring eyes, the hearth fire seeming to reflect off his weariness. But one morning the fire went out, and his only kin was gone.

Ting An had buried his grandfather himself. He still thought about the spot where his grandfather lay—on the eastern side of his mountain, at the base of two ancient ponderosa pines, cradled in the arms of their massive roots. He remembered the afternoon when he finished propping up the wooden marker with stones. Splintered sunlight shone through the underbrush and danced on his handiwork—"Chen Gwok Fai" carved deep at his grandfather's request. When the wind spoke through the branches of the tall trees, he heard his grandfather whisper through him too. The first calm he had felt since his dying. So it was true. Chinese did say that the dead come back on the third day to say good-bye.

Then it was late autumn, and Ting had been busy smoking a sackful of oysters he had gotten from a group of nlaka'pamux'sin people. They had offered to take him upriver with them to their village for the winter. They knew chinaman Chen well, and many would have gladly adopted a strong boy like him, with his pretty pale chinese face. But Ting An refused because of a vague feeling that he was supposed to wait. When he looked up through the smoke of his alder fire, he saw a man staring not at him but at the cabin. At that moment, Wong Gwei Chang was the saddest man he had ever seen.

When he had come to Tang People's Street to stay, Ting An couldn't help but feel a camaraderie with the orphan-men there; it was like a contract between faces, so to speak. People who had suffered the same hardships understood each other. Then too, since orphan children were rare in the Gold Mountains, he was lavished with attention from the A Sook-A Bak-A Gong strangers. A dried lychee nut, sometimes a nickel, pressed into his palm. Old fingers oftentimes lingered on his cheek or hair. He'd look up at the deeply aching brown eyes and smile his lovely little boy smile. In these ways, he was never lonely.

These days, Ting An had no other ambition than to stay crouched in a pedlar's wagon behind a clip-clopping horse and stare blankly into a pearly grey fogbank. He knew, soon enough, his peace would evaporate like early morning mist. His first stop was always Disappearing Moon. There, Loongan parked herself in the alley, while he went in and swished coffee around his mouth to clean it. This morning, though, crowds of men pressed up against the kitchen door. Ting An had to shove and elbow past the crabby men in order to reach the coffee urns.

Not quite six o'clock, and Wong Gwei Chang was already in the middle of this bustle.

It was going to be a long, hard day, Ting An figured as he took his first sip of the hot brew. Someone jostled his elbow, and the coffee slopped over his chin, scalding him.

"Damn . . ." He stopped and swallowed his curses because it

was bad luck to begin a day with angry words. "Why don't you watch where you're going?" he yelped instead at an unfamiliar back.

He caught Gwei Chang looking at him with such wholehearted concern that he had to turn away, embarrassed. Still, he felt Gwei Chang's eyes lingering on him, and he smiled in spite of himself. Gwei Chang was the fat-bellied boss; he wasn't an overly affectionate man, but in all these years, Ting An had never had much occasion to question his loyalty to him. After all, he was a man easily admired, easily adhered to, especially if one was alone in the world.

It wasn't as though Ting An didn't ever have a wandering heart. Sure, he'd like to leave this Chinatown, go up north, maybe work in a logging camp for a while. What was there to keep him here? A young loafer, as Yee Gaw said, no ties! Some of those camps would pay white man's wages if they were desperate enough, and when you knew enough to ask for it. One cold hard bunk was the same as another, and he could easily earn in four months what he'd been earning down here in a year.

Very tempting, yet Ting An just couldn't bring himself to face the old guy and say, "I'm going to quit! Had enough!"

No, he just couldn't; somehow, he knew a light would go out in the old man's eyes. Ting An could see a deep voiceless loneliness in Gwei Chang, and somehow this made Ting An all the more loyal to him.

Ting An knew he was expected to stand close to the old man. In his familiar slouch, hands thrust deep into his pockets, he sidled up to Gwei Chang and stood waiting for orders.

"Don't suppose you brought along one of the new trucks, A Ting?" Gwei Chang gave him his first greeting of the day. Ting An simply shook his head, irritated with himself for such an obvious oversight. Of course Gwei Chang would not reproach him, but this did not make him feel any better.

"Leave Loongan with Yee Gaw! He can take over your delivery route. Need you probably all day," Gwei Chang continued. "Another big shipment on the docks. Came in last night. More at the customs office. Today might get a bit tricky, but maybe you can ease by those customs ghosts like you did with A Fong Mei Sow, he, he, he!"

He was referring to Ting An's negotiations six years ago, which had considerably reduced Gwei Chang's soon-to-be-acquired daughter-in-law's wait at the immigration holding station. Ting An didn't do anything special—just looked a ghost full in the eyes and asked a few questions, but nobody in Chinatown ever forgot a miracle. Ever since then, he had found himself handling all the customs and immigration business, as if he were a good-luck charm.

"Know you can't be two places at the same time, but maybe A Fong Mei Sow can take over the inventory at the warehouse today. Maybe you can take her out there before you get the truck. Show her where you left off. But just the big items today. Yesterday, you two got too involved with little things. Tell her to quickly check over all the big items on the invoices first. Go into detail later. That way, we know right away if things don't add up."

At the mere mention of Fong Mei's name, Ting An's empty stomach growled.

The boss shuffled him into a quieter corner of the kitchen and lowered his voice further. "Of course, I'd like to send Nye Nye out there with her, but I've already taken away so much man-power from Disappearing Moon she probably won't be able to get away until after the lunchtime rush. This afternoon earliest!"

A nauseating wave of guilt threatened to eject the coffee grounds from Ting An's stomach. By now, he wondered how the old man could not know. Wasn't deceit written all over his face? But even if it were, how would Gwei Chang know if he never looked? This thought snuck up on Ting An and gave him an unexpected jolt.

"Of course, the old lady'll grumble about it, but we're just too busy these days to think about any of this-and-that female reputation business. She's just nervous with all this going on. You know how women are. A Fong Mei Sow does the books just as well and just as fast as you. She's one of the few people I know I can trust too. Without someone to keep track of the bills and invoices, we'd get clogged up with such a backlog that it'd cost me hundreds of dollars a day. You understand, Ting An. I know I can rely on you to handle the old lady gingerly."

With that remark, Gwei Chang strolled briskly over to a group of men awaiting their orders. Every day, the old man told Ting An what to think and do, and any other day, Ting An did it without thinking. But today, he felt severed. Today, he stared after Gwei Chang's receding back as if he were seeing a stranger for the first time. He thinks he knows me, thought Ting An. It's always a big mistake, his face turned a dark, angry red, when you think you know somebody. Why the hell, he suddenly flashed, does everyone have the notion that I can always handle people?

Loongan pulled the wagon up to the front of the three-storey brown frame house on the hill and stopped automatically. The day was already quite light, the shadows erased by the high clouds. Ting An hopped off and hesitated for a few seconds, blinking up at the last few vaporous streaks of fog flitting about in the air like shredded souls. Then, as if some unknown force had grabbed him by the front of his shirt, pulling him through the gate and around the side of the house, he found himself on the back porch, cringing, at the screen door. He knocked, removed his slouch hat, and stepped back down the steps, not relishing an encounter with Mui Lan.

Mui Lan hated him. And the reason had always been a bit obscure. When Choy Fuk and Mui Lan had first arrived in Salt Water City, she had persevered at establishing a friendship between the two teen-aged boys. She had fed Ting An beside her own boy, dressed him in Choy Fuk's old clothes, and treated him like a long lost son. Ting An, who had never before been the object of such maternal love, couldn't have been more fascinated than if she had suddenly begun to chew his food for him. Some mothers love their babies so much, they lick the snot out of their noses. Of course by the time young Ting An fell for it, Mui Lan had very mysteriously cooled in her exaggerated affections for him. Then one day, she swept him out with the debris.

He started thinking about her talonlike eyes piercing into him. She'd stand there, lizard lips tightly set, silent except for the disdain screaming out her every pore. Under any other circumstances, he'd play a cocky role in front of her. Cigarette stuck to his lips, flapping as he answered back with something like, "Lo Yeh's say-so." Usually that was enough to make her comply, but today, he was fully prepared to lose the battle. If she yelled out, "You go die! What, you trying to catch a pig? I'm not going to fall for that!" he'd probably turn around and leave quietly.

However, instead of Mui Lan's dour face staring at him as he had expected, Ting An looked up to find Fong Mei's comely smile beaming down on him. She opened the screen door with a delighted squeal, stretched out her arms, and threw herself at him. Caught by surprise, he toppled back onto the dew-drenched grass and rolled into the raspberry canes denuded by winter. She on top of him, smothering him with her soap-scented kisses.

Ting An was too overwhelmed to move, but Fong Mei sprang to her feet and pulled him into the Wongs' kitchen with surprising strength. She backed him up against the wall and held him hostage, eagerly pressing against him. His head still reeling from the shock of this welcome, he fell back onto a calendar tacked to the wall with a nail. Everybody had apparently been too busy to tear off the previous month, already long passed. It still decorated the household with a maudlin image of a ghost-boy beneath a huge, resplendent umbrella, mooning in total adoration of his ghost-girl love. On top, fat winged cherubs danced, floating in the air, cheekily testing for raindrops. The curly, golden-haired girl looked out at the prosperous kitchen with its ultramodern refrigerator, and half-smiled knowingly.

"You've been hiding from me. You haven't changed your mind since the last time we met, have you?" Fong Mei asked, unable to contain the eagerness of the question.

"Where's the old lady?" Ting An managed to puff out, his breath locked within his chest.

"Gone already!" Fong Mei snuggled closer to him. She started to unbutton his jacket, hoping to slip her arms completely around him. He knew he would have no more resistance left if she succeeded. He took hold of each slim wrist and held her back. Persisting, she stood on her tiptoes and rubbed her soft lips against the nape of his neck. With his head thrown back, he closed his eyes to enjoy the sensation of her velvety tongue roaming over his stretched neck. She was ravenous, wanting to touch everything at once. Caught up in her frenzy, he felt every pore in his body wanting to open up to her, his soul to be laid bare. Then, in spite of the hazards everywhere, he let himself sink, his wobbly knees opening up to her, and they both slid to the floor together.

IV

Ties to the Land—A Ticket Out

K A E

1986

Ever since I can remember, I've been plagued with the feeling that something was going on that I didn't know about. It drove me a little crazy! Now I wonder if that was what drove me, period! When I was little, I refused to go to sleep because I had to stay up to wait for . . . it, I guess! An event or whatever! A visitation? Oh please, yes—just a few words, and things around us would become clear. Why be so stingy! There could be a definite purpose to human existence. We could have meaning to our lives. What good is a soul, without gods and goddesses hovering about us?

As often as I could, I remained vigilant, curled up very small on our chesterfield, hoping that I'd be overlooked by Bo Mo at bedtime. I watched my father prepare his lectures for the next day as he did every evening. And my mother composed her music and played the piano as she did every evening, until I got very sleepy!

Now at thirty-six, I'm still waiting. In fact, the feeling is even stronger. I am obsessed by it. "It" makes me restless. I roam around my house and peer out of windows. I am quite uncertain as to what I need to see between the blind slats which hide and hold me in. Obviously not a visitation! I know that, but why is it so hard to get answers to questions I've been asking all my life?

The street scene in front of our house is clean and green. The occasional little old lady with a walking stick strolls by, but this doesn't placate me. I also know by now that people are almost never what they seem. Some take longer than others to reveal themselves; some a whole lifetime; some never—they have that much to hide.

My arms fold across my chest. My toes dig into my hand-knotted carpet. And my mind stretches over our little city lot, fifty feet wide, one hundred and forty feet long, from corner to corner to corner to corner. I build a mental fence around it, visualizing the high-voltage electricity fairly crackling off it, not just to ward off evil but to fry it dead.

I switch on the TV and plow through the channels. When I do not find what I want to find, I meander through the house until I find myself in the nursery where my three-week-old infant lies sleeping, his tiny mouth sucking continuously on sweet dreams of my milk. Only the odd, very rare person will expose herself totally, and only when she's become totally vulnerable, backed against a corner. What's the point of hiding herself then? She'd only look childish hiding under a chair, hoping people wouldn't be able to see her.

I stand beside the crib and watch my baby breathe. This morning, his father finally had to go back to the office. Why, I interrogated him, was he so anxious to go back to work at this crucial time in our son's life? Henry, my husband, peered at me over the metal rims of his glasses as he drank tap water and ate Oreo cookies for his breakfast. Why didn't I agree to some hired help, he asked. Was I sure I could handle everything by myself? He doubted me. I flew into a livid snit. What would I need with hired help, I insisted. I was not totally witless, was I? Then, I went back to bed in a huff. There, I worried endlessly. After I heard the door slam, I nearly panicked and called him back. I was truly alone for the first time in three weeks, perhaps for the first time in my entire life.

I am so afraid of being found out for the coward I am. All my life, I've managed to mask it with ambition and diligence. Making it as an investment research analyst for a small though influential canadian holding firm was easy. As long as I guessed right, I was in; if not, out! Read a lot! Know what to do with what you've read!

And never, never reveal your "in" in the market. And I have made it. My newest job offer waiting for me proves that I am no flash in the pan. A prestigious research position with the Howe Institute would mean no more scrambling. No more cocktail chitchat, which I despise! I've always preferred the basic things in life. Wear navy maternity business suits to shove and bull and bear in. Wool-silk, tailored; be self-conscious! Be the token, pregnant, ethnic woman; act cool, powdered, inhuman. I never lost my perspective in the business world. It was as two-dimensional as computer print-out.

My private life is what I find confusing. At home, I must work at unravelling knots—knots in my hair, knots in my stomach. Knots of guilt; knots of indecision. Knots in our dainty gold chains. Figurative knots in our children's shoelaces. Do not panic lest we get more tangled! We must pick, trace, coax and cajole each knot out. One at a time, even when we know there are hundreds more.

I realize I am very hungry, so I go to the kitchen and make my-self a peanut butter sandwich, because it is the only thing I crave. I open a bottle of beer. My aunties told me that while I'm breast-feeding I should consume as much alcohol as I can stand, implying that most women sip their drinks with their noses scrinched up and leave most of it behind. I, on the other hand, am glad of a prim ex-cuse for drinking. However, I do microwave the beer to warm it up. They told me never to drink cold. And not to even put my hands in cold water while establishing my milk! In the old days, chinese women and their babies weren't allowed to take a bath or leave the house until after the full-month celebrations.

"So what if they got a little fishy smelling," my aunt exclaimed when I deprecated her story with my western attitudes, "that's the way they healed."

They were right! I tried to go out for a walk. And I stuck my hands in cold water. These sent raw chills and shivers right through me to the tips of my nipples, and left me so full of wind that I had to chase it away with another thick, black, brewed help-ing of raw vinegar, sweet chinese cooking wine and pickled pigs' feet. I haven't challenged any more traditions since.

The baby squawks. I drop crumbs running to his side. He is about to rouse. Although it takes him five full minutes, I stand and watch it all, the soft mews to begin with, the restless squirming. I am fascinated by the rabid intensity of his rage and passion. Before all else, human beings have rage. Heart-piercing screams! Little red face knotted up with pain and anguish. I pick him up by his armpits and dangle him at eye level. His bullet-shaped head shrivels into his tiny body like a spent penis.

Lo and behold, wet yellow stains between his stubby legs. And in his crib, the brand new balloon-print sheets, with matching shams and bumper pads, are full of babyshit, painted on by restless knee strokes. I freeze. With Henry at home, this would be a major emergency that keeps the both of us running. Now, I am on my own, facing a true test of matter over mind, no matter how toilet-trained the mind.

In my vocation, one tends to accrue the most ridiculous of vanities like Hong Kong business luncheons (known to last three days and three nights) and leather limousine seats (cushioning against harsher realities). I remember not long after I started with Peters, Harley and Miika Investments, they landed a really big asian account. Naturally, my bosses figured out that it would be comely if a nice-looking chinese junior sat beside one of the senior partners at the meeting. I arrived in Hong Kong, lagging a modest number of steps behind my boss and discreetly sizing up the racially integrated sea of male faces, when who should I spot but Hermia Chow draped over a chair, against the sky-scraping window which swept around one side of the room like an IMAX movie screen. Her slim legs intertwined; her luscious lips pressed against one long finger in a gesture that suggested silence on my part would clearly be in order. And that was how the Hong Kong market opened up for me. Hermia set me up. I could have been a senior partner in a matter of a few years. I could have become an overseas consultant, cavorting about, in and out of Asia.

In any case, I walked out of that meeting, flirting with the boys, a couple of steps ahead of Harley himself. And oh, the good times with Hermia! She took us to a private club in a garden so lush and luxurious that they drove guests to their tables in vintage cars—ours being a 1959 Porsche Speedster. Hermia's a riot!

Now imagine giving up this kind of thing to face one little bare bottom out of that neverending swarm of humanity being born every day; I must have either been crazy or hoping to attain more enlightenment or something. I think back now and wonder why I never did totally succumb to Hermia's very enticing lure.

However, I now know just how it feels to sit with the new mumsies in the hospital, slurping up a baby bath demonstration. They perched tenderly on their chairs in a polite semicircle, with their full-length velour housecoats and acrylic mules. They all beamed with confidence and seemed to know something spiritually uplifting. I would flap around in mules too, but those answers, I found out, don't come easy.

However, back to the poop! I spin around, looking for something to wrap Bobby in. There is nothing except a fine, hand-stitched satin coverlet in his crib. This I grab and recklessly wrap him in it, clinging onto him as tightly as I can, but his froglike legs wildly kick and can't be contained. By now he is screaming so piercingly neither my heart nor my ears can take any more. I have no choice except to put him down and close the door.

Bringing up baby is not as easy as I thought, and I head to the telephone. Before I dial, I test my voice out loud against any indications of distress, any hints of quavering. I guess if one translates literally, what the old-timers called the telephone in their village dialect is "crying line." Their lives full of misadventure, they only used the telephone to declare tragedy or blight.

"Good morning, Mother!" Cheerful! The message would be that everything is normal. "So glad to catch you home . . ." I would affect a slightly bored, arrogant note, "Oh, baby's fine. He's so cute and adorable." Then a casual aside, "Coming to see him?"

Instead, my fingers are so shaky I have to dial three times, and then, I practically sing out, "Hi Mom. I'm glad you're still home . . ."

"We're coming right over," my mother cuts in, then she hangs up. My life is rosy again, my heart opening like a thirsty flower to the soothing rain. How my mother evokes this in me, I will probably never know.

I watch my mother's Buick sedan pull up beside the boulevard in front of my house. As the daughter of a rich man, my mother, Beatrice Li Ying Wong, was once described as "a clever girl who's sharp enough to see the other three corners as soon as you describe the first to her."

Today, she regally glides into my home and pecks me lightly on the cheek. She smells like new clothes. Her generation of women still wear wool skirts, classic George Straith cardigans and the humble two-inch pump. They still show a bit of calf. And they still like to distinguish themselves in front of the counter at pâtisseries, or in grey Mercedes purring in front of stoplights just off Point Grey Road. This elusive sisterhood of those who have made it, usually by marrying into it. And the more money, the more righteous!

When my mother stands by me, things begin to happen. The baby becomes sweet and small and darling again, instead of something which looms large and threatening. My muscles, tense from what seems to be yet another neverending marathon of life, smooth out under her artistic hands.

"All I want to do is cuddle a baby," says Beatrice right away. This I must intepret too. She means I need you as much as you need me, my darling daughter. By her clothes, I know she's in a modern mood today, and jaunty too. I like my mother. And I've often wondered if this means I am like my mother, elegantly restrained, capable, thick peppery hair, quick lithe walk, expressive face, easily taken aback. She has this defensive habit of carrying her head too high, thus her eyes tend to look down on whomever she is talking to. I notice she will do this subtly, even if she has to strain her neck backwards to accommodate a person taller than herself. And not many people are not taller than her, so there's a certain vulnerability displayed here. Today, I am so grateful for her presence that for a change I find this a charming trait.

She was once Miss Chinatown, 1942. I used to think much of this and kept pressing her for information until she became an-

noyed. Finally, she blasted me with the truth. She was chosen because of patronage, because she was the granddaughter of Wong
Gwei Chang. Besides, how many chinese girls could afford piano
lessons in those days? I remember how indignant I became, not at
the iniquity of the patronage but at her for telling me this. Ten
years old is not a good age to dash a young girl's dreams of becoming a publicly acclaimed beauty. It never made me any less superfi-
cial, just more cynical.

Oh, and behind her, carrying the heavy bundles, comes my
other mother, Seto Chi. She is my mother's housekeeper, also
dreamkeeper and protectress; my mother's barker. When Chi
stands behind me, I am confident someone is always there to hold
out a hand in case I falter.

Suddenly, my whole household is transformed. Peace and
serenity descend. A feminine order takes charge; a hearthlike
warmth alights. Magic. Chi sniffs around the crumbs and sticky
rings in the kitchen. To the clatter of pots and pans, I go back to
bed for a much-needed nap.

Chi, my old nanny, was the only one who could finally chase
me into bed, relying on her folksy, peasant image to cut through
the nonessentials. As a (trans)parent, she established an intractable
reference point for power between the two of us right from the
start. She had all, and I had none. Simple and also quite elegant, if
you think about it.

"What! This late and still not in bed! What are you waiting for,
you silly little chicken?" she used to scold. By age four, I should
have realized that it wasn't wise to argue with Bo Mo (the chinese
name for nanny), but who is wise at four years old?

"I'm waiting for things to happen, Bo Mo!" I remember pleading with my big brown eyes, wide-set and winsome.

"Nothing's going to happen!" She'd scoop me up in her big,
strong arms and trundle me off to bed.

"Lots of things can happen. You know?" I was positive she did,
clinging onto her neck, pressing my little face against her big pock-
marked one. I knew she had a tender heart beneath the jagged
edges, and sometimes these cloying techniques worked. Up close,
I touched her enormous, thick lips, which she said made her face

an unlucky one. They sagged heavily and dragged her face down when she relaxed. When she was incensed though, she could use these to good advantage, sneering with a good long snaky twist, meanly.

She'd plant me between the cool linen sheets, tucking me in like a tree sapling. There, I felt like an incubating egg, with a long time to go before I would hatch. Chi was very good at incubating, especially if she thought it was for the good of my moral fibre.

"Dream ghosts will come for you though," she'd begin abruptly, with a hiss which could shrivel backbones until they snapped—the way all good incubus stories begin. "Especially when little farts like you are busy being naughty, like when they try to keep their tired eyes open instead of shutting them tight! Dream ghosts will creep up from behind, and quicker than a wink, they'll grab hold of those eyeballs. Once they've dug into the fleshy parts, they'll shake and pound and screech and never let go! That's what people call a nightmare. People nightmare themselves! However, if you close your eyes peaceably and obediently, then they'll only be able to get in as far as your nose. There, they just tickle like ginger ale bubbles."

"How do you know this?" I'd ask, hoping to prolong the human contact before the dark gathered, the lonely night that seemed to yawn ominously and stretch forever.

"People from China just know!" She'd matter of factly close my bedroom door.

So I was very let down when I found out that Chi didn't come from China any more than I did.

In a way, she wasn't even pure chinese (as if that were important), and she had learned her chineseness from my mother, which added tremendously to my confusion. All my life I saw double. All I ever wanted was authenticity; meanwhile, the people around me wore two-faced masks, and they played their lifelong roles to artistic perfection. No wonder no one writes family sagas any more!

Although Chi was not very inclined to explain herself, I on the other hand was forever being asked to explain who she was, why she was. And out spewed this same story every time, a little too apologetically, a little too contemptuously.

SETO CHI

Chi was born in Malaya in 1927. Her father, the only son left alive of a decaying, dynastic, overseas chinese family with a floundering oil business. Chi was the first-born and perhaps such a disappointment that Chi's mother immediately rushed to the nearest and dearest monkey temple. There, she sought out a fortune teller, who told her that first-born daughters bring bad luck and that this daughter in particular would only worsen her father's poor finances. The fortune teller told Chi's mother to give her baby away. The stupid woman, obviously a grasping villain, sold her instead.

Happily, Chi was adopted by a kind hindu diplomat and his good wife, who had five sons but not one daughter. They were middling well-off. The wife was a simple woman. And Chi grew up hindu, without any hardships.

Unhappily, because middle-echelon government officials are always the most vulnerable in political upheavals, when Malaysia started to give way to the japanese invasion, these wonderful people lost everything. The father died a grievous death; the rest of the family were just lucky enough to escape with their lives, managing to emigrate to Canada with what was left of their diplomatic impunity.

The family tearfully split up to find employment where they could. Chi came to Vancouver with one brother. The mother and two brothers moved out to Saskatchewan, where they operated a Texaco garage on a long lonely stretch of the TransCanada for years.

Chi has apparently always been a little at odds with her environment. My mother, Beatrice, and her brother, John, first met her at high school—a big-boned, poorly dressed girl with an oxlike head, a flat moonlike face and a very large mouth. Her features seemed unmistakably chinese, but she had a long, well-oiled single braid down her back, she smelled of curry, and she barely spoke english at all except with a thick tamil accent. Her toes stuck out of a pair of torn sandals although it was October, albeit a warm October.

Of course, she was the object of much scorn and derision. East Vancouver wartime youths not being the most big-hearted and open-minded about the cultural diversity they called "chinks, japs, wops, and hindoos!" Uncle John wasn't much better. He called her the ugliest toad he had ever seen.

Chi probably wouldn't have stayed even one day longer in that high school if it hadn't been for my mom, who stepped up to her in the schoolyard and looked her up and down very carefully. In those days, ladies' fashions were subdued with what they called ww II utilities. Bea, a senior and always immaculately dressed, wore a simple princess-line frock with white appliqués and harebell buttons, fluffy white bobby sox and saddleshoes. Her hair tightly permed and pulled back with a big ribbon. Pinned to her chest, a mandatory button which shouted "China" (vs. jap) to the satisfaction of current social exigencies.

Finally, after some hesitation, Bea asked Chi, "Would you like to use some of my new perfume?"

Although they didn't have a thing in common, Chi and Bea became inseparable after that. Chi was a rare oddity and seemed profoundly happy to stay umbilically attached to my mother. Like a hatchling, Chi must have had to imprint immediately lest she get misplaced again—maybe permanently. Following an instinct for survival in a hostile situation, she had to assume an identity, preferably one which would nurture her back.

It wasn't as though Chi didn't have a mind of her own. In fact, she had an iron-strong will. It was just that, from the moment they laid eyes on each other, Chi existed totally for my mother. In the *Pinocchio* movie I dragged her to when I was five, the fairy touched the wooden boy with her glitter, and he sprang to life, ready to serve. Yet, even that wooden boy eventually got enough street-smarts to look after number one, didn't he? As for Chi, she has always been there to turn the pages as my mother played on and on.

Chi never married or thought to have children of her own body. She always treated me like a pet poodle, making sure I didn't clash with my mother's outfits. And she must have thought of my father as a kind of medicine which Beatrice had to take, even though some men are poison.

In my more reflective moods, I'd imagine that, for Chi, my mother was an unmet commitment that haunted her from a past life; but maybe it's simply that every Tonto has to have his Lone Ranger. Or even better, every Lone Ranger, his Tonto!

Strong string is threaded through the tiny pierced ears of a little ceramic urn to tie down its cover. As it simmers in the middle of a pot of boiling water on my gas range, the peculiar aroma of a herbal wine and beef concoction, intended to build up my blood, wafts over to me as I raise my head off my pillow.

Chi is standing over me. She is scowling with supreme disapproval, the soiled quilt that I had tried to hide in the closet in her crooked old hands.

"This is no way to treat an expensive gift," she hisses at me. "A fine punch in the gut for the guy who so nicely went out and paid good money for this. It's ruined, eh!"

"I know . . . I'm sorry," I say unconvincingly. "Where's Mom?" I ask, hoping to change the subject.

"Still in the sunroom with the baby," replies Chi. "Now, I don't know if I should let you stomp all over me and wash this by hand. Or should I just leave it for you to lug to the dry cleaners . . . my hands being what they are! Look, stiff as a corpse . . . and ache like the devil!"

"Leave it, Bo Mo!" I say too abruptly. "I can do it myself."

"Oh, you can, can you?" She throws me one of her most spiteful faces. "At least your mother is honest about being totally useless. She was openly bred to be a princess! So were you, except I guess it's fashionable these days to conceal it!"

I glare at her with all my might, as indignant as a four-year-old, all the more offended knowing that her words are true. Oh, but what's the sense of staying angry at your mother? It's soon puffed out like a disagreeable bout of gas. Besides, I of all people should know better than to hide my mistakes in the closet. Everything, especially the mistakes, it seems, will come right back to you.

"Hey Bo Mo . . . guess what!" I sit bolt upright in bed and pull her down. "Mother finally told me the whole story."

O

"When?" She fakes a hurt indifference, holding up the quilt to survey the stained landscape.

"In the hospital, the same day Bobby was born. She cried a lot."

My mind slips back to the memory of my mother in the hospital, sitting on the edge of a plastic chair like a scrunched-up piece of paper. Her face crinkled with tears, shoulders knotted together. Telling a lousy story that should have been thrown into the wastepaper basket a long time ago.

"It seems," she began, "that both your father and I come from rather dubious parentage . . ."

One born out of infidelity, the other of mercenary intrigue; as for myself, I was tainted with incest. And listen, I got away easy! I prefer Chi's version of the story. With Chi, there is no discussion; reality is what it is. Very imperfect, like our perception of it.

"Does she still cry about it?" Chi sighs, full of worried concern. "Lots of old wounds there."

"Chi, I want to know the real truth!" I announce, each word highlighted against the fluorescent daylight.

"No you don't," Chi whips back, "you want to hear about smut, and the guilt. And who is to blame for the little lost babies . . ."

In mid-sentence, Chi stops because the same idea occurs to both of us at the same time. Lost babies grow up, whether in this lifetime or the next, and perhaps they find themselves. And when they do, they come back with those little-gotten-big baby urges, looking for those who had lost them to begin with.

Two babies were born in 1926. With them sprang new hope and fresh beginnings, as symbolized by the red tissue wrapped around coins, which were then eagerly pressed into their blankets, or the red-dyed eggs lovingly rolled all over the infants' heads. And the women at the first-month celebrations somehow chanted in a peculiar destiny for them too. This destiny would watch over them and make them my mother and father against much odds.

BABIES

1926

The waitress had a beautiful baby boy in Lillooet, British Columbia, delivered in an isolated cabin by a white midwife who was pleased with the ease of the delivery. And the mother who bore her pain with silence and stoicism confirmed the midwife's prejudice that chinese are a capital breed. She had plenty of energy left over to be complimentary and solicitous, grinning from ear to ear at the tall, dark man whom she naturally thought was the father. Like most new fathers, his face drooped with humility and awe when she tenderly placed the baby into his arms. She'd seen it so many times before. Then perhaps a tiny hand, on its furtive way to the mouth, would break loose from the blankets, to create an effect of exquisite wonder on the whole paternal being.

"A Song-ah," asked the father in a muted voice, "maybe we should keep him ourselves?" The midwife was blissfully unaware of the conversation. She folded her hands together, a graceful gesture that indicated her work was finally done, now that she had delivered the infant safely into the proper hands.

"Pay her first! We can talk after she leaves," said the waitress. She was nervous of outsiders, afraid they might witness the storm that had been gathering clouds on the edge of their domestic calm, as if Mui Lan might blow through the door at any given moment.

About four months later, Fong Mei had a premature but robust baby girl, delivered by a qualified midwife and physician team in the unheard-of luxury of a lying-in hospital. It turned out to be a good thing that Mui Lan had had several unlucky dreams about the baby "being born not quite right" as she put it, because she then convinced everyone that a western doctor standing by would be worth the extra expense. So when it did become a long, trying labour and Fong Mei had to be transferred to the Immaculate Sisters of Grace Hospital, at least everyone was able to nervously reassure each other that mother and precious baby were in capable hands.

Of course, the new baby consumed Fong Mei, and she liked the idea of a sanitary western hospital at first, because she knew the baby would be out of Mui Lan's ever-grasping reach. But soon the austere rules of a foreign hospital came between her and her baby as well. She had felt less a prisoner when she was detained at the immigration station. After two weeks of confinement, she came home a very nervous, high-strung woman, so any spark at all could have sent her into a fiery rage. Yet fierceness, whether she was conscious of it or not, was exactly the artillery she needed to do battle with her mother-in-law in order to usurp the throne.

And Fong Mei certainly would upset the order of this house; her rage demanded it. From now on, things would be done her way. Never, never again would Mui Lan bring her to her knees.

Little things had become intolerable even before the child was born. Fong Mei had begun to brazenly disobey. More and more hostilities had erupted. One day the exaggerated belligerence with which Fong Mei was cleaning and gutting a wriggling fish on the chopping block offended her mother-in-law, who might have had some buddhist superstitions.

"Knock it over the head first," Mui Lan commanded, "right between the eyes!"

Fong Mei ignored her and took another vicious swipe at the fish, its juices splattering the walls and counter.

"Why don't you do as I say!" she insisted out of hurt pride.

"It'll be juicier my way!" Fong Mei sneered back.

"Black-hearted bitch!" muttered the elder woman, who stomped out of the kitchen and headed straight for her son.

"I tell you she enjoyed it! Watch yourself in bed with her!" she complained to him. Choy Fuk said nothing.

Fong Mei produced only a girl, who, tiny as she was, gave her mother enough armnipotence to vie for power and launch a full-fledged mutiny (as one can do only from deep within the ranks). First, Fong Mei learned to drive a car; next, she took her share in the family business and turned it into the most lucrative one of all—real estate. Then there was still that matter of Choy Fuk's son out in the swamp somewhere. Fong Mei didn't say so in actual words—but she gave strong indicators to her mother-in-law that she would tear her to bits if she ever dared to bring that baby home.

Not that Mui Lan ever had a chance either. When she showed up at the cabin in Lillooet to claim the waitress's baby, she found the waitress and her son nervously agreeing with each other that the baby boy should stay with his nursing mother yet a little while longer, until Fong Mei Sow was able to take care of another child, Fong Mei Sow's constitution being feverish and weak then. What could Mui Lan say to that? She was also surprised and a little disturbed that the baby had already been named Keeman without consulting her. But what could she do about that?

Fong Mei also spent much of her time chastising her mother-in-law to her husband, with a mouth as bitter as bitter melon. "And another thing, you're already the laughingstock of Chinatown. Let your slut keep her little bastard! If that old bag makes any more fuss, you'll both have to answer to Lo Yeh personally. That baby doesn't belong to her, just like she doesn't deserve my daughter either. Because of all the trouble you've both caused, the Wong name is shit—you savvy that!"

Fong Mei drove this point home again and again, if only to shift blame away from herself.

Mui Lan fought back via her son. "How can she say that! I was right to do what I did! Every family has to have its offspring. But two together, I don't know whether to laugh or cry!" She was genuinely bewildered. Not having foreseen this twist of events, she could only assume that the waitress had uncorked her son's juices somehow. "Isn't that the way of the gods though. Five years without a sprout, then this year doublefold good fortune!"

Throughout the years, whenever the issue popped up, Mui Lan came back with the same counterattack. "You're a selfish and black-hearted bitch; it was right that you should have taken it in! He's Lo Yeh's grandson, Choy Fuk's son, and therefore your son too. You don't care about this family's name. All you care about is yourself!" But she was no longer a formidable opponent—not even a force to consider.

Fong Mei had two more children, including the coveted boy, my uncle John, but his appearance was just a formality. He wasn't my grandmother's favourite, not because of all that he symbolized to her. She just preferred the girls, not that he lacked affection. He was called, and I still like to call him, "the golden boy." Maybe it was a hard name to live with, but we all know how chinese love their descriptives.

The waitress married the gambler. Mui Lan got deposed. And Choy Fuk kept his mouth shut. So, one could say that life marched on. But what about all the hidden entanglements—the corrosive mess underneath, which eventually would make the bottom fall out? Well, except for one little story that happened right after my grandmother had my mother, the rest may be just embellished speculation.

This story was told to me by Morgan Wong. How he came to know it, and why this particular incident endured, I don't know. But I believe it is true, because my mother still has the teak chest— not very good quality—decorated with plum blossoms and phoenixes, a romantic scene of a scholar with his maiden-love carved in relief, except the maiden's face is a bit lopsided.

S T O R Y

1926

Fong Mei needed more room for the baby's clothes and things, so she had a dresser moved upstairs from the basement. Mui Lan objected, mainly out of contrariness, muttering about "wind and water" and whatever village superstitions she could excavate out of memory, but she grumpily accepted the change in situation.

When Fong Mei came to put the baby's things away, she felt the dresser was not good enough for them. She said that the wood stank, and she found mice droppings in the bottom corner. The baby's clothes had to be put in the cleanest place possible, so she started to empty her teak hope chest of the last remnants of the silks and brocades and fancy embroidered pillowcases that were a part of her dowry. When Mui Lan realized what she was doing, she attacked her daughter-in-law, drowning her in a deluge of putrid accusations. Everything from her unlucky eyebrows, to her laziness, to her failure to produce a boy—all of which was contributing to the ruin of the Wong clan—was mentioned at a very high-pitched shriek. Mui Lan became so overwrought that she came to blows.

Fong Mei doggedly kept on emptying the hope chest, dropping its contents on the floor, out the window, until she reached the bottom. There, she found a pair of brand-new scissors, which she had bought in Canton City. All these long years, she had totally forgotten about them, and they were still wrapped in paper with the shop's name on it, as if waiting for this precise moment when she would finally need them. These she picked up with a rather deliberate gesture, then turned threateningly to her torturer. Mui Lan took fright and flight. She almost made it out of the bedroom, but Fong Mei dragged her back with the strength of ten madwomen.

Realizing that she had made herself very vulnerable, Mui Lan took refuge in a corner while Fong Mei fingered the sharp, pointed blades like a well-fed cat toying with a cornered mouse. An intense pressure surrounded them and made the room expand and shrink wildly. Fong Mei got up and sliced her and her husband's bed quilt neatly in half. At this bit of profanity, her mother-in-law said not one word. They stayed in this position until the baby started to cry, wanting to be fed. Then Fong Mei dropped the scissors with a heavy thud and went to her child.

Poor Fong Mei! For her, it was very poetic and very true that
> Yesterday's dreams are empty drawers,
> littered with mice turds!

HERMIA

1971

My face was a little lopsided after I bounced my head off the wall. I was amazed but not amused. The noise of the impact was so loud it echoed down the vast empty halls of the An Men district middle school, which I was visiting with a group of twenty-five foreign students who would spend their summer touring and working in the countryside. For a long, dangling moment, Hermia thought I had really hurt myself. Our official chinese hosts immediately crowded around me to fuss and show their concern. Hermia started to giggle, and so did I.

Could I have been not concentrating that much as to walk into the underside of a huge staircase? Hermia teased me by saying that travel was like that. One had to have the presence of mind to negotiate unfamiliar pathways. So, where was I?

I was thinking about something else, obviously. I had been saying to Hermia, "I know I love melodramas, but this is beginning to sound like nonstop hysteria."

Then Hermia said something that sent me into total introspection. She said, "If you were a little child, desperately trying to cling to somebody who refuses to nurture you, you would get quite hysterical too."

"What are you talking about?" I asked. "I'm talking about my grandmother and great-grandmother at each other's throats. They were grown women." I rubbed the tender new egg on my forehead.

"Grown women are orphan children, are we not? We have been broken from our mother's arms too soon and made to cling to a man's world—which refuses to accept us—as best we can, any how we can. And of course, let me tell you, many of us are just barely hanging on by the skin of our teeth."

Hermia eyed the commune leader, whose village we had been assigned to. Comrade Zhou had already singled us out, as though he could spot the troublemakers a mile away. She turned back to me and added, "I don't have to tell you this. Kae, your chinamen stories are about, how shall I say—trying to fit in any way we can.

Next, Hermia's pretty eyes settled on Bo Ming, who was an overgrown, overseas chinese boy from Japan, intent on watching females. He was obviously very taken with Hermia. He grinned from ear to ear.

"Sweetie, why don't you write about women trying to fit in any how they can do it?"

"Who? Me? Why me?" I replied. "I'm going into economics. Why don't you?"

"Because, *chérie,*" drawled Hermia, "I am not the one who walks into walls."

That night, at the commune, we could not sleep because of the sweltering heat. Hermia and I had been relegated to an airless room with one door facing a tiny, boxed-in courtyard. Because the chinese tend to play favouritism despite other claims, Bo Ming got lovely, breezy sleeping quarters, facing the western plains, probably because his father was an important dignitary. Hermia simply decided that Bo Ming's room was big enough for three of us; it being after liberation and all. We didn't mean to oust him, as we were trying to explain to Comrade Zhou the next morning. I guess we did embarrass Bo Ming a little. He didn't want to leave his spacious room for a closet full of mosquitoes, but he knew he couldn't sleep with us unless he could produce a marriage certificate or something like that. He did mumble something about keeping (did he say his or our) reputation. But, as we emphatically told Comrade Zhou, he wanted to go. Bo Ming came to our rescue by stating that he did indeed want the smaller room. Of course, Hermia and I were ever so solicitous of Bo Ming after that, looking after his every little whim whenever we could.

Comrade Zhou very patiently told us that our thinking was not right. I think he was trying to tell us to be more patient and more loyal, although I wasn't sure to what! He couldn't complain about our work though. Being young and strong, Hermia and I both got something out of our re-education-through-labour program, although I'm quite sure it wasn't more loyalty.

BEATRICE LI YING WONG
1939

In 1938, my mother, Beatrice, was sent to one of the best British-run young ladies' finishing academies in Hong Kong. She and her younger brother, John Soon Him, went to stay with Ai Goo Mah, her great auntie, Gwei Chang's elder sister. At the time my mother was barely thirteen, but my grandmother doted on her and was quite unabashedly preparing her for a prestigious marriage. By then Fong Mei had money and a very fine sense of herself; listening to her talk, any one of the great Shanghai banking or textile "hundred surnames" would have done. So what if they didn't speak the same village dialect!

She used to say that there was absolutely no future for Beatrice, John and Suzanne in Vancouver, growing up dark-skinned and as wild as indians in this backwater settlement. She herself was too busy with business to tend to them. And, of course, who could argue that there were few opportunities at all for chinese here? However, the truth was that Fong Mei had always been ten-parts nervous about the smallness and the intimacy of Tang People's Street. Her plan was to eventually transplant Beatrice, John and Suzanne back into China.

Unluckily, even before a year had passed, Beatrice and John were back in Vancouver. Beatrice was once again the undisputed belle of Chinatown. In fact, she hadn't even missed one Chinatown Freemasons' picnic, held every summer at Lumberman's Arch in Stanley Park.

"Those pesky, troublesome little japanese 'turnip heads' have been making so much trouble in northern China," Fong Mei explained at the picnic, her leaf-shaped fan flapping. "Now they've gotten so far south they're starting to make the Hong Kong business cliques nervous."

Actually, China, including many loyal overseas chinese, had already declared full-fledged war on Japan in 1937. Fong Mei, having participated in enough auxiliary women's volunteer war efforts, should have realized this.

"But who would have thought they'd get so far south?" exclaimed my mother's mother, whose singular pursuit of happiness for her three children had left her perception of history in the making somewhat distorted. However, she had money to hide behind, and often that was what really counted. The women around her in their flowered dresses nodded sympathetically.

Suddenly, her fan stopped. Fong Mei's eyes darkened, although she was careful to keep her face smooth and smiling for the sake of the ladies in the shade of the bushes. She reached into her straw bag for her sunglasses; these she put on the high bridge of her nose with such elegance that it must have been a pleasure for her companions to behold. Stretching her slim neck, she asked, "Isn't that the Woo boy that Beatrice is with?"

All of the women's faces turned to trace her gaze. Far away in the shimmering heat, on the far side of the green expanse, two figures broke away from the tight huddle of their children. A tiny speck of a white dress followed close behind a boy in dark clothes—too dark for the glaring heat really!

"Ahh yes, that's Keeman all right. I can tell by that pair of hand-me-down pants," someone confirmed.

"He's a smart boy! Came in first in his class again. Won that ten-dollar prize that people made such a fuss about." The conversation veered so easily.

"Isn't that a shame! Some people are so mean. Imagine trying to keep the prize away from the boy when he earned it fair and square. And such a poor boy too—patched knees, mended elbows."

"This is it. They don't like to treat tang people like human beings."

"Well, they say his teacher put her job on the line for him." People kept crowding into the conversation.

"I'm not saying they're all like that but . . ."

"Keeman delivers groceries for me. When he's working, there's never any trouble with the customers."

People soon lost sight of the two children, but sharp-eyed Fong Mei never did. She remained silent, brooding. She had hoped that Beatrice would have matured more, but obviously not enough. A year abroad was not enough, especially when Fong Mei had been hoping for a whole lifetime.

Oh, that stupid war, she thought. And that stupid boy, her afterthought.

Keeman Woo finally stopped at a small tree where he had parked his bicycle, but he didn't turn around because he knew Beatrice would be right behind. He stared over Burrard Inlet at the smoky blue mountains north of Vancouver. The green sea rested his eyes.

Beatrice had a chance to catch up to him. She looked hot and flustered. With a dramatic sigh, she brushed her hot-iron curls to one side. They relaxed from the moisture on her forehead.

"Why are you mad at me?" asked Beatrice.

"You've changed since you've come back. Who wants to hear about servants and dumb stuff like how rich your relatives are? I'm going swimming . . . by myself!" retorted her friend since Mon Keang kindergarten.

"They haven't even gotten to the ice cream yet," offered Beatrice.

"Naw, don't want any!"

"Want me to save you some?"

"You can't save ice cream!" he said wryly.

"Can I come? You can double me?" she asked hopefully.

"What about your mom? She'll get mad as a hornet!" Keeman watched as she clasped her hands behind her back, a worried look on her face. The soft material of her dress drew back with her arms and delineated the pair of small buds on her chest. She had changed in more than one way, and these changes confused him; he felt torn between wanting to stay and wanting to run as far away as he could. They both glanced nervously over her shoulder at the group of pastel ladies watching them from a great distance.

"Yes, I guess . . ." Bea had to agree, but she looked so crushed that Keeman relented a little.

"Well, I'll probably be back in time for some ice cream."

"Will you run the three-legged relay with me too?"

"Nope, don't want to lose!"

"Please!"

"Maybe." The boy rode away on his old bicycle, hopefully out-fitted with new white-walled balloon tires. It was really too tall for him, and he had to lean his body dangerously far over both sides of the crossbar in order to ride it.

Beatrice watched Keeman acrobatically swerve onto the sea-walk and disappear behind the granite wall. Behind her, she could hear high-pitched baby shrieks gaining on her. She turned and saw a troupe of little girl messengers racing towards her, their crinolines flashing, pink bows bouncing, baby blue sashes trailing.

"Bea Bea," they mimicked. Beatrice hated it when her mother called her Bea Bea in front of others. It sounded like "baby" in chinese.

"Bea Bea," they squealed with delight, "your mommy's calling you, Bea Bea." They yanked at her hands, all wanting to be twirled around and around on the grassy slopes, until they dizzied, tottered and fell.

With Keeman off pouting, Beatrice had no other choice but to wander back to her mother and sit with the other ladies. There, she was so beautifully demure when they plied her with compliments and attention that Fong Mei herself almost squirmed with admiration.

"A Bea-ah, we've heard that you've become quite the lady since you've come back from Hong Kong."

Beatrice smiled as politely as she could, knowing her mother would soon take over the reins of the conversation. Sure enough!

"Well, if there weren't all this trouble," her mother stepped in, "we would have all gone back to the village for a visit. I haven't seen my elder sister in so long. And it's getting more difficult to go back these days. All that talk of bandits and soldiers roaming the countryside! Have you been finding it more difficult to send money home? I find myself having to bother Lo Yeh more and more about it these days . . . "

Left to herself in the middle of a crowd, Beatrice wondered how Keeman could have thought she had changed. In fact, she had changed little. Instead of cultivating sociability, she had only solidified her inborn solitude. She'd always had this dreamy quality about her and maintained as thin a relationship to the world around her as she could get away with. In Hong Kong, this had been even easier for young Beatrice to do. Away from her overbearing mother and grandmother for the first time, in her great aunt's prim house on "the hilltop," as they say in Hong Kong, she had been more or less on her own. Her great auntie was the export half of her grandfather's flourishing import business across the ocean; Beatrice and John were pampered like royal offspring.

In the mornings, when Beatrice awoke, a tiny porcelain teacup of fragrant tea stood waiting on a lacquered tray beside her bed. Slippers miraculously appeared before her feet. Polished shoes whenever she expressed a wish to go outside. Pretty umbrellas to keep her skin pale. Curtains and blinds drawn by unseen forces. Dirty towels left in a heap no longer drew criticism but were simply replaced by clean on the rack. Fresh linen every day. White cotton blouses starched and ready for school. Food in bowls came; dirty empties went. How long could it be before the inevitable happened?

One night, she dreamt that her hands and feet dissolved; the next night, her arms and legs as well. Then her trunk. Finally, everything, until she was nothing more substantial than a puff of smoke. Instead of running up and down the halls and stairs whose black lacquered floors, glossed with a purplish undertone, stretched into a gleaming infinity, she floated. She was not awed by this alteration. She felt comforted and happy that this world had especially opened up for her. Around her, the woodwork glowed, the glass shone, the mirrors reflected lightness. She played in a courtyard so cared-for that not one dead leaf dared to rear its ugly, parched self on any rim of the ceramic planters neatly displayed row upon row. The floor tiles, symmetrical perfection, sent her into a mesmeric trance. Bird cages glittered in the sunlight, their kaleidoscopic coloured contents fat and happily chirping, well-loved, innocent of the ways of a harsher life. In this museumlike poignancy, she could have stood forever. Her legs never tired because she had none.

Versions of this dream kept repeating, until one day she awoke and realized that this was the home she was destined to escape to. No, not an oriental palace filled with antiques and baubles! Material concerns could not have mattered to Beatrice. Big house, small, here or there; these details were incidental. Her house had to be an ethereal realm; she needed to build spiritual perfection around herself.

Beatrice came from a home where two incredibly strong-willed women had fought over her since the day she was conceived. While the two battling titans trampled the household to pieces, Beatrice got used to doing things quietly, her own way. As soon as she became illuminated in Hong Kong, she turned towards the clear blue horizon and never looked back. With her usual elegance, she let her mind simply float away. She forgot there was anything else, like a stroke victim whose left side of the brain forgets that the right side ever existed. Oh, but the goddesses were good to her! They gave her lots of wind to fly by. Privilege would always be Beatrice's divine right because she had no concept of mediocrity, neither her own nor the rest of the world's.

Mother never understood poverty, not even when she married a poor man. Convenient perhaps, but she could not grasp the reality of underwear greying with use and time. She would always need someone else to fret over the petty details of our human condition. My mother was an *artiste*. Eternal beauty and exaltation became the only qualities which could be valid for her. Along with her meandering music, eurhythmy would be her sole dedication to her intimate little world. Towards that esoteric end, she was given first Chi, then my dad, and finally me, to do the mundane, oftentimes trying tasks like picking up the pieces.

Fancy words to excuse my mother's helplessness. As a child, I used to look up from my play when the music stopped, to watch her at the piano. And there, behind her shut eyelids, was a kind of insanity—sometimes bleak but also full of creativity and possibilities. I knew she was happiest there, in that faraway place she had finally escaped to.

Funny how I can still get protective of the women in my family, how I can give them all sorts of excuses for their littering. In the telling of their stories, I get sucked into criticizing their actions, but how can I allow my grandmother and great-grandmother to stay maligned? Perhaps, as Hermia suggested, they were ungrounded women, living with displaced chinamen, and everyone trapped by circumstances. I prefer to romanticize them as a lineage of women with passion and fierceness in their veins. In each of their woman-hating worlds, each did what she could. If there is a simple truth beneath their survival stories, then it must be that women's lives, being what they are, are linked together. Mother to daughter, sister to sister. Sooner or later, we get lost or separated from each other; then we have a bigger chance of falling into the same holes over and over again. Then again, we may find each other, and together, we may be able to form a bridge over the abyss.

"I was there when her mother first tore her heart in half," Chi once said protectively, of Bea, to me. "And I was there when Sue took the other half."

"So were you, I guess," she generously included me afterwards. And I thought, at the very least, Chi and Bea will be eternally loyal to each other.

And who's Sue? Suzie was my aunt, who died with the final irony—the last male Wong child.

BEATRICE AND KEEMAN
1946

At twenty years old, most couples right after the war would have been married already, but Beatrice and Keeman wouldn't have married as young as they did if their families with their hysterical antics hadn't forced them into it. They would have been just as happy to maintain a platonic relationship—she from her big house high up on a hill, he from a run-down one on Georgia Street. They were like that, meeting in some heavenly headspace as only a math whiz and a classical pianist could do.

News of their timid engagement resulted in Beatrice's mother fighting with her grandmother, one screaming and fainting, then the other screaming and fainting all over again. And the way they both descended on Beatrice's dad was terrible to behold! Her grandfather had already passed on, thank goodness, before he could witness the screeching all the way out onto the street. Astonished onlookers stared at Fong Mei wielding a shotgun, grappling with her son, John, who was trying to get it away from her. There's still a ragged hole up there, just under the eaves, from when the gun went off. Of course, the roof's been repaired and the scandal patched over since. She was determined to go down to Chinatown to put a hole into Keeman's mother's head. Her husband cowering inside the house, sweating it out!

Naturally, Mrs. Woo wouldn't have anything to do with the Wongs either.

"Son, don't go near her any more! Her whole family's cracked in the head." She never knew how close she came to getting cracked in the head herself. "Go find somebody else."

A sound piece of advice, but twenty years too late. And how could he find somebody else anyway? There was such a meagre number of young people—no new immigrant blood. What few there were, were native-born. Since 1923 the Chinese Exclusion Act had taken its heavy toll. The rapidly diminishing chinese-canadian community had withdrawn into itself, ripe for incest.

In 1946, Keeman had just come home from overseas, and he wanted only peace in the world and a quiet environment in which to go on to his doctoral degree. He came back a survivor, a WW II veteran—a man of the world, because he had become an expert on the dehumanizing experience of war, and terror, and despair. He had been a part of the wanton technological genocide that humankind had finally consolidated into history. Back home, this qualified him for compensation, so that he and men like him could rebuild their ruptured lives the best they could.

Chinatown welcomed its returning war heroes with as much gusto and fanfare as any small town. They wanted to validate them as individuals again, precious because each young man was an important part of their small-town lives. Not a nameless death, diminished even more by that vast desolation over there. Chinatown would have given Keeman anything to show their eternal gratitude. He chose wisely. He claimed the love that had matured out his childhood with Beatrice. And she consented to an engagement with him by strolling up the street in Chinatown with him, hand in hand. The more modern of the young people were starting to engage themselves. They stopped and chatted with a few of the shopkeepers who were sweeping their portion of sidewalk clean. People were ecstatically pleased with the fairy tale—a warrior-hero and a beautiful princess. It even made the local newspaper a few days later. Of course, the darker side of the story stayed in the dark, privy to family members only.

On the way back home that evening, Beatrice and Keeman, their hands still pressed palm to palm, fingers tightly interlaced, stopped in at Chi's brother's house, to tell Chi first. They lingered a few hours and listened to CBC radio broadcasts on Chi's brother's upright Vitrola. They all had lots of time for leisure, since Chi had been laid off from her job at the Mac & Blo sawmill on Marine Drive. The three friends made a tranquil scene in the living room, content just to be with each other.

"I wish I could have frozen the three of us right then and there," remarked Chi. "Bea would have like that too. We all could have stayed fresh, and dreamy, and in love forever and ever. The perfect ending for your mother. If I had known, I wouldn't have let her go home that night."

After a program of Beethoven's forested symphony, Keeman and Beatrice left in a hurry because Beatrice began to get quite anxious about telling her family.

Unexpectedly, that very same evening, Bea was back at Chi's home again. The left side of her face terribly swollen and bruised with red-hot finger-shaped welts from her mother's right hand. Her eyelids puffed out like overripe apricots. Chi had to get out of bed to answer the banging at the back door. When she opened it, Beatrice fell into her surprised arms and sobbed like her insides were coming out. Chi reached for the leftover popcorn bowl, thinking that she was about to throw up.

"Mother slapped me," was all Chi could get out of her for the longest time.

Beatrice shivered out of control as Chi guided her up the stairs, to her bedroom. Chi peeled off her sopping wet dress, stockings and underwear.

"My mother's . . . never . . . never . . ." Beatrice stuttered as Chi sat her down on the bed and threw a quilt over her quivering shoulders. Then Chi went to get a towel for her wet hair.

"No one's ever hit me in my entire life!" she wailed afresh, as Chi rubbed and blew on her cold white hands and hugged her as tightly as she could. Finally, Chi urged her to lie down, under the covers, and climbed in close beside her.

As Chi held her, Bea told the whole story. ". . . And the terrible things she said. I can't believe them. Oh Chi! . . . Oh Chi! I can't ever go home again. I can't bear to face her."

All night they whispered, and she wept. ". . . I wish I were dead. Where have I got to go now? You know, I almost passed out on the train tracks on my way over here. I tripped over them because it was too dark to see. I should have just lain there until a train came. She said that . . . she said that Keeman's my father's bastard son!"

FONG MEI
1946

Shocked, Fong Mei couldn't believe what she had just done! She looked first at her mother-in-law, who was swaying and clutching onto the doorjamb, then she stared vacantly at her youngest daughter cowering and sobbing in the farthest corner. In the background, she was dimly aware of Beatrice clattering out the door, down the porch. The glass in the front door rattling. In front of her eyes, the image of fear on her baby's face still swam, after Fong Mei had slapped with all her might, again and again, wanting to kill. Her beautiful Bea, her first-born! Yes, she would rather see her dead.

"You could see that I've always hated him. Why him?" she hissed at her surprised daughter. "Didn't I ever count for anything?" Year after year of tightly knotted lies—what she had had to endure. All that she had worked so hard to avoid. She would not have it destroyed. Blind rage consumed her. She kept striking out. Her daughter's soft, tear-streaked face, so compliant, so sweet and dumb, round and so unsuspecting. She suddenly hated it with all her heart, enough to blot it out of her life forever.

This fateful evening had started out with an electrical storm—

flash lightning, followed by booming thunder and a heavy downpour. As was his habit, Choy Fuk, before parking his Buick Roadmaster in the garage, let his wife and mother out near the back porch. Mui Lan went on ahead, but Fong Mei stood for a few minutes on the wet driveway, listening for the studied notes of a Chopin nocturne. But the house was dark and obviously empty. Beatrice must have gone out. And without the eldest at home, the two younger ones would have weaseled out of their evening routines in a flash. Feeling piqued, she waited for Choy Fuk as he came up the walkway to express her dissatisfaction.

"I told her to call us at the store if she was planning to go out. Her little sister is still too young to be left on her own," she said, her breath steamy against the damp night air. "I don't know what's gotten into her. She's going out all the time now!"

That was a nervous lie on Fong Mei's part. She knew all too well that Keeman Woo was back in town. She just didn't want to spell disaster out loud. Who wants to wreak havoc on themselves?

Suddenly, a bicycle whizzed by, and a familiar bell tinkled at them.

"Hi Mom! Hi Dad!" their third sang out to them from the dark. "Turn on the porch light when you get in, will you please, Mom?"

Choy Fuk watched the unhappiness evaporate from his wife's face, just as he'd seen it broaden with pure bliss countless times before, whenever she spotted any one of her children.

"A Suzie-ah," she scolded the girl with plenty of indulgence in her voice, "what are you up to, bicycling in the dark and rain?"

To Choy Fuk, she ordered, "Hurry up! Turn on the porch light! And go boil water in the kettle for hot cocoa!"

Fong Mei waited by the door to hug her daughter. At least one is back, she thought to herself. When Suzie finally bounced into the big kitchen, her mother clasped her cheeks and stroked them gently.

"Aie, how chilled you are! Where were you, my pet?"

"I was just standing on the corner, talking to Judith and Lily. I saw you drive in. I would have asked them to come in, but you don't like them, do you?" Suzie pouted most effectively.

"The less you see of those white girls, the better off you'll be. They don't make good friends. Just be polite enough to get along with them at school!" Fong Mei said out of habit, fingering one of the young girl's braids. "You've lost another ribbon."

Suzanne Bo Syang Wong fairly bloomed with pubescent charm. She had the same clear features as her older sister, and she was already taller. Many people would claim she was in fact more beautiful than Beatrice because her demeanour was more coquettish. Where her sister was a bit too serious and aloof, Suzie was a bit too free and easy, the way she moved a teensy bit too fluid.

When she spotted her father, she sprang at him from behind and flung her arms around his waist. Choy Fuk chuckled and chided, "Well, let me at least take off my coat, you little monkey!" Like Fong Mei, he particularly doted on the youngest one. She was after all the last one for them.

"Now, tell your mother where your elder brother and sister are. She's very worried about them." He touched his index finger to her forehead, a gesture as stern as Choy Fuk ever got with his children.

"John's over at the Dart Foon Club. And I'm never, never going to tell you where Bea Bea's gone. Never, ever, cross my heart and hope to die!" The twelve-year-old girl broke into a dance around the kitchen table, her braids flipping back and forth, as she shook her head.

"Now don't be silly," Fong Mei demanded and grabbed one of her arms, "and tell me!"

"She's gone off with our soldier boy, Mummy. And they were holding hands. I saw them." The girl slipped out of her mother's stunned grasp and ran off.

Choy Fuk tried to sneak out of the kitchen too, the kettle blasting like a siren, but not before he suffered the full impact of Fong Mei's deadly scowl aimed at him from across the room.

Fong Mei made enough hot cocoa for everyone and left it to keep warm on the stove. Then she went upstairs to sit in the dark of her room and to wait for Beatrice to come home. But old memories came to visit instead.

In 1926, Choy Fuk's whore must have been five months gone before she confirmed her pregnancy to him or his mother. In actuality, she didn't have to open her mouth at all. Mui Lan seemed to know already, and strangely enough she remained calm. In fact Fong Mei remembered that time to be the calmest she had ever experienced in the Wong household. Choy Fuk was calm, and Lo Yeh was, as always, away. More importantly, she herself was in love and living a splendid dream.

Every day she flitted about, looking radiant, as if in full bloom. She could feel her body lighten, soften. Where it had been silent before, it began pulsating the most exhilarating messages to her brain. She was not aware that people were remarking upon how womanly she had become. Some even went so far as to suggest this to her mother-in-law, who reinforced their observations with some of her own creations, such as how picky an eater her daughter-in-law had become, how she'd been needing more time off on her own, probably to rest. Ironically, Fong Mei seemed to be doing all the right things, for a change, and Mui Lan had suddenly become very protective of her. And she'd been losing a little weight, didn't they think?

"Of course, to begin with," people smiled, "of course." Of course, nobody would bother to discuss this openly with the daughter-in-law herself.

Fong Mei was well aware of what her mother-in-law was whispering into every ear she could bend, but she just didn't care any more. Let Mui Lan think that she had everything carefully mapped out, that she knew exactly how to manage people! Let people draw their own conclusions. They're all so clever—for now!

In fact, the waitress was too slim for her time. Soon enough though, Mui Lan would be sending her away. She'd already had Choy Fuk make all the secret arrangements. And soon after her, Mui Lan, with Fong Mei by her side, would be going up to supposedly see about one of their stores in around Lillooet. Mui Lan told everyone in Chinatown that Gwei Chang had talked about selling it for a long time. Of course, it could be inconvenient with Fong Mei's health the way it was, but if all went well (and from one peasant woman to another, why shouldn't it?) they'd be back in plenty of time.

She would change the story afterward. She would take all the blame of overestimating "A Mei Mei's" capabilities. Fong Mei would supposedly fall ill. Then they'd have to stay because they were warned against travel until after the baby came. By then, it would be winter, and such a trip would be far too hazardous for a newborn infant. Since they were already nicely settled in a cozy house up there, with Choy Fuk running in with supplies and out with what Mui Lan told him to report, why not stay until the baby was stronger? This way, the waitress's baby could be easily passed off as Fong Mei's when they got back to Chinatown.

Mui Lan had no qualms about being lashed together in a lonely cabin with two desperate women—one who was being forced to give up her infant, and the other one who was being forced to take it in. But then, why should she? She was the matriarch, and she considered them both daughters-in-law.

On the day of departure, their trip was interrupted. Ting An was the driver, with Mui Lan packed between him and Fong Mei. Much preparation and planning had gone into this automobile journey. Gwei Chang was only too happy when Mui Lan suggested to him that Fong Mei needed some kind of woman's holiday. Not only was he a lenient man, but he was the first to "leave women alone to be women." Mui Lan was the one who fussed endlessly over this and that. She made a great display about Choy Fuk having to stay behind, as though the whole business would fall apart without him as overseer. Actually, Gwei Chang's ever-expanding business would just idle in neutral for a while, at least until Ting An came back; and he was just supposed to drive them and stay long enough to see if the Lillooet store could be sold. No one in the cab of the truck spoke except for Mui Lan barking out orders. They didn't get as far as New Westminster before Fong Mei was vomiting so much they had to stop.

Fong Mei felt no shame, retching and gagging, grovelling in the dust. This was the last time she would ever grovel. Mui Lan, angered, stared down at this female inconvenience on the side of the gravel road, and kept insisting that they continue on their way. Ting An stubbornly refused, saying he didn't want to take the risk of dirtying his truck.

In the middle of the argument that followed, Fong Mei blurted out that she might not be able to go on, that she had missed her moon. Mui Lan didn't believe her right away. She stared at Fong Mei, unable to refocus on what to do next. Was it true or ploy? She looked ahead; the road was wooded, unfamiliar. She couldn't have foreseen this one.

If Fong Mei hadn't been as sick as she truly was, she would have laughed with glee, watching her mother-in-law topple, a wrench thrown into her works. Anyway, whatever Mui Lan decided in the end had little consequence; Fong Mei's accomplice, whether he knew he was or not, was already turning the truck around, carefully avoiding the soft shoulders of the road.

How unfair to make Fong Mei reflect on her infidelity twenty years after such a simple fact! If one were to argue her case at the gates of heaven, one could say that she had not been at all disloyal to her husband and lord. Three beautifully behaved children who had brought nothing but delight and distinction to their parents and grandparents certainly could not be used to condemn their mother. And how shameless a hussy was she, with this unwholesome fate soon to be hoisted upon her? She being a young women in perfect health, and as such no doubt vulnerable to the droplets of male potency found teeming in the air from the sneezes of so many overanxious bachelors around her.

She might not be innocent of infidelity, but Fong Mei's kind of infidelity had come about innocently enough. At any rate, at the time she had had very little time to consider her deed—or misdeed, depending on one's point of view.

Fong Mei's pregnancy saved her from unnecessary travel (or should I say travesty) in the nick of time. It also saved baby Keeman from what probably would have turned out to be an unhappy and bewildering childhood. It supported his mother's decision to keep him. Imagine the battle the waitress would have had with Mui Lan otherwise. And it definitely enhanced Choy Fuk's mangy—oops, sorry, manly—reputation. He surely must have guessed, but he didn't say anything. Last but not least, it left Mui Lan in a bit of a dilemma—in fact, hanging by the skin of her teeth, one might say, for many, many years—but everyone had invested too heavily in their own little secrets to ever have mercy on her!

After Keeman was born, Mui Lan tried again and again to stake her claim over him as her rightful grandson, bearing gifts and toys and promises of an inheritance. Time and time again, the waitress-woman rejected her. Mui Lan threatened and cajoled and tried to pay, until finally her efforts culminated in an ear-splitting fight right after the waitress married the gambler. Keeman was the most beautiful, robust four-year-old boy by then. Ever since then, the two women hadn't even looked at each other. Not even when their little ones graduated from the one and only Chinatown kindergarten; at their high-school graduation, they ignored each other with a livid passion.

When Beatrice came flying home with Keeman and news of her engagement, she had no way of knowing about the family's twisted past, nor about her mother who was intent on forgetting. She crowded Keeman and Sue together on the chesterfield and eagerly ran about the house looking for her elders—her dad missing for some reason. When she reached her mother and found her sitting alone, outlined in the darkness of her room, Bea had a fleeting thought that her mother might object. She always had objected to Keeman before, probably because he was poor. But the war was over, for goodness' sake! He was alive! Her time was now! And she loved him to the ends of the earth!

"Mother," Beatrice was quite breathless, "come down quickly. I have something wonderful to tell everyone."

Even before her eyes adjusted to the darkness, Beatrice felt the chill. An unfamiliar snarl froze her as she stepped up to the dark form of her mother.

"You get that bastard out of my house right now. I won't have him here. Dead girl-bag, how dare you bring him into my home!"

KEEMAN
1946

My father is a gentle man. He's kind and honourable; on many matters, he's also a bit dim-witted. No imagination whatsoever! I suspect that it was this quality in particular which saved my parents' love for each other, led them through the rank sewers which threatened to flood their lives. With his steadfast strength, they endured until they were able to climb out, quite unsullied.

When Beatrice left him in the parlor, he very patiently submitted himself to Suzie's, and her grandmother's, scrutiny. Suzie's giggles were easy to read, but the old woman stared at him so hard that he got quite unnerved. He found he couldn't look at her; the most he could manage was a couple of glances in her direction to make sure she wasn't actually stone.

Being a hometown boy, Keeman had never left home before except to go die in the war. There, he had learned to always expect the unexpected. So when Fong Mei came screaming down the stairs, with Beatrice totally distraught trying to hold her back, Keeman stood up and put his cap neatly down on his seat. Maybe this was the way that mothers acted when their daughters got engaged. Having survived the war, he thought that he had seen the worst—until he looked deep into Fong Mei's eyes and saw the deadliest fury and hate there. That he was apparently the source of all this distress shocked him.

Here was Beatrice's mother, who, as far back as he could remember, had never acknowledged his presence, screaming at him to get out. He looked to Beatrice, who kept pleading with her, asking over and over, "What is it, Mother? Tell me what's wrong!"

Then Fong Mei came up to him and tried to shove him out of the room. But he just stood there clumsily and waited to see what Beatrice would do. He was aware of the roomful of addled women, quite beside themselves, multiplied, bumping into each other. There was confusion; he knew he was under attack, but he couldn't pinpoint the enemy.

Before he could sum it all up, Beatrice took his arm and told him that he had better leave.

"No," he said. He wouldn't leave her.

"But you're only making things worse here."

He had to agree, so he said he would wait for her outside.

"No, please go home," she begged. He could see that she was ashamed, crying so hard his heart felt torn. She pushed him out into the pouring rain.

Keeman would always regret that he had hung around long enough to get soaked but not quite long enough to see Beatrice flee from her home.

Early next morning, Chi sent word to Keeman, and he went to get Beatrice, then he escorted her all the way up to the front gate of her house. It was a hard thing to do, even for a ww ii veteran, he being just as confused as she was. He ignored Fong Mei, who stood and wept on the big front porch, aching to have her daughter home with her again. While she waited, shivering from the cold, or trembling with remorse, he held Beatrice back for a moment longer.

He said, "You don't ever have to go back in there. I can take you away right now."

Bea said, "It's O.K. I'll be all right. My mother and I have to talk. I'll see you later!" She smiled nervously.

Still reluctant to let her go, he added, "I'll wait out here a little while longer, just in case." For a split second, his eyes met Fong Mei's. Even with the sun in his eyes and she far away in the shadows, he could spot the eyes of an adversary. They had a certain glint to them that stirred dangerous reflexes in him.

"No," replied Beatrice, "you really don't have to." Behind her, as she spoke, he spotted the curtains in not one but two of the second-floor windows move deliberately. Instead of a weapon in his hands, he had Beatrice, and he had no other choice than to place his trust in her.

After patrolling the Wong premises for much longer than was necessary, Keeman decided to go straight to the horse's mouth.

"Mother," he said, "Beatrice and I seem to have a problem."

"Beatrice?" questioned his mother, raising the hoe beside her like a question mark. She had been weeding the snow peas beside her house. He still stood on the sidewalk, in his uniform. He looked very handsome and troubled. She gazed upon him, as she had always gazed upon him, ever since he could remember. Now back from the war, more than ever a look of infinite adoration and eternal gratitude that he still is—that he exists!

To Keeman, his mother looked much older, worn out. He knew his going to war had taken another huge chunk of flesh out of her. When chinese sent their sons off to war, they did not expect them back.

"Wong Li Ying," he rephrased himself.

"Oh," she sighed, "her." Suddenly, she felt very tired. Her story was also a long, trying one. Before she would begin it, she had to ask one more time.

"Son, are you very sure that it has to be her?"

Then she began. His mother was like that. She never wasted anything. She wasn't going to waste her breath until it proved to be absolutely necessary. And she wouldn't, he was certain, waste any self-pity in the telling of it.

Yet, in the end, she had to say, "Who knows for sure? It could have been him, but I'm inclined to think your real father is the right one. You look like me, you see. I haven't thought about it in years. But I remember when I used to, there was always this doubt in the back of my mind too. I used to think that it wasn't important, but now I guess it's suddenly gotten very important."

She turned her face away. In one fell swoop, she had lost all of it in front of her son. It was as if she never should have dared to hope for any bit of his love. When he was born, she had nothing to offer him. The least she could do for him was to not hinder his prospects. Left to himself, she knew Keeman would triumph. That was why she had dared keep him. She would not have let anything interfere with that promise, not even herself. However, now it seemed that she would not even be allowed that one pure wish.

She wouldn't apologize. So what if she was dismally sorry! There was nothing that she could do or say to help him.

Keeman saw things differently. She needn't apologize. She had nothing to be sorry about. That was the way things had turned out. So what if he found out about it a little late! He couldn't see humility in his mother any more than he could see humility in himself. But he did see the sadness wash softly over her features. She withdrew from him by closing her eyes as if she had a headache.

"Mother," he said quietly to draw her back to him, "don't worry! Bea and I will sort things out."

Keeman was being optimistic, of course. Beatrice and he never did sort things out; they merely married out of desperation. You see, when Keeman was finally told his mother's story, he couldn't have known that it was nowhere near the whole story.

V

Identity Crisis

MORGAN

1968

"Why don't you give up, sweetheart?" Morgan mocked a festive mood. "All talk, big deal! Why talk? What the heck, nobody's listening anyway!" He was drunk. "A story full of holes . . . no, wait! A family full of assholes . . ." he giggled, "assholes plugged with little secrets!"

We were both drinking in a New York eastside bar. We had been there a long time. Even after more drinks than I'd ever had, Morgan was still looking pretty disgusting to me, his face askew, wrapped around his own inner misery, sentimental tears drying on his thin lashes. Clinging onto the bar for dear life, he couldn't see me.

I'd driven three thousand miles, six days of speedometer fatigue, to sit on barstools with him, filthy cavelike arches over us. Dejected, I sipped out of fear. The way he fell on that bottle terrified me. Like the ancients who fell on their swords, he aimed the booze straight for his heart. A day later, we fought. Then I left him for dead in that dead city-arena. Sped out of that scene in my little red Mustang time capsule, but not until he wounded me, sabotaged me for life, because I loved him. Wore my little old heart on my sleeve for him to burn cigarette holes into. After I'd told him my most precious secret.

"So you wanna be a writer," his lips smeared with venom. "What for? That's not very pristine chinese! Remember, if nobody speaks of it, then it never existed. Damn clever, those chinese. Like I don't exist. Never have, have I? Damn clever, our sly little Beatrice mommy!"

Not long after our car accident, Morgan had told me he was going to San Francisco, but maybe even that proved too close to home. From there, he headed back to Columbia University, which was where he had come from when I met him. How easy to say that once he got away from home he lost what little sense of identity he had and went downhill! But if the truth be known, he worked hard at getting lost. He wrote me twice. The first time was a long, dramatic apology; the second a postcard with handwriting sprawled downward.

My father had bought me a car as a graduation present. He wanted to buy me a new, '68 Mustang, but I chose the red '64 and a half on the car lot instead. Even as early as then, I was able to recognize a good investment. It was a beautiful little machine, and I knew my father would take good care of it. I wrote my heart out to Morgan. I didn't know that he wouldn't take care of it. His to have and to hold, and to shred. Suzie had been seventeen, same age as me.

That was how I landed up in New York. One day, I was looking at my one ninety-four horsepowered pumpkin, gleaming and waxed, its bath water still steaming off the driveway, thinking about the long, hot, empty summer. Thinking about university in the fall. Thinking about going out to find a summer job that would look good on my résumé. I got in and backed it out of the driveway.

Driving it out on the open highway was such a pleasure, I discovered sheer ecstasy in the car's hypnotic rhythm of freedom. It was like something unthrottled in my head, and the vehicle flew through space that wasn't distance and didn't matter any more. The TransCanada a satin ribbon trance. It beckoned me on and on.

Wait a minute! I went back to my bank, then I went home, left Chi (my parents were in H.K.) a daring note that said I would phone from wherever I was going to be that evening, sneaked some things out, and then started on my journey to find the elusive Morgan.

I don't know how much of Morgan I found left in the stewed carcass I met, but at the end of my quest I found somebody else in my place. Somebody who was more enduring than I, more inquisitive, even when the truth stung. Somebody who could log the thoughts I didn't even know I had in me. Somebody powerful, who had stood alone on the edge of a great expansive wheat field, with the morning sun at her back, watching a new rising, a new life roll hill upon hill in from infinity. Weeping as wave after wave of sweet-scented wind blew crisp and clean through my soul.

I grew up suddenly, and I was only gone for just over a week and a weekend. Driven, mostly. But that little venture, which Chi still refers to as the time I ran away, changed my life. I had managed one small glimpse into what it was like to release one's being, to let it slip into the other realm where all the senses explode. And that was enough to set me off on a lifetime quest for more of the same.

The rising heat of the pavement during a NYC hot spell dried up the odour of mildew in Morgan's apartment. I was afraid of cockroaches, so he propped up the boxspring on four folding chairs. Precarious for making love, especially the way Morgan made love to me, in desperation, grinding against me as though he wanted to punish himself. Then again and again, as if he couldn't be satisfied. I fell asleep, exhausted by his turbulence. I woke up, my energy drained by the mere grasp of his hands around my midriff. Those weary eyes, staring relentlessly at me, haunted by Sue.

I wanted to put my hands over them and gently close them like a dead man's. I wanted to tell him that I recognized him in spite of his camouflage. We were looking for the same answers. Given half a chance, I could communicate with him and his ghosts, but he'd only be offended. And with the tension already built up, we would both end up screaming at each other, neither one listening.

"I know what you are," I hissed. "We all have our little demons! You're no different from every other egotistical mama's boy whose big wish is for people to weep for him!" I was too young, but Morgan was also too young.

"Go die!" he would mimic the chinese hatefully.

For the moment though, I let him prop his head against the outer wall of my heart and listened to yet another version of another story.

In 1949, Sue was barely fifteen, and Morgan was sixteen. And the way they met, pure destiny. At a bus stop, waiting for the Oak Street bus that never came.

"I'm going to get me a car!" Morgan declared. Lean and tough, like the black leather jacket he was wearing. He didn't exactly say this to her, but since there was no one else around she felt it would be impolite not to make some kind of reply. She was curious as well.

"What kind of car?" Her words, the beginning of the end!

And by the time her mother looked up from the entanglement that was the older daughter, it was too late to save her younger one, or herself for that matter. Their insular little world—an ivory sphere, protected by layer upon layer of filigreed lies, all revolving independently of each other, finally collapsed like a decomposing melon. Those who could cling onto the wreckage clung; those who didn't spun away into oblivion.

To her son, the waitress had finally revealed her part in the twenty-two-year-old scheme with Choy Fuk. Keeman told Beatrice, who naturally went to her mother. Fong Mei was amazed because it had never occurred to her that Keeman might not be Choy Fuk's son, but she still held Beatrice back, holding her hostage with a tenacity which could not be justified by maternal motives alone. She continued to maintain that if there were any doubts at all, then Beatrice could not marry Keeman. So Beatrice, still gangly and naive, was kept torn between Keeman's protests and her mother's hardness of heart.

Beatrice got thin—she became too weak to move, too confused to think, cried out all the time. Any other mother would have relented, but Fong Mei was immutable. She simply could not admit that Keeman might not be Choy Fuk's son without casting suspicion on her own children's patrilineage. And on that she would not give an inch! Keeman and Beatrice must absolutely never marry.

Besides, Fong Mei thought, if she could just interrupt their marriage plans long enough to get Beatrice back to the flourish and glitter of Hong Kong, that toady Keeman would soon be forgotten.

One generation between mother and daughter, and already how far apart their goals and sentiments. They shared a common experience, but while Fong Mei hated this country, which had done nothing except disqualify her, Beatrice had grown up thoroughly small-town canadian. While Beatrice hardly knew anywhere beyond the quiet streets of Vancouver, Beatrice's mother hated this pious town, which kept her bored and labouring like a poor woman. After Ting An had finally ejected her from the last bleeding shreds of his heart, she hated him too. She hated her marriage, and her mother-in-law especially. She longed to leave them all and go back home. Beatrice was once her one-way ticket out of this backhog wash, and still could be if managed correctly. What was the use of all her money if she couldn't get back to civilization? And she certainly wasn't going to leave any one of her darlings behind either. Suzie would be no problem at all, and John, who was in medical school, would have a brilliant and heroic medical career in China, of course.

However, there's an expression that pertains to Beatrice:

> You can take the girl out of Chinatown,
> but you can't take Chinatown out of the girl.

Racial prejudice helped disconnect Beatrice from the larger community outside of Chinatown. Then, the old chinamen added their two cents' worth by sneering at the canadian-born: "Not quite three, not quite four, nowhere." Everyone had a hand at drawing circles around Beatrice and telling her to stay in. But what Fong Mei did not understand about Beatrice was how fiercely loyal she was to the little circle of local-born friends left to her. Friends growing up in Chinatown were allies, necessary for survival; for those times they ventured out of "their place," and came back fractured. They nursed each other, offered each other protection; their comminuted humiliation not easily forgotten; their bonds against it sinewy and strong. Together, Beatrice and Keeman could stand firm, and keep reaching for validity. And because Fong Mei did not understand the strong tie between Beatrice and Keeman, she ultimately made the mistake of underestimating it.

Fong Mei bullied Beatrice with all of her might. In fact, by 1950, she had almost succeeded in bullying apart this almost perfect devotion between Keeman and Beatrice for four years. Also that year, Beatrice finally agreed to steam back to Hong Kong with her mother on an Empress ocean liner, naively believing she would be allowed to come back to her beloved. Luckily, like her mother when she was the same age, Beatrice was also saved from unnecessary travel in the nick of time. This time too, the reason was pregnancy.

"You and Sue were awfully young, weren't you?" My comment flung carelessly out of my thoughts. "Babies really, to have gotten into so much trouble!"

Morgan stirred, moving away from me in bed. I was surprised by his face, which could express a thousand shades of shame and confusion in a split second. Irresistibly touching! But I realized my tactless choice of words too late. His bedroom was filled with the heaviness of her ghost. She possessed us like the heat wave pressing down on us, shimmering off the cars and pavement. The din of the sidewalk clamoured through the window, along with the smell of frying grease and seared meat. All this made us perspire. I felt sickish.

"We weren't the troublemakers," he answered, immediately on the defensive, "we were just fucking around!"

But I was insistent. "I meant . . . I just wondered if you still blamed yourself, that's all. I mean, you were just a seventeen-year-old kid when this happened. And you couldn't have known very much about Suzie's family, or anything."

"Oh sweet Jesus! I have been redeemed," ejaculated Morgan. "And here, for eighteen years, I thought I had waited in vain for a member of the Wong family to come and forgive me. To pat me on the head and say, ' 'Twasn't your fault you banged up my aunt. Just don't do it again, boy!' He, he, he."

Then I clued in; I realized how much he hated me—as much as he hated himself. I thought maliciously, I know you Morgan. You're a runaway slave, with one bare foot on floating ice, the other on another chunk swirling in the opposite direction. But you like it there.

Suddenly, all the anger and disgust I had been harbouring against him came flooding out.

"You're so emotionally clueless!" I cried. "I bet you still look back and think that it was two horny kids pounding flesh!"

I could see the guilt smeared over his mouth, like a kid eating a stolen chocolate bar, but I couldn't stop myself. "What did you think? Not enough Guidance in school, right? You go right ahead and use that excuse! Blame yourself! Drink yourself to death over it!" I gloated when I added, "You didn't even scratch the surface. I don't think you knew anything about Suzie! So why bother drowning in guilt?"

It felt good being one up on him, and I didn't care that it was a creepy thing to say. Neither did I care that I didn't have a clue about what I was suggesting at the time. After an exchange of a few more colourful words, I found myself half-dressed and my suitcase half-packed, thrown out on the filthy stairwell.

That was eighteen years ago, and I haven't seen or heard from Morgan since. I know he's still alive, probably. All I can say is he sure gets nasty hangovers!

After a breakup like that, it's usually best to submerge oneself in work. In my line of work, I have learned that prosperity is an illusory thing. One can be enormously rich and still have no easy sense of it. But what is scarier—that or slipping into bankrupty in total flamboyance and ignorance?

The postwar years were very prosperous ones for my grandparents. Not that they did very badly during the war. The shipping blockade just made Choy Fuk look elsewhere to spend his tightfisted family fortune. He chose Texas long grain rice. Up until then, China rice, from China of course, was the popular staple to import. Again, due to circumstances beyond him, Choy Fuk stumbled upon a better quality, cleaner, cheaper commodity. The rest is local history.

Fong Mei and real estate didn't do too badly in the postwar years either. There was a cheap-housing boom happening, and the lure of easy money was too tempting. That was why Fong Mei hung on for four more years, when she should have refugeed out of the Wong household long before disaster caved it in. Her intuition surely must have told her to flee with her money and children right after the waitress's story collapsed one side of the crumbling walls. True, she did try to make plans to wrap up her business ventures, but she was too greedy, wasting more time trying to keep as much as the family holdings out of Mui Lan's grasp as possible. Then, in 1949, China closed—no, slammed—its doors to the west. Fong Mei never did accept this separation from her beloved sister. I like to imagine Fong Mei as this cold war cartoon character I once saw in a magazine, with no other option than to stand in front of those bamboo curtains, banging her fists on them, with what she didn't realize was an empty suitcase at her side.

BEATRICE

1950

By and by, Mui Lan came to hear about the waitress's story too. She went a bit crazy. She heaped a mountain of abuse onto the dead-boy, traitor-bitch's head. She threatened to cut Choy Fuk out of her will. That's what one does to one's own rotten flesh, isn't it? Amputate! Her pain! Her wounded pride was too painful to endure.

For two days, Mui Lan locked herself in her bedroom. Fong Mei dutifully brought in her congee and pretended to be concerned about the old lady's health, her long eyes mockingly innocent against her mother-in-law's cold, stony silence. Whenever she could, she listened intently at the door as Mui Lan whimpered into her thin gruel and moaned sporadically in her sleep. She swayed in her bed, making it creak, oftentimes a screech or two for effect. And what effect! Choy Fuk was so traumatized that even Fong Mei could take no pleasure in bullying him. He wandered about with a weird vacancy in his eyes, and Fong Mei was forced to be kind to him because she couldn't take the chance of pushing him over the edge completely. Embarrassed, the children scuttled off wherever they could. They ate at the restaurant.

In her abandonment, Mui Lan started to imagine things. She began to get suspicious. If Keeman, then who else! No, she made herself stop though. She could see for herself that her grandson John was the splitting image of Gwei Chang. It was obvious that John was his grandson. Everyone said so, but nagging doubts still bit all over and made her skin crawl until she couldn't stand any more.

One morning, they found her gone. Her royal bedroom torn apart. Clothes and photographs strewn all over. She had signed a promissory suicide note with her tears, then taken one of the cars and a hired driver to San Francisco. She vowed she would die there. Thus, the whole household was hurtled into noisy chaos.

Choy Fuk had no choice but to doggedly follow his spiteful mother and try to persuade her to come home. He knew she still had some "outside" relatives in the Chinatown there, although he suspected that, with his mother's knack for antagonism, they were a lot closer than she claimed. Under more normal circumstances, she would have avoided them like a plague of locusts. These, however, were not normal circumstances. Fong Mei thought of this crisis as an opportunity for a shopping spree. Beatrice and Sue could come too.

"You come." She spoke harshly to Beatrice, who of course felt guilty. "You started all this. You're to blame if the old bitch dies."

Actually, Fong Mei was more anxious about their future inheritance. Ever since Gwei Chang's death, Mui Lan had gripped the family fortune with an iron fist. One didn't carelessly leave a broken-hearted old money-bag just anywhere, and especially not with greedy relatives. More than that, Fong Mei was enjoying herself immensely. During times like these, she found miserly satisfaction in consorting with Choy Fuk and Mui Lan's troubles. After all, a bad relationship with the family she hated and had never felt a part of was infinitely better than no relationship at all.

"Suzanne-ah," Fong Mei said to her adored one, who could do no wrong, "you pack a few things too."

"No, Mummy," answered her prettiest favourite. "You know how carsick I get." It was true that she suffered a great deal on long car rides. "And I've got school and things. Can't I stay home? I'll cook for Johnny!"

Since Johnny was in the throes of medical school, he certainly couldn't be expected to take care of himself. Fong Mei was touched by little Suzie's thoughtfulness. It showed maturity, and she made a point of saying this to Beatrice, who kept quiet.

That evening, however, in the adjacent rooms they shared, Bea said to Sue, "Come with us, please!"

"No, I won't. And you shouldn't either! But I know you, you'll go! You do everything they tell you to do." Alone with her sister, Suzie's disguise dropped to the floor in an unkempt heap.

Beatrice paused to think about that. In her self-conscious way, she knew she gave in to her parents too much. By parents, she naturally meant her mother and her grandmother—two powerful women, like bone-crushing "Iron Chink" machines. Yet wasn't it the most sensible thing to do? She hated hysterics, especially after a whole lifetime of being made to watch their grandmother's soulless pettiness day after day, to witness their mother's terrible bitterness translated into endless bickering.

"I don't think it's very safe to leave you behind," Bea said unswervingly.

With a metamorphosis as spectacular as swift, her little sister's eyes sharpened. "You couldn't possibly be thinking of suggesting that to Mom, could you?"

To pay her back, Bea changed the subject. "And you won't even consider doing anything crazy, would you?"

Oooh, Suzie hated that word. But she was too easy for Beatrice to read—the way she gripped the railing at the foot of the bed and leaned over her sister, both arms supply pivoted, fully displaying the white undersides with their arborescent blue veins.

"I'm sure I don't know what you could possibly mean!" Suzanne's elegant contempt to the bitter end; magnificent with her chiselled neck stretched over a chopping block.

They looked alike, except one was so intact, the other scattered; one so safe, the other so dangerously suggestive.

"I mean that I don't trust you alone in this house with that Morgan what's-his-name hanging around. And you'd better promise me that you'll behave, or you can just bet that you'll be coming to San Francisco with Mom and me tomorrow!"

At this, Sue did not have a ready answer. She touched her long fingers to her lips and looked off vaguely, her eyes trailing out the dark window as though there were someone or something waiting out there. Beatrice had been undressing, and she suddenly felt menaced for no apparent reason; she didn't dare cross the room to close the window and draw the curtains. A cold dread seemed to brush against her skin.

"Suzie, will you please close that window?" she asked. "It's getting chilly."

Sue popped up and did as she was told, her face brilliantly happy again.

"Oh Bea Bea," Suzie gushed, "why do you always think the worst of people? Morgan's not at all like that. People think he's a hoodlum, but he's not."

"I don't think anything of him in particular. I've never met him, have I? I just go by what you tell me." Bea tore a hairbrush through her waved hair, a hundred-times dedication to beauty. "Did you see him today?"

"Sure! We met in the park . . . and talked. Bea Bea, you believe me, don't you? We just talk . . ." Sue didn't want to say "fool around," since it sounded childish. "Gee, the way you act, I sometimes think I'm a criminal or a mental case or something like that!"

The hand holding the hairbrush stopped against hair so black that it glowed bluish; static made it crackle in the silent room.

"I believe you, Suzanne," the voice reserved but reassuring; the voice swept out of her mouth and was lost in a great wind.

SUZANNE BO SYANG WONG
1950

I wanted to tell you how we talked, my dear sister. Just saying that Morgan and I talked was a lie, flat and purposely kept so. Because how we talked . . . but you already know that, my antimatter twin, don't you? How could you not know? After all that we've been through together! There was no escape, Sister! Our little balancing acts; two little girls, glued to a seesaw in the park by the seat of their pants! When you were up, Sister, I was down! And it made you nervous, didn't it? Your face averted, as though it had been disfigured by what you and I faced every day in this house! You must have known how Morgan and I talked. We chattered endlessly. We couldn't take our eyes off each other. We talked without speaking. And how we played on words, with ideas; we fairly frolicked over everything and everywhere. We talked as if we'd known each other a hundred years ago. Isn't that how children play? As though there wasn't ever a time when we didn't know each other?

On cold, wet days, Morgan and I huddled on benches, eavesdropping on what people said. Sometimes we'd whisper to each other, and sometimes they'd whisper to each other. Other people's lives seemed so meagre compared to the enchantment that overflowed within us.

When we got too cold, we'd go into every little shop and business we could find and look carefully over everything from plumbing joints to carnations. We didn't buy, we never repeated, and we kept track of the faces—the thin, tight lips completely powdered in, the pale glass eyes, the huge cheeky smiles.

On sunny days, we romped all over the city and delighted in the places we visited. Like the huge graveyard we found, totally deserted, high up on a hill! Perhaps from the shock of stumbling across an entire segment of the earth devoted to sweet, eternal rest, I felt drawn to this new idea of death. That day was windy; a strong breeze swept in from the horizon. It was sharply scented and had a strong cleansing effect on me. For a minute, I could almost believe it would topple all the ridiculous ideas that people had been foisting on me year after dreadful year. I couldn't help thinking that it was a continuation of a strong wind from another dimension that I could only guess at.

Then, there were days when I didn't dare play any more hooky from chinese school, and Morgan would wait for me at Maclean Park. There, we could meet for a few precious moments before dusk crept in around us. You know, Morgan never stepped into Chinatown. He crouched outside, on the fringes, parked on a park bench by the cement wading pool. There's nothing more dismal than a wading pool in the middle of a grey winter, but he was more afraid he might get mistaken for a chinaman himself.

We were hanging around one day, keeping to ourselves, when some white boys came by and called me "chink" to challenge him. Morgan tried to lure them closer for a fight.

"Come closer and say that, toilet-face!" he snarled. "I want to piss on it when it's down!" Boytalk.

They backed off, sensing Morgan's fierceness, intimidated by his good looks, shy of me.

After a few more sightings of Morgan waiting alone in the park, they skirted a little closer each time. Muscled in on a bit of territory, he on one park bench, they on another, nearby enough to brag loud and big-shot to each other. Pretty soon, they shared a cigarette, played some basketball under the ring. Morgan made friends easily. When I came along, they watched, fascinated that he would walk out of their game to be with me.

Why me, I'll never know! Morgan could have had anybody. Droves of white girls hung around him. With them, he wouldn't have to be chinese, but he said that he couldn't talk to them. That made sense to me. If he had said that they weren't his type, I would have been worried. There was a way in which he refused to be sucked in. He could see that I wouldn't play the game either. Bea, you could play their game, but I couldn't. Remember when Mom told us to smile, you used to smile the widest? Nope, for me, it was too much like selling my soul!

Morgan said that his father was dead. When did he die, I asked, but Morgan refused to talk about his father. And the strange way he said "dead" made me wonder if he had even lived. I met his mother, saw that sad, sloppy expression of hers that made Morgan bristle, then finally brittle. I saw his baby pictures in her parlour, layered with dust and grime; the whole house smothered in the same. There was a time, Morgan said, when she mustered enough energy from her hate to tear photos of his dad into a million little pieces. He didn't think it was such a good idea for me to meet his mother. But I had to. I told Morgan that I had a very good idea of who my enemies were, that I had already made up my mind to face them relentlessly and fearlessly. And part of that meant witnessing what they did to themselves, what they did to corrupt their love. He looked at me funny, but I knew he'd be my confederate.

Bea, I don't know how we got out of control. Maybe we never were in control, but we just didn't realize it. When I try to explain, it gets all distorted like the reflection from a shattered mirror. Maybe I felt too pure, too naked; like a fresh petal, too easily bruised. We finally crushed each other with this desperate need to be one. When Morgan and I met, it was like we had each finally found the piece that had been missing all our lives.

Oh this hunger, Bea! It was terrible. My dearest, honestly, we didn't know the beast was there, straining at its leash, furious in a strangled silence. I don't know why we were like that. But you do see how I couldn't have gone back to that limbo any more, not after the freedom I had taken from him? Do you know what I mean, Bea? Do you? I'm sorry, Bea Bea, I'm sorry!

KAE

1968

"Was it the wind?" I asked Chi.

"What?"

"That moaning."

Chi was looking relaxed. Her thick lips puckered over a salted melon seed. The big house on the hill had been empty for a long time before it was finally sold in 1968, which was not exactly in accordance with my grandmother's will. Haunting sounds still echoed off the long, dingy halls. Chi and I had come to look it over one last time.

The silence behind my grandmother's death was breathtaking. At that time, 1962, I was old enough to sense the numbing effect her death had on my mother. I remember visiting Poh Poh when I was very young, and even then I could feel how trapped she was as an old woman. She kept filling my mouth with sweet, sticky preserved plums, until my mother led me away. After that one glimpse, my mother never again took me along when she went to visit her.

"Maybe it's a ghost," Chi said. "They say that houses have a way of absorbing turmoil. My God, I guess this one has had enough of that." She spoke hypnotically as always, the dough of her stories ever rising slowly, tantalizingly yeasty.

It was late summer, but a grey, cold day. University in less than a week! And I could finally talk to someone about what had happened in New York. From the second-floor window, I looked down onto a few straggling raspberry canes, which had come back again through a greener patch of more recent grass. I wondered about that, about the sobbing echoes of words that should have been spoken a long time ago, but had not.

Chi said of Morgan, "So I'm not surprised that the bottle-boy is drinking himself to death!" She picked her teeth behind cupped hands. " 'Cause he never really knew what hit him. They never do, I guess. All you need to do is look at his father." She paused.

I gazed out the window. Chi stared at the room.

"And then his father's father," she added.

If hate is wounded love, then I hated Morgan for sure. And I would have nothing to do with his stories. His stories reached for his forebears, but never went beyond himself wallowing in self-pity. I thought, why should I be his tragic heroine? I could be my own consummate tragic heroine, in my own way. I could find my way in my own stories about Suzie.

I said to Chi, "Tell me about Suzie."

Chi never could pass up an opportunity like that.

"Your aunt Suzie?" sighed Chi. "Where can I begin? I guess she was desperate to break out. But this is easy to say after the fact. At the time, nobody realized how desperate she was. How can one say for sure? On one hand, she ran around with a crowd of mixed-up rich kids. Four years after the war, everything was exploding—money, population, attitudes. Maybe she had these dreams about rebel romance, and the hell with everybody else! Hollywood movies were full of that crap. You know—restless, wild and lost! Maybe Morgan was the wild rebel, and she was the only one who could love him, and their only home was in each other's arms."

Chi lined up split and sacked melon seed shells, one after another, along the window ledge.

"Don't you think you're being a bit hard on her?" I had to take the side of rebel romance.

"Maybe," admitted Chi. "Maybe she wanted to get pregnant, to get married, to get out. To this day, I'll never forget the way she waltzed into my place looking for an audience, and the breezy way she talked when she told us that she was pregnant by Morgan. I was living in a rooming house on Odlum Street, and your mom visited there with me a lot. Suzie had come straight from Candy Leung's birthday party, for chrissake! You know, the south Chinatown-in-Kerrisdale social event of the year! She was probably four or five months pregnant by then, all dressed up in taffeta bows and crinolines. It looked funny, the little miss in a tenement building that her mommy owned, pregnant. And big and obvious too! She was radiant though, like she didn't have a care in the world."

"Ugh, ugh . . . uh hem!" Chi, clearing her throat of a stray bit of the nut, had to add one more thing. "Poor kid, maybe she was crazier than a bedbug by then."

"Remember your trip to San Francisco?" Suzie looked into her big sister's open mouth and gushed. "That was when. And it was so beautiful, Bea! Our love made everything else so trivial. School,

Mom and Dad, and Granny's dumb China rules! All crud! None of that's really as important as they say. They just want to con you into the same crap they got conned into. Money, money, money! That's what they're really after. That's all they ever think about. Look at Mom! I don't want to land up like her—dried up and hateful."

"My God, Suzie, do you know what you've done?" Beatrice, horrified, yelled at Suzie's belly. "You're going to have a real live baby!"

Suzie ignored her and went on. "We had the house all to ourselves. You know, I don't ever remember being alone in that house! Mummy and Daddy sail away often enough, but Granny's always home. Anyway, when we first walked in, the house was so cosy and warm, and do you want to know what I thought?"

"It's going to be illegitimate . . ." Beatrice aghast.

"Well, I thought gee whiz, I've been going steady with this guy for more than six months and not once have we been alone together in a warm place. Sure, in the library or at a party it'd be warm, but there were people around. All the rest of the time, we'd be freezing in some park or out pounding the pavement just to keep warm. I said to him, 'We don't have to be out in the cold any more.' "

Suddenly, Beatrice broke down. Great, heaving sobs, and Suzie sat there plucking at the ruffles on her lap.

"Bea Bea, don't cry! We're going to get married." She looked almost desperate for a second, but her face quickly spread into a grin. "It was like playing house for a while," she mused. "It was funny. I asked Morgan, 'Have you tried instant coffee yet? Do you want some?' And he said, 'Is that a little like instant intimacy?' Then I asked, 'So what about a slice of chocolate cake, darling?' And he quipped back, 'A slice of the good life, of course, my sweet!' Cute eh? We were both a little nervous, I guess."

Suzie was still chortling to herself when Beatrice flew at her and grabbed her by her shoulders.

"Do you know what you've done?" she shouted at her. "You've ruined your life! How can you marry him? He's only seventeen."

Suzie twisted away, and her little cashmere wrap fell off. She rubbed the finger marks on her skin as she backed into the nearest corner. Then she started to scream too.

"You're not listening to me! You never listen to me. Do you want to know what Morgan said about our house? He's really on the ball, you know! Look at me, Big Sister," She came back and clipped her fingers under Beatrice's chin, yanking it brusquely over to face her. "He looked at the stupid knickknacks all over the place and said that we were too many females climbing all over each other, all suffocating each other. I hate it, do you hear? I hate all of you!"

Beatrice looked thunderstruck. Suzie broke down into tears.

"I want out! Out! For God's sake, let me out!" Suzie still hollering, while Beatrice held her down and hugged her the best she could. Suzie's face buried in the hollow of Beatrice's neck; both of them collapsed into a huge heap of taffeta, crinoline and gabardine plaid.

Chi said, "They clung to each other on my cracked linoleum floor, rocking, trying to keep each other from drowning. After a while, Suzie tried to whimper something. Everyone was too shaken up to even think. I couldn't figure out what she was trying to say. But Beatrice knew right away. Beatrice turned to me, and I realized too. I was sure she said, 'Help me, Bea! You're the only one who can help me.' "

"Anyway," sighed Chi in the end, "that's also the story of how your mom and dad finally got up enough nerve to register at city hall. Your mom, trying to be as cool as a cucumber, had this strange idea that she had to protect Suzie from her mother. So they got a cheap, ugly apartment in Fairview Heights, which was a white, working-class neighbourhood, as far away from Chinatown as they could manage. Then they bought an old clunker, a beat-up Nash or something. Ten years after the start of that goddamned war, and good secondhand cars were hard to come by. Anyway, without your mom's grand piano, they were

○

all moved in a day—pregnant little sister included."

"You know, I bet anything, Bea must have been surprised to find out just how easy it was to get married and finally make a stand against that mother of hers. After four years of procrastinating, nothing to it really. The hardest part was probably piling Suzie, Keeman and herself all back into that old jalopy to go back to her mother's to explain."

VI

The Writer

KAE

1986

To see one woman disintegrate is tragic, but to watch an entire house fall—that has the makings of a great chinese tragedy. I know I've had to turn my face away many times. In front of me, there is nothing to speak of except torpid text and a throbbing cursor on a black-and-white computer screen—electric shadows—but even this is too evocative of the old pain. I am afraid to look intently. I might turn to stone, petrified by the accumulated weight and un-relenting pressure of so many generations of rage. But in front of my mother, I could imagine there was something more immediate—her mother's ravaged face, manicured fingers trem-bling as they crept over her pencilled brow.

I could ask my father how it happened, because he was there, faithfully standing beside my mother. Was it a cold day? Which room were they in? Was my great-grandmother still snivelling in her room? And my grandmother! Was she happily dusting off empty suitcases, getting ready to blow the scene, when they all walked in to shatter her handiwork?

I could create another scenario, with handfuls of hair torn out by their roots, with brutal language to roil the blood, but these points of reference no longer count. And that which should be included in the final reckoning is deeply buried within my mother. She will not speak of it. Chi will speak, Morgan is all too willing to tell his version, even my father will say a few words if I ask it of him; but even after so many years, my mother still needs that margin of silence from the guilt and the pain.

Like my mother, I will speak of other times only if they were happy ones. Yes, yes, Hermia agreed wholeheartedly with me, only happy mentionables for the family record; another unspoken chinese edict among so many.

I wonder. Maybe this is a chinese-in-Canada trait, a part of the great wall of silence and invisibility we have built around us. I have a misgiving that the telling of our history is forbidden. I have violated a secret code. There is power in silence, as this is the way we have always maintained strict control against the more disturbing aspects in our human nature. But what about speaking out for a change, despite its unpredictable impact! The power of language is that it can be manipulated beyond our control, towards misunderstanding. But then again, the power of language is also in its simple honesty.

Oh Mother, Mother, tell me the truth! What did you feel when you brought your own mother to her knees? If you had to do it over again, would you? Could you have saved your sister from your mother? Or your mother from your sister! Which one, Mom?

You must have had to remind yourself over and over again that you knew this woman. She was your mother who was devoted to you, who had clung to you. Beneath her mask, you'd seen her raw desperation. And you'd even wondered what it was that drove her so relentlessly. You spoke quickly, didn't you, brusquely getting all the information out before the tears that you knew would come, came. Your timid heart shrivelling with guilt. You knew your mother could talk circles around you, so you gave her very little to hold onto. Then there was Keeman, whom you held out in front of you like a protective talisman on a chain.

I imagine that my grandmother in her cold rage might have stared right past Beatrice like she was absolutely nothing to her. I can also imagine her oh-so-calculated reply.

"Well, I only wanted the best for you . . . I worked so hard, sacrificed so much for . . . the both of you." Fong Mei glancing a blow first at Beatrice, then staring hard at Suzie. But her indignation would have gotten the better of her. She would have struck out in pain.

"But you had to sell yourself short, didn't you!" meaning Keeman.

"And that one," meaning Suzie, "she had to make herself a piece of garbage in some white devil's pig-sty bed! Who was it, you stinky slut!"

Even if Suzie had had enough guts to stammer out a name, her mother would have been too overwrought to hear. From her winged chair, in her mind, she had already conjured up a big, red-furred caucasiatic rapist. Who else would dare offend the Wong name? Sooner or later, Fong Mei would have shrieked at Suzie again.

"Who is the father of that bastard swelling your stomach?"

Sooner or later, she would have heard Suzie speak up, with Beatrice close behind.

"His name is Morgan Wong, Mummy. We're going to get married right away." Suzie thought this would surely placate her.

"His chinese name is Wong Keung Chi, Mother. His father is chinese, and his mother is french," Beatrice added on Suzie's behalf.

Fong Mei closed her eyes. There was an exaggerated silence. Both sisters watched in fascination as she staggered under the weight of their words.

What a mean writer's trick, to drag Fong Mei kicking and fighting back again, this time to face the day she had sworn everlasting love to Ting An. Especially now, when she thought she had gotten far enough away from her own days of torrid passion that they should have never caught up with her. She was young then, and she still thought she had that promise of purity to life. It wasn't until later, when the love affair ran aground and she callously abandoned ship like a sinking rat, that she stopped looking at what she had become! She often swore that he would never touch her again—in any way. When she heard of his death, she allowed herself no feelings, no thoughts other than the hope that he had not tainted her children with his obvious tendency for short life.

FONG MEI

1925

It was an isolated day of warmth in spring, during that period when her life was so bleak that her whole body ached for days on end. Fong Mei cringed on the far edge of the hard bench in Ting An's wagon as it rattled over every pothole and mud puddle on the road to the warehouse, her bones already crushed by Mui Lan's constant criticism. She felt too faint to go on.

Ting An felt a slight touch on the sleeve of his coat. He looked over at Fong Mei's drawn face, and understood right away. He drew back on the reins. She jumped down even before the wagon came to a full stop and headed towards an old tree in the middle of an empty patch of land. There were a few houses not far away; their roof tops and attic windows peeked at them from over the overgrown bushes. As Loongan edged over to the new green shoots beside the road, Ting An checked over the muddied wheels of his wagon. He was hauling a full load, and the road was unfamiliar and bad. He had to concentrate on his driving, but he knew there was another reason for his silence. Out of the corner of his eye, he had watched the young woman sink into her own silent desolation, even as she now sank onto her haunches under the shade of the tree.

When she lifted her head off the crook of her elbow and opened her eyes, she saw Ting An standing over her. He looked so humble, not quite daring to face her; his eyes wandered off in every direction except hers.

"I . . . I'm a bit tired," she lied, a little embarrassed by her lack of restraint. "This beautiful old tree suddenly reminded me of the ancient banyan tree back home. Do you know of banyan trees?"

Ting An shrugged.

"Of course, you wouldn't know. How could you?" When she lifted her eyes to look up at the branches, her silky hair cascaded back. Tears trickled along the thick hairline, which refused to absorb them, and into her ears. "I don't know why. They don't look at all alike, actually. What is this one called again?"

"Oak," said Ting An in english.

"Ook, ook," her voice trembled, "what a painful sound! Like weeping!"

Her sobbing sent waves of delicious pity coursing through his body. He leaned against the tree and immediately felt its strength, its shelter from the downpour. She need not be stranded as long as she rested in its bower, he thought.

He patiently waited until she finally cried herself out, then he solemnly asked her, "A Fong Mei, what do you need to make you whole again?"

Her reply was very solid, "A child . . ." as though she had answered this question many times, "a little family to . . . take care of."

Fong Mei felt him creep close by her side. Then he reached out for her hand; his palm flat against her palm, he lifted it up as if he were reading a precious book. A light caress; not once did his fingers close over hers.

"Then be my wife, Fong Mei," he whispered into her ear, his breath like hot mist brushing against her cold creamy skin, "because I love you and I will give you anything you want."

She closed her eyes to let herself float upwards into sun-drenched waters. Her whole body tingling at the sudden sensation of warmth; the rush of blood overwhelming. But even as she basked, her shame pulled her back down.

"I'm a used-up woman, A Ting. Another man's dirty cast-off! Old before my time! What good am I to you?" She added, as he opened his mouth to protest, "My life is finished."

"No," Ting An interrupted, "it's just finished with him! Start life over again with me!"

The urgency in his voice made her shudder in ecstasy. She,

who'd been abandoned for so long; she clamped down on his hand, because she desperately needed his touch to release the pent-up intimacy within her.

"Help me then!" she cried. "Hold me!" She was about to enter into his arms. Ting An braced himself, ready to be seized by her feverish passion. That time in the wildflowers, by the side of the road, under Loongan's munching mouth, Fong Mei tore into his body like a starved woman. Wave after frenzied wave of pure pleasure consumed her; she couldn't stop until she felt him spent inside her. And afterwards, there was more hunger.

Like the ten courses at a wedding banquet, Ting An surrendered his whole being to her. In childlike delight, he exposed his most tender parts to her alone. And Fong Mei, perhaps already a woman of the flesh, supped and drank and utterly gorged. She could not stop because she was driven by need. And yet, in the end, she never did leave her husband for Ting An.

See there, another example of the unpredictable power of language! A glib sort of statement to sum up decades of suffering out of a man's life. It especially sounds worse in reference to Ting An. On some people a few years of a bad love affair can look as dignified as a jade on their fourth finger. It enhances their appearance with a touch of luminous pathos. Unfortunately, Ting An being an orphan didn't have a secure enough framework to cordially absorb rejection, filing it away under the you-can't-win-'em-all category of his memoirs. He suffered disproportionately. Not that the unsatisfying affair left him despondent—nothing as melodramatic as all that. It merely left him without a leg to stand on, so to speak. No protection whatsoever, except for the true grit Ting An rubbed on like exterior paint, year after year. Only the two people who knew him intimately later on in life—his wife and his son—knew that his house was built on sand. He died in 1942—of drink, or so the rumour went.

Life is always tragic in the end. So I should give Ting An famous last words, like, "But what do I know of women?"

Well then, I should try to tell him. Ting An is my grandfather, after all. A poetic dirge for his soul's repose, belated. That's the advantage of fantasy that writers have at their disposal, plucked straight out of life itself. On the other hand, we also have some distinct drawbacks, like emotions shrinking and expanding between people and themselves, between people and others, between people and their stories. In writing, I feel like a drunk weaving all over the road. The air can be made wavy and warped, hot with tension, full of mirages. Or details can be made to distract extravagantly, cling possessively. Information can cringe from pain, or reply in a cold, detached manner. How many ways are there to tell stories? Let me count the ways! For example, love is a fragile subject matter, too easily corrupted, often beaten dead. Let's take an opinion poll: the many and varied ways to destroy love! Oh, come on! We should all be very good at it. It'd be fun!

FEEDING THE DEAD
1986

I could begin with Suzanne (Wouldn't you love to imagine her being interviewed on a wintry Vancouver street for the six o'clock news? Black-and-white TV. Nineteen-fifties dress. The most beautiful asian woman you've ever laid eyes on, especially knowing how invisible asians are in terms of the media.) saying: "Money."

"What can I say? She sold out to a whole generation of vipers." She might add, referring to Fong Mei, "Women who are never satisfied, who throw away happiness with both hands. And she especially had a choice of turning her back on it and going off into the sunset with the one guy she really could have learned to love. She turned her back on the wrong guy. She got scared of being with an orphan. She got scared of being another waitress. Yet, she pursued Ting An to the bitter end. I bet she never forgot him for a minute for the rest of her life. Just like how she kept on going back to her sister in China, she kept on coming back to him too. How else do you think that she could have had three of us over eight years?"

Myself: "I would say jealousy," referring to Ting An. "Keep in mind he finally dumped her out of pain. I wonder how he felt having to watch her strut in and out of his life, looking more gorgeous each time. I bet, deep inside, he burned with many furies! The abandoned child, the chinaman, tied to women, not understanding women, feeling cheated."

Beatrice (if she was willing to talk, I'm sure would respond in a brief, essential way): "Love is the most fundamental and at the same time the most exalted purpose we have in this life. You"— probably meaning Mui Lan—"can't ignore that noble principle, to breed men and women like they were cattle or pigs." Then she'd go back to her grand piano. "In fact, it's dangerous," she might add.

Chi: "Since when has that ever stopped anyone?"
  I bet Chi's answer would, as a matter of fact, be very uncharacteristic of her. "Have you ever stopped to think that love is actually impossible? Maybe it's just something which people have invented to torture themselves with. Love is elusive, doesn't translate well into reality. When you have two people in so-called love, what do you really have but two people busily trying to enslave each other? The more in love they are, the more compulsively they strip each other of dignity, self-respect, identity, until there is nothing left."

Poor, pathetic Morgan: "What are you trying to get at? You're trying to blame me! She just ups one day and slits her veins open. And it's my fault? Well, let me tell you," he screamed, "you don't know fucking shit! They drove her to it! With their filthy lies! They wouldn't let me near her," sobbing drunk. "They did it! Not me!"

One cold, dreary day in Peking, I came back to the dorm and found Hermia had packed my bag. She announced that we were both spending chinese New Year '72 in Hong Kong. New Year is the one and only annual holiday in Asia. One of the eeriest experiences in my life, seeing one of the most energetic cities in the world almost deserted and emptied of its infestation of antlike people, because in H.K. everyone with funds either joins the exodus back home to pay obeisance or goes as far away as they can get to shirk the ridiculous family rituals. We met Hermia's latest stepmother with her father at the door, on their way out "to Singapore for the holidays." I remember the shock of being confronted by a tight, gold lamé jumpsuit, platform shoes, and Cleopatra make-up under tiers of stiff black ringlets after the cultural austerity of the really chinese chinese. Hermia's father was short, stout and bald—a stereotypic sugar daddy!

"Think of love as something free of remorse and restraints," advised Hermia after they left. "No ulterior motives. Try harder, Kae! Imagine, nothing to explain; no need to justify! Genitalia coming together because it feels good. If you think real hard about it, how could something that quintessential have gotten so screwed up in people's minds?" I loved the way her brows knitted together. "I think the world's drying up!" Such an angelic face floating wet and free in her daddy's swimming pool!

"Anyway, I'm telling you this for your own good, sweetie. So you won't go on and on about it. I'd hate for people to think you're boring."

I gulp, but I'm afraid I still feel obliged to give Fong Mei the last word. (She is the dark, shrouded lady who has been lurking in the corner of a twilit room for years. My mother, myself, Chi, Sue, Hermia, my other grandmother, my two great-grandmothers—all the women wailing around a timeless circular table; we sense her presence long before she deigns to speak. She is resentful that her worldly deeds have been misunderstood. But Grandmother, aren't we all misunderstood in this life?)

Finally, Fong Mei speaks: "I was too inexperienced when these deeds were done, and I wouldn't have been able to explain them then because I didn't understand them myself. But I am speaking to you from beyond the grave. And I have had plenty of time to dwell on these matters since."

(I want a classic scenario of wailing women huddled together to "feed the dead." Lots of eerie mist. I want to make them weep from their own time periods and, at the same time, in harmony with each other.)

They all chant:

> Mui Lan lived a lie, so Fong Mei got sly.
> Suzie slipped away; Beatrice made to stay,
> Kae to tell the story,
> all that's left of
> vainglory.

Thus, Fong Mei is encouraged to recant: "When the Wong family snubbed me, I should have farted in their faces. But I was a coward and wasn't willing to give up their money and position. There I was in Chinatown, a lovely young female with a body that hungered beyond my control, surrounded by this restless ocean of male virility lapping at my fertile shores. I could have gone swimming, but instead I felt so ashamed, guarding my body so stiffly that the muscles shrivelled and ached. How I hated my woman's body; encasing it in so much disgust, I went around blind, deaf, senseless, unable to touch or feel. That was how the old lady got the better of me."

Mui Lan sighs: "A rather minor tragedy made major!" But her role in this domestic melodrama has long since faded.

Fong Mei continues: "Imagine, I could have run away with any one of those lonely Gold Mountain men, all without mothers-in-law. This was a land of fresh starts; I could have lived in the mountains like an indian woman legend. If men didn't make me happy enough, then I could have moved on. Imagine, I could have had children all over me—on my shoulders, in my arms, at my breasts, in my belly. I was good at childbirth. And in turn, they could have chosen whomever and how many times they fancied, and I would have had hundreds of pretty grandchildren. I wouldn't have died of loneliness."

Kae asks Hermia: "Is this what they call a forward kind of identity?"

Hermia asks Kae: "Do you mean that individuals must gather their identity from all the generations that touch them—past and future, no matter how slightly? Do you mean that an individual is not an individual at all, but a series of individuals—some of whom come before her, some after her? Do you mean that this story isn't a story of several generations, but of one individual thinking collectively?"

(The ghost signals for silence. She wants to go on.) Fong Mei: "What if I had refused to have children for men and their namesake? Then my daughters would have been free to have children for their own pleasure as well, and then how free we all would have been! What little inkling I had of this at that crucial time; I threw myself totally into the same malicious meddling that oppressed women excelled in. And for what? What is this Wong male lineage that had to be upheld at such a human toll? I once thought it was funny that I could take my revenge on the old bitch and her turtle son. Another man's children to inherit the precious Wong name, all their money and power. I forgot that they were my children! I forgot that I didn't need to align them with male authority, as if they would be lesser human beings without it.

"Women, whose beauty and truth were bartered away, could only be mirrored, hand-held by husbands and men; they don't even like to think that they can claim their children to be totally their own. I was given the rare opportunity to claim them for myself, but I sold them, each and every one, for property and respectability. I tainted their innocence with fraud. Even more contemptible, in order to do that, I had to corrupt the one chance at true love I ever had."

(Suzie suddenly breaks down into tears. She wants to run away. Everyone else strokes her as she screams. We all hold her back, knowing her spirit is the most restless, most at risk.) "Knot after knot after knot!" Sue cries. "All this bondage we volunteer on ourselves! Untie them! Untie me! Don't tie any more!"

(However, there is more.) Fong Mei says: "Even after this list of my crimes, I still have not told you of the worst of my cowardice. The worst was when I willingly gave up the love of my woman's body to the poisonous oppression of woman-haters. I can see clearly now that I was put into this life to be tested. At every turn, I failed miserably. I can see now that it didn't matter that the ignorant, brutal men around me leered and had a dozen different ways to threaten and beat down women. In the end, their impotent violence was nothing in the face of love."

(Silence follows. As the ghost recedes, she seems to want to say that she wouldn't love any of us less if we lost the same fight and went with her; we all cower at this except Suzie, who knew it was all rhetoric after all. She never could be detracted from what she knew she must do.)

K A E

1986

"You know, you look just like Suzie! Has anyone ever told you that?" asked Morgan at that fatal cocktail party long ago. I looked up at him and almost peed my pants, he was so handsome. And I wanted to look so grown-up with a drink in my hand.

"No," I breathed at him, "who's Suzie?"

I still want to know. Who is Suzie? Chi told me she was the most uncompromising person she had ever known. She said, "Suzie was one of those types who couldn't be contained."

I don't know why I remember that description of her over all the others. Probably because it was, as per Chi usual, the most direct and elegant. I realize now that I was impressed by this statement because it is one of the most satisfactory explanations of why she killed herself. Maybe we'll never know who she really was. At seventeen, when she died, she probably didn't know who she really was; we are all too busy testing our limits at that age, either going splat all over the ground too close, or going too far beyond; rarely anywhere near the mark.

There was a time when I too was too young—specifically after I came back from New York, when I was ready and willing and as a matter of fact anxious to spit out blame and frustration for what I thought were silly intrigues and conspiracies but were really my own hurt feelings. I almost yelled at my mother, "Why didn't you tell me! What's the big secret? Look at the identity crisis you left me with!"

However, I would have had to get past Chi first. She towered over me even though she was no taller than I, blocked my way with what I thought was infallible wisdom and barked, "Identity crisis! Pah! What's your real problem? What have you got to complain about? Being overprotected, overcherished, or just spoilt? It was your own ignorance, so what if you didn't ever think to ask until now!"

My mouth pressed against the side of a fishbowl, opening and closing, little helpless bubbles of protest floating up to the surface. Who could argue with logic like that?

I should have known that would happen when the clock struck the Suzie hour. Where my deceased auntie was concerned, I was entirely on my own. No one to tell me the truth; plenty of unresolved grief to speculate upon; lots of intepretations, but so what? I can interpret well enough for myself. I can sift through the embossed family albums and get a sense of a sad smile, attribute motives to a twisted necktie. I bet I could write an entire novel about a hand flung carelessly over a woman's shoulder. Remember, a great work of art is supposedly prepared within the silence of the heart! Or is that what they said about the act of suicide?

My favourite photograph of Suzanne is not specifically of the black-and-white portraiture variety which has decorated many a plant stand and coffee table. The subject perfectly posed, dressed up in layers of cloudlike tulle, heavily powdered shoulders; a perfectly lovely exposure by stark, white stage lights, but a total fake as well. Nothing there to sink your teeth into!

Instead, it's my unwholesome curiosity surrounding her demise that leads me to examine a group photograph, which had been neatly slotted away in my father's mental filing cabinet, "chinese-canadian veteran's fundraising—1951," scrawled on the back. Suzie is but a barely discernible face-dot among many smiling ones, including Keeman and Beatrice and their usual circle of good old buddies whom I'd readily recognize, even today. Back then, all the faces shone like freshly washed porcelain, but if you look really closely, you'll see that Suzie's face is crumbling, chipped stoneware. It was the year she died. I used to half-heartedly wonder if this photograph had been taken before, during or after all the horrendous events of that year, but I guess the important point is that a lot happened in that one year, not the least of which was my birth.

VII

The Suicide

SUZIE

1950

My feet felt heavy and stuck, as if they were melting, shoes and all, over her hardwood floors; my eyes riveted onto my mother's face. There was insanity there. Without one speck of doubt in my mind, I could see it as clear as day. It looked eerie, like the last rays of sunlight snuffed out by bleak clouds gathering on her face. She must have felt them too, because her hands reached up and swept over her brow. It surprised all of us when she just turned and staggered out of the room. None of us would have thought that our news would have an impact like that.

I turned and looked to Beatrice to know what to do. She stared down the hallway at Mom's receding silhouette. Bea's white poreless complexion, her mouth hanging open. She was just as puzzled by this sudden change of events as I.

"There's something terribly wrong here," I heard her whisper to Keeman, so that I wouldn't hear. But I heard everything, especially anything that Beatrice had to say. We were listening attentively to our mother; her high-heeled shoes toiling up the carpeted stairs as if she carried a ball and chain. Each step crushing one pink plush rose after another all the way up the stairs. The gaudy scent of her rosewater wafting back at us.

"Yeah, there's more than meets the eye here," Keeman

193

whispered into Bea's ear. Thank you, Keeman! You can sit down now! Those two little smarty-pants were beginning to get on my nerves. I thought they were awfully stupid for having a few more years of so-called life experience than Morgan and me. I should have come with him and declared ourselves, like real adults. Not this timid snivelling.

I wandered off into the drawing room towards the piano to tinkle on a few keys.

"So, what do we do now, Sis?" I asked, not in a fainthearted way, but loud. Not in an intimate way, but from far away.

They looked at me, startled, as if I were the lunatic! I stared right back at them; Beatrice about to open her silly little oh-so self-righteous mouth again.

"Well, I don't know about you, Suzie," her patronizing tone, her snowy white peter pan collar, "but we have to go and see Granny now."

"Oh no," I said, suddenly alarmed, "not me!" I had mercifully forgotten that old bag heaving about upstairs, and I certainly didn't have it in me to face her now.

"What do you mean, 'not me'!" Beatrice almost took a step in my direction, but Keeman grabbed her by the shoulders.

"Maybe we'd better go a little easier on her this time," he said. I wasn't sure if he meant me or Grandmother. I felt like I couldn't hold back the tears any more, ticklish little things that they were, so I swept myself off the piano stool and headed towards the front door.

"I'll wait in the car," I muttered as I almost ran past them.

Out on the porch, the door slammed with a terrible finality behind me. It felt like leaded glass splintering against my face, because I knew that door would never open up for me quite the same way again. In my mind, word drills kept up as I ran down the stairs—Let me go! Please let me go! Let go of me!—as if there were thousands of invisible hands holding me back.

Out in the car, I could hear Beatrice and Keeman talking to my granny, upstairs in her gloomy bedroom. I slapped my hands up against the sides of my head and pressed as hard as I could, but it was no use. I could still hear every word, even smell the sickening odour of her withered body.

She was lying down as she did all day long, her deadening spirit seeping over the entire house. She got up when she heard Beatrice calling, "Ngen Ngen-ah!"

"A Bea Bea-ah, so you've come to visit Ngen Ngen. Who have you brought with you?" The old woman squinting at them from the far side of her four-poster bed, shaking with the exertion of having to get up.

"I've brought Keeman Woo, Granny! We just got married yesterday. We've come to tell you."

The old woman got up and tried to walk, wobbling unsteadily. Beatrice flew to her side, and the old woman pointed to her armchair by the front window. Beatrice led her over, and as they limped along, both of them started to cry.

"Don't marry him, Bea Bea! Brothers and sisters can't marry! You'll ruin your life. This family is falling apart, and I won't be here much longer. Please listen to me!"

She sank into the chair, and Beatrice knelt in front of her, crying in her own delicate way. As the old woman stroked the black hair on her lap, ancient tears coursed down a beaten face, and fell in.

"There, there. You and Suzie are good girls. Always obedient. You only need to go right up to him! Tell him that you can't marry him," her words melting Keeman against the doorway like an atomic shadow. "Granny'll find you someone better to marry, all right? You'll have the biggest banquet in Chinatown. People will remember it for years to come. And Suzie next, when her turn comes. Where is Suzie? Why hasn't she come to visit Ngen Ngen?"

Out of habit, the old woman looked up from the piles of bills and invoices on the desk in front of her, and brushed aside some lace curtains. From the upstairs window, her sharp eyes could scan practically the entire street. There in the yard across the street, Suzie, a lonely little girl in pigtails, squatted, her tricycle beside her, staring intently at a squashed insect or something on the sidewalk.

Out in the car, I immediately dived down onto the mildewed back seat, overwhelmed with a nausea that pricked more tears out of my sinuses, as if there were a whole stinking ocean back there. There I stayed hidden, lying in a heap as the old woman's eyes passed over me again and again, like a lighthouse beacon.

The trip back to Keeman and Beatrice's apartment was in a total silence that sucked at us like a vacuum. I kept thinking the whole passenger compartment of the car might collapse inward, onto our heads. I sat behind Bea and stared at the back of her head, looking for diamond teardrops in her curls. Suddenly I felt a wave of sorrow for my sister. I had imagined such a beautiful wedding for her; it would have splashed romantic glitter all over Chinatown. Double happiness overflowing their banquet tables! Surely not this pathetic state of affairs!

There was Morgan waiting for me on the fire escape. I got out; he came down. I flew over to him, pulling at his sleeve, wanting to get away, about ten thousand miles away.

Instead, Morgan dragged me back to Keeman and Beatrice.

"Well, what happened?" he demanded. An abrupt approach, a wide stance for railroading, but deep down, Morgan was skittish. One side of him wanted to bolt.

"My mom's willing to sign," he added quickly. "She's not happy, but she's got no choice." He grinned down at me under his arm. I wanted to snuggle into him, he was so wonderful. But I caught him off balance, and we swayed.

Keeman hesitated, but his eyes watched us unerringly. "Gee, I don't know," he admitted, "Bea's mom acted really strange. Locked herself up in her room."

"So what? I just want to know if she's going to sign." Morgan's body tightly strung. "Did you even ask her?"

"Well, no. We didn't get around to that."

"Oh shit! What the fuck else is there?" His voice an explosion which ripped through me. I jerked back, or Morgan pushed me away.

"Listen, you greasy little punk," Keeman's short hairs bristled, "when there are ladies around, you don't talk like that!"

Morgan shook his head and sighed as if he needed to drum up

more patience. "We've got to get married, you know. Suzie's my wife, whether they like it or not. We're not going to sit around and wait for nothing!"

"Take it easy, will you! Things like this take time," Keeman growled from the pit of his stomach.

"We don't have time to spare, Big Brother." Morgan always had to have the last word. "Will you lend us your car for a while?"

"But you don't even have a licence."

"So what! I know how to drive."

I could tell that Keeman was about to refuse, but Bea Bea took the keys out of his hands and headed towards the old Nash, dangling the keys under Morgan's nose.

Just as Morgan was about to start the motor, Bea leaned over and asked him through the open window, "Didn't you say that your dad's name is Wong Ting An?"

"Was. Yeah?"

I caught my breath. Morgan was always a bit touchy when anyone mentioned his dad. Bea Bea watched my mouth.

"He used to work for our family, didn't he?"

"Yes ma'am, he sure did," Morgan answered with a delinquent grin, and Bea stepped back from the car.

About a week after that, I was sitting in my parents' brand-new Pontiac, our faces lit up green in front of the dial cluster dashboard. They bought a new car almost every other year. As usual, I was snuggled up to Morgan as he drove down the Ninety-nine. It was dark countryside around us, and we were about to get caught at the border.

Not that I thought for one minute that we might have looked a little bit suspicious to that big, fat, american border guard. Being chinese for one thing, being chinese and looking even younger than we were for another! Driving an expensive late model and having a steamy little bundle of about one thousand, three hundred bucks, give or take. Enough for a ticket out of this mess, anyway.

He didn't know how much we had to begin with, not until the Vancouver cops came and got us. If we had really thought things out, we would have decked ourselves out in a tuxedo and evening wear and told him that we were headed for a very exclusive party in San Francisco—Chinatown, of course. I bet he would have been too impressed by rich chinks to see anything else.

The way those cops swooped down on us, amazing to see! We were told to park, then to wait in this holding room while they checked out a few details, or so they said. Morgan must have known something was up, because he said that we never should have gotten out of the car, should have just floored it through. It happened so fast, we didn't even know we were being held until we saw a lot of flashing lights.

Suddenly, Morgan ripped the door open and leapt over the counter. And it was a high counter. He yelled back at me, "Run for it, Sue!"

But I stood there, stupidly surprised that he was going to leave me behind like that. The hordes of cops caught him in the parking lot though, pinned him down like a dangerous animal. They all ignored me. When they saw Morgan screaming for all he was worth, kicking and writhing, they all rushed to muscle in on the action, like a pack of starved dogs. They probably already knew that all I would do was whine like a lost pup and stay as close to my master as I could get.

My mother threw the book at Morgan. Who knows what kind of strings she pulled. She knew the chief of police. Oh sure, real good friends! Madame Wong this, Madame Wong that, Madame Wong what a laugh! She sold him a downtown eastside tenement building. Sure, found him a chinaman bossboy to collect the rent too, made it real easy for him. Chinese New Year? Dinner? Sure, as long as she did the inviting, why not? He'd been thinking about investing in another one, you know, on the side.

I couldn't believe my ears. Morgan had been in trouble with the law before, B & E's, petty theft, tried to burn his mother's house down. He had his own probation officer. They blamed him for everything—theft on two counts, even though I told them that I took the money and the car, and that they belonged to my parents, so it wasn't really stealing. But Morgan insisted that he did it. What was he trying to prove—that he was gallant? Didn't he know he was going to reform school? What would happen to me? And the baby! They wanted to pin contributing to the delinquency of a minor on him, unlawful flight, resisting arrest, and the penknife he had on his person. They wouldn't believe that he was just seventeen any more. They were going to double-check his birthdate just in case they could squeeze him into criminal court.

Suddenly, I had this terrible thought that they were going to electrocute him. I couldn't help myself, I was so wired up. I started to yell out loud. Who cared if the whole police station heard me?

"I'm pregnant! I'm going to have a baby! Can't you see?" I jutted out my stomach with its slight pointiness. "We were just on our way to get married."

I heard a cop sneer, "Somebody shut her up, will you!" Even Morgan threw me a disgusted look.

"What's the matter with you guys?" I barked as loudly and clearly as I could, as though they spoke another language. "Let us alone! Let us go! We haven't done anything wrong." A policewoman came and started to pull me away from the table, out of the room. I fought with my skinny, match-stick arms, shrieking with all my might, but Morgan slumped behind the desk and looked away. I thought he would spring to my rescue, but someone closed the door.

For days afterwards, I thought if I fixed my eyes on each locked door, any minute he'd burst in, grab me, and we'd make a run for it together. I kept waiting and waiting. My baby kept growing and growing.

I was kept in the dark about a lot of things. I knew that much, but I couldn't have cared less. After I realized that Morgan wasn't going to come charging through the dungeon walls on his white steed, I settled down. My mother no longer had to lock the door. She went back to selling her soul. I wasn't allowed to go anywhere, but I didn't care. I liked sitting in my dark little room. I wouldn't even go downstairs until I was sure everyone was gone. In fact nobody ate meals together in that house any more. John had a huge fight with my mother and wouldn't even come back to sleep. I wouldn't have put it past my mother to try and convince him to do a little operation on me. I played records to drown out the old-woman sounds down the hall, read a lot, sewed all these neat summer outfits for when I would get my figure back. I daydreamt.

I remembered when I told Morgan that I was going to have a baby. His face lit up, as though he had just discovered a deeper meaning to life.

"Is that true?" he asked.

"Yeah," I said, "it's in my belly."

"Really?" I could tell he was spellbound.

"Really," I answered him, laughing, relieved that he wasn't . . . wasn't inconvenienced, I guess. In fact, he reacted as though it was the most natural thing in the world, like the Morgan I loved to play with.

"Look, sometimes you can feel it move." I pressed his hand against a particular spot.

"Wow," he exclaimed when he felt its punch. "It's true then, it really can happen."

"Now, you'll have to marry us," I teased.

"Oh wow!" He leaned over for another kiss.

That seemed so long ago; maybe I imagined the whole thing.

In front of me, Beatrice looked plumb awful. Tired, sick, thin and worried. Granny was threatening to die again. This time, she even had Dr. Gunn making house calls every day. Beatrice came back home every day to take care of her too, just as though she had never got married. We sat at the kitchen table drinking Coca-Cola, my hair up in rollers.

"Bea Bea," I whined at her for the hundredth time, "why can't I come to live with you and Keeman?"

"I told you, I'm trying not to get Mom all riled up, but she's acting strange these days, and she won't talk rationally any more. I really can't figure out why she won't let you marry Morgan, even if he is a criminal. I'm really at my wit's end with worry!"

"What are you so worried about? She'll have to let us marry. It's as simple as that."

Bea looked away. I stared blankly at her. Then I stared blankly at the wall. Then I wondered why I was staring blankly.

"Aww, she's just giving you the silent treatment," I said finally, perhaps more to console myself, "because she's peeved at us, because of those wasted boat tickets, but that can't last. You should have heard her last night. She's still real good at the good old ear-piercing, screaming-at-Dad number. Last night, they had a whopper!"

"What was it, the same old going-home-to-China one?"

"No, it was more like Daddy and his slut-waitress bringing eternal shame and whatever nasties Mom could think up onto this family. She said that if you have a baby by Keeman, it'll be some kind of horrible cripple or retarded mental case. Nice thing to say, eh?"

Bea Bea jumped up from her chair, her hand clamped tightly against her mouth. She started to head one way, changed her mind, and flew down to the basement. There, she retched and gagged and coughed. It was awful! When she recovered, I helped her up the stairs and sat her back down.

She said, "Suzie, I think I'm already pregnant." I was flabbergasted.

"So soon? What happened to that bride's year that was supposed to be the fun part after you get married?"

Poor Bea Bea. She started to heave up, then she started to cry her eyes out again. I was sick to death of tears, endless tears.

After a while, I asked, "So, does Keeman still think that the government's anticommunist witch hunt is really an excuse to take away the chinese vote?" Oh well, I was only trying to make conversation. She was supposed to laugh! Looney tunes, right Bea? Just laugh! Who cares!

My sister Bea, such a nice girl! I thought it was awfully unfair that these horrible things should fall on her shoulders when she really deserved nothing but the very best. Watching her reminded me of another time she had cried her eyes out, after she was not only refused a scholarship but also entrance into music at the University of British Columbia. They said that her english marks were not good enough, but I was sitting out in the hall, waiting for her. Nine years old, and I could see that stinking old man who was supposed to be the head of the department couldn't even look at Bea without hate oozing from every pore. Pure envy and jealousy that a mere girl, and chinese to boot, should be so gifted. One professor after another came up to us afterwards and apologized to Bea, telling her that she was musically very promising and that it was a shame such talent might be wasted because of prejudice; but one couldn't do anything about it because he didn't even have tenure yet, and another one wasn't on the selection committee; why didn't she consider study in the United States?

The hottest part of summer passed slowly. Beatrice turned out to be definitely very pregnant; she kept throwing up and lost so much weight that they put her in the hospital. So, there was no one else to tend to Ngen Ngen except me, and even though she was getting very feeble-minded, she used to lecture me endlessly on the right way for a girl to behave, and the wrong way, of course. I got so bored that I sneaked out of the house more than a couple of times for some ice cream or a magazine or two. I was careful to avoid anyone I knew, not because I was ashamed but because I didn't want to talk to anyone. What was there to say?

A couple of days later, Mom drove home in the middle of the day. Right away, she marched into my room and started to tear out my hair. By then, nothing she said or did surprised me.

"Are you crazy? Have you no shame—no shame at all?" She slapped and slapped, and when I tried to crawl away, she dragged me back by the hair.

"Parading yourself up and down the street! Dead girl, dead girl-bag!" The words edged out through her tightly clenched mouth. She wasn't going to stop until I conformed to her fierce will, but I wasn't going to do that any more. She never cared about us. She never loved anything but money. I hated her for all the years of dressing us up like monkeys and telling us to behave like good little girls in front of fat men and their high and mighty wives because it was good for business.

"What have I got to be ashamed of?" I shot back. "I would be married to Morgan by now, if it hadn't been for you. And I'd be out of this crazy house."

I was aware of a tiny bleating noise in the background. Ngen Ngen was standing there, clutching onto my doorknob for support. She must have crawled out of bed when she heard the commotion. Now, she was pleading with Mom to stop beating me.

"I'll see you dead first. You'll never marry him. You're going into Greenwood, a prison for cheap sluts like you. I've already made all the arrangements. And that thing in you is a deformed monster, so I'm giving it over to the government to raise."

I staggered back onto my bed; my heart lurched out of my chest. I kept thinking, this is what people call déjà vu. I'm reliving an old nightmare. But I still couldn't bring myself to believe her.

Ngen Ngen was whimpering, "A Fong Mei, don't do this! Don't do this terrible thing!"

But my mother had become medusoid.

"Why, Mui Lan, you old bitch," she hissed at my old granny, who wobbled as if against a great wind, "how good and kind and decent you've become suddenly. How blameless you can pretend to be, now that you're near death!"

Shoving the old woman aside, she ordered, "Now get out of here. I'm locking the door."

"Mother," I asked quietly to disarm her, "are you in there, Mother?"

For a brief instant, the faintest flicker of recognition made her hesitate, but a shroud of pain descended over her face again. And the door clicked to a close.

Before they would let me into the Greenwood Home for Wayward Girls, I had to see a house doctor for a checkup. She was a conscientiously stiff lady doctor who asked me blunt questions and looked concerned. By then, I had become a desolate nothing, locked in my room for days. I had been disintegrating. Although I didn't know they had a real neat term for it—nervous breakdown. So, I was having a nervous breakdown, and the doctor was talking as though I wasn't the only one. That perked me up; the idea was so compelling! So, when you willingly fling yourself towards death—at about a thousand miles per minute—it's called a nervous breakdown. When you just sit there and pee on your chair, you are having a nervous breakdown. Some people don't have nervous breakdowns; they just die early.

After the questions, Dr. Pastega gave me hope. That one look of concern on her plain round face was good medicine. Her crisp, confident tones made me feel human again,

"O.K., Miss Suzanne Wong, here's the story. You've broken your bag of waters. That's the bag of fluid that holds your baby. Not only that, I think you're going through a bit of a nervous breakdown. I'm going to put you in the hospital right away, so we can keep an eye on you, sweetie."

And then, to be transported down the tiled halls and gleaming corridors of a great institution to be saved! A whirlwind of white faces. White social worker face. White nurse face. White cleaner face. All of them gave me the illusion of hope. Please, please tell me, I only want to know one thing, I felt like asking them all, can I keep my baby? But, as the days passed, I began to worry afresh. The isolation cell might have changed, but the isolation had not.

Dr. Pastega didn't mince words. "I've spoken with your mother. She doesn't want you to keep the baby. Now, what's your story, young lady?"

And after my story poured out.

"I see, hmmmm. I'm afraid I can't answer that question. But Suzanne, you must think about what is best for you and your baby. You're only sixteen, and you'll want to start life anew. Finish school, get married eventually. You'll soon forget about this bad mistake. No one need ever know about your past. Your baby can be adopted, and it need never know about its past."

But that wasn't the answer I wanted to hear. I wanted my baby.

"You don't understand; you don't know my mother," my voice shaking with desperation. Real fear seeping in, as the cracks deepened. My mother was still the one calling the shots.

Strike one, I thought, and the props came tumbling down. I

knew as I felt my precious baby coming on that I had no way of protecting him. No way at all!

"Suzanne, now, I have some bad news to tell you. I think you're in labour much too soon. This puts your . . . THE baby at risk."

Strike two.

Beatrice and Keeman
sitting on a fence,
K-I-S-S-I-N-G.

Beatrice to Keeman: "Mom has a legal right to sign away Suzie's baby?"

Keeman to Beatrice: "Don't you think it's for the better?"

"Do you?" Beatrice suddenly sprang out from under him.

"I don't know." His eyes dogged her.

Beatrice toyed with the fringe of some heavy drapes as she stared out the window.

"Keeman? I just figured something out. You know, it's not you and I who are brother and sister. It's Suzie and Morgan."

Beatrice was always Mom's favourite. She talked to Beatrice a lot more than to me, but I find that being your mom's favourite can work against you too. Beatrice used to have to listen.

In the face of Fong Mei's determination, Beatrice felt very insignificant. Yet in the face of Beatrice's cleverness, Fong Mei literally fell apart. An elegant course of tears, brushed aside; a geisha's white powdery mask, washed away. A folded handkerchief pressed against a trembling mouth.

"Mother," Bea's voice trembling, her knees weak. "You can't do that! I won't let you."

"Please, try and understand what it was like for me," Fong Mei's impassioned eyes pleading for mercy. "Believe me, you couldn't know what I've been through because of that. But nobody can know. It's too disgraceful. Just help me! Help your mother." Beatrice hesitated, but Fong Mei pressed on, "What good will it do to let her keep it? She can never marry that boy. And our family will be destroyed, Bea. The baby is going to be a monster, don't you see! Just let it go, and nobody will know. After that, Suzie can come to Hong Kong with us. She can marry someone else, have servants, more babies. We won't ever come back to this town again. You can come with us. Keeman too. I was wrong about him. Please."

Beatrice was shaking her head because she didn't know what to do. She was very sick still. Her head in a thick cloud; unable to think things through. She didn't want to let fly this shocking bit of news. Her first thought churning around and around: she's our mother after all.

Fong Mei could see Bea weakening, so she doubled her efforts. "We'll all lose. Bea, we don't have a choice."

Bea felt ripped apart.

Suzie is on the verge of death again; her labour long and hard. Suzie is worn out, gasping for air; I got slurped in.

"I can't take any more," my dark, clammy moan. But Dr. Pastega is much smaller now. She doesn't loom as confidently as before. There is another doctor in the delivery room, a little man with hard, glassed-in eyes that don't really look at me. They bolt and duck.

The baby is struggling, pitching about inside of me. Oh, this pain! If I had a razor, I would slit my wrists right then and there. I can't scream. Screaming won't help! He has metal scoops in his bloody hands, he keeps shoving these into me again and again.

You're hurting my baby! I don't have a voice. Little legs pounding against me, little hands scratching to get out. My little deformed monster, what have they done to you?

"Knock her out! Why isn't she knocked out yet?" screams the irate doctor.

I am drifting, drifting up high. There in the dark room, near the window, my body on a narrow bed. Oh, but it's so white and shrivelled—no, not just shrivelled, flat as a leaf, flat as those sheets.

In this dusky light, I see eternal peace in that blue-grey little face. Oh, but I feel free and light, like light, soft and shimmering white! Quiet . . . Shhh! I hear someone coming.

Why, it's big Chi coming down the hall!

Chi looks determined, but then she can get away with that. She always did look older than she was. People don't readily cross Chi with an argument, just like they don't readily look for trouble. Nurses point her down another darkened hall, their fingers pressed to their pursed lips for silence. Chi's shoes are rubber soled. At the end of the hall, there is a special little nursery with bright lights that shine all night long, every night. Chi raps on the window. The youngest nurse comes out.

"May I see Suzanne Wong's baby?" asks Chi.

"The Wong baby? Well, I don't know. Are you a relative?"

"No, a good friend."

"Well, then I don't know." The nurse looks back into the nursery. The other nurses are working at the back.

"What do you mean?" demands Chi.

"Well, all right. But the baby's very sick. It's not expected to live. A Dr. Dean special! And you have to put on a gown. And if the nurse-in-charge asks you, say you're related!"

Chi quickly dons her cover-up, muttering to herself to help ease her nervousness, "All chinese are."

"Pardon me!"

"Nothing. What do you mean, a Dr. Dean special?"

"Nothing! Shhh. Come with me!"

Chi can't hold back her tears when she finally looks into the incubator. Her shoulder collapses and starts to shake. The three nurses standing together, whispering, watch her with extreme sympathy. Finally, one breaks from the group and approaches Chi.

"What happened to this baby?" asks Chi. The nurse gazes in at the tiny face concentrating on its great pain. The little chest panting arduously. The beaten-up head has ballooned into a massive medicine-ball bruise. Its eyes press out against their bluish lids as if there isn't any room for them in their rightful places. The baby can't completely close its eyes.

"The baby's head is hemorrhaging."

"What do you mean?" Chi repeats.

"Well, it was a very difficult delivery." By now all three of the white-winged angelic forms have drawn near. They look at each other meaningfully when the nurse-in-charge says, "I mean, what happened was that the baby was facing the wrong way, so it would have been difficult to deliver. The doctor tried to turn the baby's head with forceps. In order to do that, he had to lift the baby's head out of its stubborn position. But I guess he punched it a bit too . . . much." The midwives shoot each other warning glances, and her voice trails off.

"Listen, who did you say you were again?" the nurse asks, nervously trying to reassert herself.

"Somebody who cares a lot," answers Chi, and the nurse blinks.

"Poor little lamb!" she sighs, busying herself with an easier thought. "Wouldn't you know it though?"

"What do you mean?" Chi sounds bone-tired.

"That this would have to happen to a baby that nobody wanted. Like it was an act of God or something. The mother's an unwed teen-ager. We don't see many of those from your people . . . I mean, people of your race."

Chi can't decide to say yes or no, so she says nothing.

And I. I flit back to Suzie's drugged sleep. I hover over her limp form for a while, and then whisper into her ear, "Strike three, you're out!"

K A E

1986

"Chi," I am ecstatic. "I've got the perfect title . . . *House Hexed by Woe*. What do you think?"

"Get serious!" Chi chopping chives.

"I am serious. I've never been more serious in my entire life." I am standing at the counter beside her, staring hard into the woodgrain of my mother's cabinets, trying to imagine an enticing movie poster with a title like *Temple of Wonged Women,* in romantic script: "They were full of ornament, devoid of truth!"

After many months of pondering, I've finally made a decision. And it's a good one. I've just finished a letter to the Howe Institute, regretting that I am unable to accept their position.

"Look at my horizon, Chi. Not a cloud in sight. The sky's the limit. I am free. Isn't that how the prophecy goes? After three generations of struggle, the daughters are free!"

"What prophecy?" asks Chi.

"The prophecy you once told me," I reply.

"Oh brother, that was just a story."

"Chi," say I, feeling protected and confident, "in the end, entire lives are nothing but stories."

There is a terrible, earth-shattering crash behind us. Chi and I both spin around and look. There is my sweet little Bobby on the floor, into the pots and pans. He is pleased, and he also turns to us, looking for approval.

"He just discovered your pots and pans," I warn her.

"Lucky none of them clipped his precious little fingers," she coos at him. The thought of how easily his pink little tadpole fingers can be crushed makes us both walk over to check out the possibility.

"Oh my gosh, Chi," I exclaim, "I just thought of something."

"What?"

"That means that I am the resolution to this story."

"What do you mean?" We listen to Bobby, who is exuberantly celebrating the idea of pot lids as cymbals.

"It means that I have to give this story some sense of purpose."

"So? You knew that all along, didn't you?"

"No, I didn't. I just realized now."

"Huh?" Chi is one of those people who has actually become more attractive with age. With features which were too exaggerated in youth, she has designed a dignified and beautifully intelligent face for herself in her sixties.

"Don't you see?" I gesticulate emphatically. "I'm the fourth generation. My actual life, and what I do in it, is the real resolution to this story. The onus is entirely on me. Yipes, what do I do now?"

"Aren't you taking this a little too seriously?"

"Chi," I say patiently, with half a dozen or so superior tones to my voice, "you should know better than to ask a question like that in this family."

"O.K., O.K., so it's a neverending story! So, big deal!" she clucks pugnaciously at me. I feel undermined by her. But never mind, that is precisely how I got as wily as I am.

"Oh, big deal eh?" I shoot back. "And when was the last time *you* were called upon to give meaning to three generations of life-and-death struggles?"

By now I know I'm ready to make another journey.

I last saw Hermia in Hong Kong. She was living in a tiny makeshift suite of two rooms with a hotplate, on top of her "Healthy Women" medical clinic on Nathan Road in Kowloon. We were waiting for the bathroom; there was only one, downstairs in the clinic which was open for service eighteen hours a day, most days.

Hermia had changed, although I was quick to note she still had the same way of arching her neck when she was under strain. I leaned forward and pressed a long kiss against the thin nape of her neck.

Herm's face blossomed into a million smiles. Her eyes met mine, and we held each other. There was happiness as our hearts opened, then there was a quiet understanding as I read her face, and she read mine. We basked in the first few minutes we'd had alone together in years. My hands sneaked up behind her shoulders to start a massage. She leaned back for more contact. I complained that she had cut her hair too short, leaving me less to play with.

"You definitely have a bit of a dual personality," I said to her.

"Kae, maybe all free women do," she replied with cheek.

I laughed at her. "Are you free?" I teased her.

"As free as my bathroom, *ma chère!*" she always quick of wit.

SUZIE

1951

There was a peculiar sort of sunlight streaming down on the kittens. They tumbled and frolicked all over each other, batting one another with mitts of fluff. They rolled over and stretched out their soft underbellies to its warmth. That light attracted me as well; I too imagined myself rolling around on that section of the floor, exposed to light, not cold. I started towards them, but I found out too late that my feet could not feel, could not move, could not hold me. I found myself hurtling down. The startled kittens scattered.

Sprawled face down on the floor, I was disappointed to find that section as bleak and cold as stone. The mother cat prowled the shadowy edges and suffered my intrusion with stoic dignity. Her eyes gleamed at me with absolute clarity.

I rolled over and checked my nose. Snubbed but not bleeding. Make-up intact. Dress not ripped. Nylons? It was then I realized that I had neglected to put on stockings. I sat bolt upright, furious with myself for forgetting my nylons. It's details like that which give you away, you know! Disguise, I thought, is an act of war.

I figured it must be midday. The dust in the air was making the light gleam at me like that. So strangely. Last night, I got up, staring at the phosphorous green hands of my alarm clock at twenty-three minutes after two o'clock. So far, it had taken me approximately ten hours to get up, wash and dress—without my nylons—for Keeman and Beatrice's big veterans' affair tonight. I had another eight hours yet. Well, five, maybe five and a half, before Beatrice and Keeman came checking up on me. John might come home too. I had been careful to leave dried coffee rings in the bottoms of cups, bread crumbs on plates, potato chip shards on the counter, because no one must suspect that I can't eat any more. I did eat a bowl of rice sprinkled with soya sauce three days ago, in front of Keeman and Beatrice, to keep them happy.

I had no sense of time any more, so I relied heavily on that round Little Ben face, but it was getting very hard to remember to keep it going. All the rest of the clocks in the house had already died peacefully, which was more than I could say about Granny. I had a vision of her lying in her coffin, black and unsettled and buried— very much as when she was alive. I almost giggled, but that would have been profane. And I was still afraid that she might yet find a voice for herself. I didn't go to her funeral, but then neither did my mother. So, who was the more likely to get spooked? I shivered.

Being alone felt good. Solitude gave me different senses about this old house. The dust muted its gaudy colours, the unwatered plants turned brown, the cold silenced me. I would sit down to rest, not because I felt tired—my mind kept journeying on and on, prodding up a squalid hillside—but my body felt limp, drained of feeling. So I would just sit on the sofa, and the light would change subtly around me. Every day. Living had gotten to be a big problem, harder and harder to cover up.

Footsteps. I immediately plastered a smile on my mouth, just in time as Keeman and Bea strolled into the parlour. Evening so soon! Poor Bea, she looked worried. I knew it was hard for her to leave her new baby every day just to look in on me.

"Dressed already!" exclaimed Bea. "Have you been waiting for us?"

"I've been looking forward to it, but I haven't been waiting that long," I said, smiling widely at her. My lipstick felt dried on. I didn't stand up though. I hadn't moved in five hours and was afraid I would collapse again. Still, I knew I would have to eventually, so I started to wiggle my toes to get some circulation going.

"Brrr! It's cold in here." Bea looked at my thick cardigan over my dress. I caught and held her eyes, my face unstained. I liked to dress thickly, to hide myself. Lots of underwear to give myself shape; no, depth. I smiled uncannily to myself.

"Do you like this dress?" I asked innocently, knowing full well that it was too fancy for Keeman's crowd, that it was my mother all over again. My mother, long gone! Ran away and hid, she did, she did!

"You look nice. Now come on! A few of us are going to Ho Ho's first." Beatrice already marching on, anxious to get going. The house got on her nerves now, but she didn't get beyond the front door. She came back with a pile of letters in her hand.

"Didn't you notice the mail, Suzie?" she asked me, riffling through them. I suddenly felt defeated, real life just one step beyond me. "Look, a letter from Daddy!"

She tore it open, and read for a while. "Look at the dates, my goodness! He's arriving on the twentieth." She counted fingers. "Oh my gosh, he's probably on the boat already."

Now if that isn't enough to throw a scare into anyone, I thought. Beatrice read on. "He doesn't mention Mom though."

Oh yes, Bea, let's pretend that nothing happened! By now I was ready to wobble onto my feet. Take it easy, I said to myself; Bea in never-never land, but Keeman watching ever so closely.

"Oh Bea Bea," I fairly gushed as I went for my coat and purse, "can't we go to Keeman's mom's house and play with the baby first? We've got time, don't we?" My voice sounded so normal; I looked back into the parlor, and there on the sofa, Suzie was still sitting. She looked startlingly fresh and relaxed, waiting in sweet anticipation. We both knew that once we got Bea together with her baby, she wouldn't be able to tear herself away until the very last minute. Mrs. Woo would land up cooking chow mein for the whole bunch of us, and no one would notice if I didn't eat very much.

"Can we, Kee?" Bea asked Keeman.

"Sure," he agreed. I knew he would not deny me that.

LETTER TO HERMIA

February 12, 1987

My Dearest Hermia:

As they say, you're the doctor! I will bow to your greater knowledge of these things. Funny though, all these years I thought Suzie's "pneumonia" was a euphemism for that unspeakable crime of hers. Funny, all these years I have been obsessed with uncovering the truth. Yet one of the few facts I was given, I completely refused to believe. I suppose it's natural to want to believe that she died with the same passion with which she lived. Who wants to know that she botched it, succumbing instead to a slow, ignoble, wheezy death. My uncle John still remembers telling her how to do it properly.

"Slit along the veins, all the way up," he said in jest of course, "not across. Nobody'll be able to save you then." Of course, knowing Uncle John, he would have generously demonstrated as well.

He emphasized that he had said this when he was still in high school, years before the actual incident. I asked him as tactfully as I could how long she took to die, but he clammed up tight. Chi chided me for such disrespect; she said that John and Suzie were close in their own way. And she was right. It was an awfully sneaky thing to do, catching him unaware at a family dinner, flushed out with a couple of drinks. Good old Uncle John! He never quite forgave me for bringing Suzie up like that. I wonder if he's as well adjusted as he claims to be. Three daughters, all in the various chrysalid stages of medical school! Aah, Toronto is far away, and he has conveniently forgotten.

Death is a great inspiration, don't you think, Herm? Especially if you face it brutally. Well, for myself, I'd like to die with as much integrity as I have left. That's all. Sounds simple, but let me tell you, sweetie, I think I have to be pretty inspired to come up with a constant like that for my life.

Grand declarations like that are too easy when you've arrived at the end, but I'm only thirty-six (with a young child, no less). Especially these days, when there seems to be such a lack of moral choices. Lucky for me, I've been hoarding my integrity all along, the way children hoard candies. Good investment, ha, ha!

The young, they're easily overwhelmed by the incessant waxing and waning of reality. I mean, reality (life, whatever you prefer) is sordid enough, but at least if it just stood still and allowed itself to be examined and cross-examined, then the young would be able to get a handle on it. They'd be able to take aim and hurtle themselves through life with some degree of accuracy.

How many people realize how we stagger about in life? Either emotionally overdoing, or emotionally half-baked. Shrinking from things or expanding. Like love makes us expand in our relationship to life, and to each other. An extreme case of how we shrink would be suicide. Let's face it, Suzie went splat in a big way! But the young make beautifully tragic corpses.

Of course, I don't mean to sound so callous. It's my way of shrinking, so I won't be overwhelmed by the same bleakness. Where did I read that suicide is a declaration of ultimate bankruptcy? Hey, something I understand very well! Who can feel immune to that kind of intense exhaustion of funds, so to speak? If I could, wouldn't I have fun creating a stylish suicide scene with blood-red funereal roses and high-class despair. Nope, I am afraid that I am just as vulnerable as Suzie to having my first real creative expression thwarted. Aborted. Then, like her, where would I be but nowhere? Dead broke. Out of fortune cookies.

All my love
Kae

P.S. In case you're wondering why I wrote to you instead of the usual phone call, especially after all my past mumbo-jumbo about hating to write letters and all that. Well, I'm trying to save money now that I've finally made up my mind not to take the job at the Howe Institute, now that I'm going to be a poor but pure writer, now that I've got a ravenous little mouth to feed, now that I've impetuously decided to blow the last of my own personal bankroll on a voyage to you at long last (maybe, just maybe, I'll show you how big a-little-mouth in person). Anyway, sweetie, see you at the Kai Tak airport twenty-one hundred sharp, Hong Kong time, Tuesday, March fifth. Bring you' limo!

And remember, don't phone! I can't afford to call you any more.

TELEGRAM TO KAE

20/02/87

ARE YOU KIDDING stop AM ECSTATIC YOU TAKE ADVICE AFTER SIXTEEN YEARS stop YES HAVE BEEN COUNTING stop YES HAVE BEEN WAITING stop PLEASE PLEASE BRING BOBBY stop WE COULD LIVE HAPPILY EVER AFTER TOGETHER stop AND SAVE ON PHONE CALLS stop IMPORTANT QUESTION NEED URGENT REPLY stop WOULD YOU RATHER LIVE A GREAT NOVEL OR WRITE ONE stop

OVERSEAS PHONE CALL TO HERMIA

I relent. I get her at her clinic.

"Dr. Chow here."

"I'd rather live one," I say. I hear wonderful, robust laughter over the phone. And click, she hangs up. That Hermia, she's crazy as *la lune*!

EPILOGUE

New Moon

GWEI CHANG

1939

Gwei Chang didn't have the energy to fight any more, nor the instincts for ducking and dodging. It was all too futile. Maybe it was an elaborate excuse after all, but when you are old, you see the grand plan all to clearly. Details become like the women who waste their entire lives chasing specks of dust.

Whenever he felt sorry for himself, he used to say, and it didn't matter to whom, "You can be just sitting there, minding your own business, but the flow of time has a way of settling dust all over you, greying your hair, stooping your shoulders, bloating your stomach, clogging your lungs, until you choke."

He didn't know how he'd got old. Maybe he wouldn't have if he'd hung himself over a clothesline for women to beat like a smutty rug. But they don't even do that any more. They use vacuum cleaners with more neurotic spite.

Why did he feel like this? There was nothing worse than being sick of life, unless it was feeling cheated at the same time. What had he done to accumulate all this remorse now, especially as the twilight of his life gathered? Where was the peace he had expected? When he opened his dim, old man's eyes, he saw his garden was in order, everything as it should be. Summer warming his well-kept house. A sprawling lawn, covered with grandchildren who played, noisily self-conscious. Shaded women bent over servings of food. His son, middle-aged, dozing on the other recliner. But when he closed his eyes, he saw submerged violence. He had fought the hand on the back of his neck, pushing his face down into murky waters of memory, but he stopped struggling, his body preparing for the breathless impact.

THE HOUSEBOY
1924

"Lift him out!" someone yelped, his voice thrilled by the savageness of what they were doing. Hands reached over the wet shirt, and the houseboy crumpled onto the sopping floor, but he did not start to breathe again. Not right away. Someone kicked him in the stomach, and then Foon Sing coughed and sputtered, wheezing long and hard for air. He couldn't get up, not with his elbows and wrists tightly strapped behind him. Instead, he was forced to press his face harder against the floorboards, like a hurt child against an unrelenting mother. He still looked blurred, as he had when his face was just under an inch or two of water. Nice touch, plunging his head backwards into the tub so that Gwei Chang and his men all had a good view of his tortured face. But more importantly, he could gaze up at his own mortality, the tip of his nose just below the surface of subsistence, his mind rapidly seeping away.

Gwei Chang could have stopped it. One word from his mouth would have absolved them all, but even by then the dark state of his anxious mind was not opposed to murder. They were like cornered animals, bent on their own survival. The young upstart had become a mere pawn.

Of course, they persecuted the dog, although Gwei Chang doubted very much that his men would have actually allowed him to die, but then who can hold back wild boars? Gwei Chang watched him pant, his legs pulled up to protect his underbelly. He knew the boy's pathetic little story. He was young, and she was young. And who can keep young people apart? They attract like magnets, don't they? The gun went off by accident. And the boy was caught next to her. Nothing very interesting, except the boy turned out to be one of Chinatown's. At first, the chinamen could only sit very still and wait. At first, nothing happened, then they heard of the girl's clans rising up. There was nothing they could do except prepare themselves for battle.

The boy's guilt? Of course, Gwei Chang was interested in whether or not he was guilty of taking human life. If accidentally, then Gwei Chang would have asked how accidentally. But tang people's defence came first, and one of the weapons that they absolutely had to use was the boy's pure and naked innocence, regardless of the truth. Foon Sing was not a stupid boy. Under the circumstances, he learned the version of the one and only story that he was to repeat rather quickly, even under torture.

"Foon Sing, you are our soldier," the elders taught him, when he was ready, soaked and softened enough. "You fight for all of us." By then, he was terrified of them.

Hah, Gwei Chang laughed when he thought back. They'd been coolies all of their lives, dogs of famine. But in the freedom of this young land, old coolies could almost make-believe that they were generals. As though they had a say in their destinies. As though they could throw numbers onto the table and challenge them against the odds. As though they could win.

Just as the chinamen suspected, as soon as they let Foon Sing go, some white men grabbed him off the street and pushed him into a car. At first they thought he was a dead man at the hands of vigilantes, then rumours filtered through that it was police-ghosts who had taken him.

What would Foon Sing say? That first night of his abduction was the most perilous. All Chinatown mobilized; information came rushing back to the elders, as they sat up all night at the back tables of Disappearing Moon. They knew that if the houseboy broke down under pressure, he would seal not only his own fate but the fate of Chinatown. Yet what could they do but wait and discuss strategy to while away the darkest hours?

The morning found Foon Sing still alive. His kidnappers turned out to be a couple of half-hearted cops out for a little "third degree." Foon Sing had done well.

"At least, we know now that we've got a chinaman's chance," they told each other.

That morning, Gwei Chang sought out Ting An. He was sleeping on one of the lower shelves of the storeroom. He had been up all night, overwrought like everyone else, running here and there, on the lookout for mobs with torches. In his memory, Gwei Chang could see Ting An clearly—a grown man, tall and lean, slightly underfed—but at the time Gwei Chang couldn't really see him for the life of them.

"Hey, half the morning's gone already. You gonna sleep all day?" Gwei Chang nudged Ting An and watched him stir, grunting, long limbs unfurling. He had his mother's strong, beautiful face. Gwei Chang used to watch for her shadow on his face, like a witch haunting.

He should have told Ting An then. He was feeling good and expansive that morning. The sun was already high in the sky. What made him let another opportunity go by?

Too cowardly, too scared to tell him, if the truth be known. How could Gwei Chang tell Ting An that he was his father, that he had abandoned the woman who was his mother? All these years had passed, and one day—the day Ting An left—it dawned on Gwei Chang that, whenever he looked at Ting An, he never saw a son, only a sore reminder that she was gone, and maybe he just kept Ting An around to torture himself. If only he hadn't been so full of self-pity, he would have seen the hurt on Ting An's face, and the knots of anger that hardened around the hurt, year after year.

Maybe Ting An knew Gwei Chang was his father, but for sure Ting An refused to be Gwei Chang's son. That realization was what finally broke Gwei Chang in the end. He threw a pile of guilt money after him, just so he could die with some face left. If only he had said to Ting An right from the start, "You are my son." Excuses after all! And life is but a dream, right?

Instead, he said, "A Ting-ah, lots to do today." Every day he made Ting An work for him all those years for nothing after all. That particular morning, it was, "We're going to have to find someone who knows how to deal in their laws to defend the houseboy. Maybe you can look into that for the associations. Also today you can drive a few of us over to have an audience with the consul. But we'll have to see how the day turns out. Don't want this trouble to take too much time away from the business. The new warehouse gets its roof started today. Someone has to see that that's done right." Every day, every day, too busy being the big gun!

There is never any way to know what lies in the heart of any human being, and that is how Gwei Chang knew that the secret of the white woman's death would never be fully revealed. How could it be, when it sailed away with the houseboy? As for Gwei Chang, he'd lived in a belly full of doomed, deserted chinamen long enough to know what had always crouched in their hearts.

Under the strain of bigotry, they were outlaws. Chinamen didn't make the law of the land, so they would always live outside of it. In fact, it was a crime for them just to be here. The result was submerged, but always there: violence, with the same, sour odour of trapped bodies under duress. That could be why the whites complained that chinamen were unclean. Sinister, they said. But imagine their fresh-faced, thoughtless innocence beside the seething rage and bitterness in chinese faces! They grew uncomfortable in the presence of chinese, without even knowing why.

The houseboy had paid five hundred dollars, head tax, to enter the numbing, claustrophobic world of single, chinese men. He was thirteen years old, much the same age as most who came around 1912. Shy and tender, torn from their adoring mothers' skirts, they knew about stark poverty and hard work, but that was just about all they knew.

○

What boy wouldn't have dreams to sustain him while he toiled in the filth and stench of a laundry? Wonderful dreams of adventure and prosperity in a big land; maybe a smart-looking, pointy moustache and a few other frivolities. He had meant to learn proper english right away, but when he arrived he found everything too overwhelming. He spent months staring into space, at the same time able to wander about only in "safe for chinamen" areas. Beyond his grinding work routine, the most he could do was loiter on the outer reaches of Chinatown and stare at caucasian pedestrians. Sometimes, he felt flattened like an insect on the limited horizons of Chinatown.

He grew older. And Foon Sing was the stylish type who picked up manners very quickly, so he did well as a houseboy. The trouble began when he was still a houseboy at twenty-five, with each year of smiling servitude stitched deeply into his face. Each hoarded dime! What he must have found utterly sickening was how much of his life and dreams he had had to give up! Worse still, each year got harder and harder. He wasn't allowed to have his wife or his family with him. He was only allowed to sink deeper into the mire when he tried to support a wife and family in China. Not even the most modest dreams of happiness could come true for the houseboy.

Then one day, into his futile existence came a fair-haired demoness, a perfect example of their fresh-faced innocence. To him, she must have been dazzling. And why not? Her life full of human promises, she would have everything that he was denied. She was careless with her freedom; she smiled widely, even at a chinaman. He must have noted that she took everything that she was given, like a child, without forethought or after. She was also lonely, uprooted as he was once. He understood this and could manipulate it for her attentions.

Did he fall in love with her? There was no way for him not to be obsessed with her and all she represented. If that were so, did he come to hate her? Yes . . . well, that was more the essential question, wasn't it? A white woman would remind him of his alienation, her nearness exposing the raw intensity of his desperation. In the dehumanized structure of his life, murder might even have made sense. A youthful smile flung carelessly across the chasm of racial mistrust could have confused either one, perhaps harassed either one. But to the point of killing? Easy to see that there was no happy ending here, but why did it have to end in death?

All consuming at the time; now it was trivia, dusty details. Gwei Chang used to think that his part in this drama had been vital to the outcome. It turned out that he was only masking the truth, and then wearing the mask even when it stifled. And to think that he had given up a son, even lost long-time friends, over this silly affair.

Whenever Gwei Chang thought of the dead, blonde demoness, he used to remember that August Moon Festival story about the spinner and the cowherder. The old chinamen loved to recite this story because it was evocative of their loneliness. Except Gwei Chang changed their professions to be the nursemaid and the houseboy.

The nursemaid was from heaven, and the houseboy a mere earth-bound mortal. Then, they met and fell deeply in love. The gods or the powers above were very displeased with this liaison between unequals. Worse still, the young lovers' pining after each other adversely affected their work. So, the powers-that-be split them apart and created a racial chasm between them, as impossible to cross as the heavens themselves.

By August Moon Festival of 1924, Foon Sing had already sung his way through the first of what turned out to be endless hearings and trials. He was still the most obvious suspect, but nobody had charged him, so the elders bided their time and watched. For the first time, chinamen had to keep an eye on white people. Before, the old ones were too embittered by the injustice and saw only what they wanted to see. They were surprised to find how much alike chinamen and white people were.

In the white daily tabloids, strange rumours about spiritualists began to fly about. Theories that the girl was murdered during a wild party full of rich people started to divert attention away from Foon Sing. The idea of a rich playboy as the murderer seemed to entertain the whites much more than a dumb chinaman.

Gwei Chang and his clique were pleased with this unexpected change of events. With whites pointing fingers at each other, the chinamen thought they could breathe a little easier. In fact, they even began to enjoy the theories. Over their coffee and cigarettes, people in Chinatown discussed the possibilities. And they were endless. Poems were inspired by this one.

Of course, Chinatown wasn't off the hook yet. Before long, another attack, this one on another front. The whites were coming at Chinatown not with clubs and stones this time but with the way they'd gotten them every time. It was dubbed the "Janet Smith" bill at the legislature.

Already, the law forbade chinese men from certain kinds of employment if it meant that white women would have to work in close proximity to them. The Janet Smith bill was proposed as an extension of this law. At this critical time, such a proposal not only blatantly implied that Wong Foon Sing had murdered the girl but made criminal suspects of all chinese men.

"We can't let them get away with this persecution." Wong Loong spoke at the table. "We called this meeting to discuss how to fight back. If we don't protest loud and clear, we'll lose a lot more than face. We . . . some of the younger guys have already discussed this, and we feel that we may need to go to drastic measures, maybe as far as a . . . boycott! That is why we have come to you . . ."

Gwei Chang sat at that meeting. He looked around the table and saw a lot of new faces—younger faces that had just joined up, conscientious faces full of self-importance. But he also saw resistance from some of the elders who thought that these young fools needed a bawling out for letting their emotions fly at a moment's notice.

"Boycott! Boycott means our people starve!" someone roared. The swear words took their usual places at the table.

"Boycott, that cracked-brain! Wow his mother's cunt! Go eat shit!"

"If this bill is passed, we won't be allowed to earn any kind of living at all. Look around you! All the chinese who are unemployed. More of us will starve!" Wong Loong yelled over the din.

Surprisingly, Ting An came to his rescue. Ting An spoke so rarely that many people were shocked into rethinking the situation.

"It's obvious that with this law they will be able to hang Wong Foon Sing first and the rest of Chinatown later," he said.

"So, how come the Wong boy hasn't been arrested and strung up? No need to ask questions of a chinaman!" said Lee Chong.

Old Chu snorted in agreement. "We shouldn't do anything until they arrest him."

"Are we afraid to stand up for ourselves?" Another young hothead fanned the flames. "Look at them. They certainly think enough of themselves to clamour for justice at all costs, even over one girl."

"Pah, that's them! Who would have thought that one dead female could stir up such a fiasco?" An old hothead. "No white one ever blinked an eye for the countless dead chinamen 'murdered accidentally,' but one of their own catches it, and they all go crazy."

"Exactly," Wong Loong burst in. "How come they stand up so well for themselves? How come we don't stand up for ourselves?"

"You little upstart!" Lee Chong slapped his hands on the table for attention. "What do you know about what it was like in the old days? Sure, you think you know a bit of their devil tongue, and you start to think like them. You younger ones have no idea of the odds against us. If we hadn't stood up for ourselves, do you think you'd be here chattering your silly little heads off now?"

"We want to speak up for our rights to jobs. That's all," said a young one. "No work, no eat. Plain and simple. What are you getting so steamed up about?"

"Why?" roared Lee Chong. "You cracked-brain young ones want to venture outside of Tang People's Street, to work, you claim, and this is exactly the kind of shame you bring back with you. Maybe those ghosts are on the right track. Maybe you aren't fit to wipe their asses."

Nothing like a common cause to bring men together, Gwei

Chang thought, as he watched the younger cliques wind up for an equally foul-mouthed rebuttal. As expected, the point of the meeting was totally knocked off the table, to the farthest corner of the room. In the end, it wasn't the white hysteria that frightened him as much as what chinamen had allowed themselves to become in the face of it—pitiful men, with no end for their self-pity in sight. All the more pitiful because they once had divine authority, if only over their downtrodden women. Even when they all had to go into their desperate little hovels alone every night, they would still cling onto the precious little they had had.

Gwei Chang could have kept his loyalties. The old ones were wrong in this case, but year after year, right or wrong, they had always been loyal to each other. How many lonely, softhearted nights, respectfully attentive to the would-be heroics of laundrymen and gardeners, they had all played surrogate wives to each other. The biggest boasts from the lowliest kitchen helper came to life for few precious moments.

He looked over to Lee Chong, whose lips still snarled like a dog over a bone, and thought: he is my oldest friend, the one I talked into risking his life flying over river rapids with a load of human bones over thirty years ago. He's the one who brought me the news of Chen Gwok Fai's death. We go back that far.

What if Gwei Chang had kept silent? The elders would have kept their power (or their powerlessness), and the outcome might or might not have stayed the same—what did he care? But he would have been able to keep friendships intact, and the secret of their eternal cowardice. Maybe that was more important. However, when young and old turned to him, they all seemed to challenge him.

"Hey, you're the big-shot! Transform the moment!"

Well, Gwei Chang played the big-shot, all right, and he transformed the moment: "The community will stay together at all costs, even through a boycott."

He threw the entire weight of the patriarch behind those choice words. Lee Chong's mouth fell open; the old ones could hardly believe their ears. Old Chu, Duck Toy—their eyes clouded in shame, thinking that their lifetime brotherhood had been betrayed.

"Whites wear collar and tie now," Gwei Chang declared. "They don't like to dirty their hands, so they use their laws against us. Tomorrow, Wong Loong will make arrangements to visit the chinese consulate. You young ones say that you aren't afraid to open your mouths, like us old ones. O.K., this is your chance to prove yourselves then."

Lee Chong never forgave Gwei Chang that. Their friendship changed. Gwei Chang hurt himself the most, because he lost a lifelong friend, a brotherhood, an entire way of life. He asked himself if it was worth the trouble. Were mere words worth such pride? Yet, with words, he swept away the coolie generals, himself included. The back tables were given over to waiters who sat and smoked and gossipped while folding napkins.

By the time the houseboy was kidnapped again and finally charged with murder, a whole new set of Chinatown leaders had stepped in. They were statesmen, smooth liars in good english. The white press loved their boldness. They wrote letters, said the correct phrases. Even the new chinese consul worked better with them. The Janet Smith bill flopped and became Chinatown's first real success story.

This murder case blew up into a scandal beyond everyone's wildest dreams. Big-shot whites took pot shots at each other. That was how Foon Sing got away. There were libel charges, and kidnap charges; police commissioners arrested. Flying accusations from government department to government department landed on the attorney general's face, like so many cream pies. Scotland Yard got involved, even Peking. All very mind-boggling to a loitering chinaman on Pender Street, his toothpick in his mouth, who would always wonder why they didn't just lynch the houseboy. Easier, and who would have given a damn, back then!

GWEI CHANG

1939

When Lee Chong heard about Gwei Chang being laid up, he made a special trip to visit and to reminisce, perhaps to apologize in his own way. And Gwei Chang in his own way, because who can say who was right and who was wrong.

"And how 'bout that theory of the mad-dog son of the lieutenant-governor raping and murdering her?" Lee Chong offered.

"Yeah, that was my favourite one." Gwei Chang was grateful. Lee Chong's visit meant a lot to him. More than Lee Chong knew. More than he himself knew.

"What a crazy waste of time!" Lee Chong allowed himself to relax a little more.

"Yep, a crazy waste of energy."

"And money!"

"And money," Gwei Chang chuckled. They were self-conscious with each other. They had drifted apart, but somehow, thankfully, they had never lacked an excuse to come calling on each other once in a long while. Lee Chong still lived alone in Chinatown. One tiny room, kitchen and toilets at the end of a long, narrow hall. That was the way he lived. He wasn't a destitute man, but business setbacks ten years ago had widened the gap between them even further. Gwei Chang realized how difficult it was for a rough old Chinatown bachelor like Lee Chong to manoeuvre around wife and daughter-in-law prodding him with the necessary teacups. One grandchild after another to "he, he, he" at before he finally reached his old friend's bedside.

Lee Chong kept slipping off the horsehair armchair. Finally, he propped himself up on wide-set feet and looked anxiously at all the foreign things around him. Doilies behind him, plants with enormous, speckled leaves dangling over him, carpet at his feet; it would have been easier if Lee Chong had been a houseboy. But he never had been.

"You got enough to live on, Elder Brother?" Gwei Chang asked him, since they were on the topic of money. Gwei Chang asked him that whenever they saw each other, like people nowadays would say, "How are you?"

"Fine. I'm getting along fine. And you. You got enough?" Lee Chong laughed at the silliness of this fine old ritual, then added, "You have more mouths to feed. As for me—well, old men don't need too much to eat." A breathless pause, then he asked what he had come to ask.

"You very sick?"

"Yeah," Gwei Chang answered very quietly, watching Lee Chong's old fingers slide over the rim of his hat.

Lee Chong had been shocked by Gwei Chang's appearance when he came into the room. But Lee Chong was a proud man. He probably wasn't going to accept Gwei Chang's dying without a fight.

"Your strength has always been a brittle kind of strength. No endurance. You should have realized that and taken better care of yourself," Lee Chong scolded, clucking his tongue against the dry roof of his mouth.

"Here I always thought you were the brittle one," Gwei Chang teased.

"Nope, I was the stubborn fool. Fifteen years is too long to hold a grudge, especially between brothers."

"Not long enough, if you knew you were in the right." Gwei Chang's mouth always full of niceties.

"I was wrong. You were always right," Lee Chong grunted back.

"What does it matter, old friend?"

"Matter? No matter . . . you," his edgy reply, "because you always hated wasting time and energy."

"And you hated wasting money . . ." They laughed at how easy it was. They laughed until they both wheezed and coughed.

"Ah, A Chang, you knew!" said Lee Chong, with a sigh. "What were we but ignorant labourers? Couldn't hardly read or write in our own tang language, never mind theirs. It wouldn't have done us any good if they got slick, and we didn't. You were right. You always could see way ahead of any of us. That's why you're a rich man." Lee Chong's eyes glanced around the sun-drenched room. By now, the grandchildren had slithered in, prowling around the tea things. They were accustomed to such liberties. Their play helped their grandfather pass many a weary hour.

"After all these years, what if I told you the truth?" Gwei Chang offered up. "I got too tired, too lazy to play their silly games. And why did we have to anyway, with all those young hardnecks all panting to jump into the scuffle? Was it so important to you to keep a hand in it?"

"Not now," Lee Chong admitted, eyeing the grandchildren, elbows on knees spread wide apart, probably thinking about lighting up a cigar, but not daring to in front of a sick man.

Gwei Chang was getting tired, couldn't keep his eyes open. Fong Mei came in to arrange a pillow or two. He fell back with a heavy thud. The children shooed away. She was always very kind to him, chattering as she opened one window and closed another. Gwei Chang noticed Lee Chong staring at Fong Mei a little more than was necessary. She noticed as well. It was true she had come a long way from a village bride. Glossy and perfumed, she was a rich woman now.

"I should go. You need to rest and get better." Lee Chong started to get up after she left.

"No," Gwei Chang almost gasped. "No, stay! I sleep all day long. Tell me some news." For some strange reason, he almost felt like crying. He squeezed his eyes tightly shut to lock his fears in. After a while, Gwei Chang heard those old bones of Lee Chong's creaking towards him; an old hand crept over to Gwei Chang's shoulder and hung onto his neck. Lee Chong sat down on the edge of the bed.

"You're younger than me," he said tenderly, "you're bigger, smarter, richer; you can be stronger." His hands pressured, and Gwei Chang glanced up at Lee Chong's doleful eyes trying so hard. Gwei Chang managed a small smile for his old friend, and for their old and uncomplicated friendship. Lee Chong understood Gwei Chang only so far, but that was enough. Only words separated them.

"Tell me news about Ting An. He still won't come to see me, you know." The pain of that statement made Gwei Chang's head fall back, his heart aching.

Lee Chong scratched his head and spoke plainly. "Ting An drinks too much, I hear. I also hear he has trouble with that ghost wife of his. But that's to be expected, right? His warehouse isn't doing too well. Let's face it, Ting An's heart isn't in it like the old days, leastways not like Choy Fuk or your daughter-in-law now."

Gwei Chang sensed the omission then. He looked up at Lee Chong, whose face strained with indecision. When their eyes met, Lee Chong smiled a bit too widely, too quickly. There was a conspiracy in that smile.

Gwei Chang said, "Tell me what you know, Elder Brother!" The power in his voice surprisingly sharp.

Lee Chong's face fell; his jaw slackened. "Who knows? It could all be stories. People delight in maliciousness . . ."

Dying was a privileged situation to be in; Lee Chong would not hold out on his old friend. Gwei Chang listened without a word.

After Lee Chong left, Gwei Chang slept. After he slept, he thought. He thought back seven years, to the last time he had had words with Ting An. Did Ting An hate him that much? Gwei Chang tried to think, his mind circling and circling with endless thoughts—thoughts to the end.

TING AN

1932

What is the price one should pay for being a do-gooder, a blind old fool? Blind to his own flesh and blood! Hardened against the people he loved! What possible excuse could he have had?

Gwei Chang pleaded, "What do you want me to pay, A Ting? Tell me how much? Your own warehouse, Son? I could set you up in your own business. Tell me!" He was begging for the first time in his life, his hands kept reaching to hold Ting An. Ting An knocked them aside, again and again. He was in agony.

"Don't touch me!" he screamed. "I have to go. I have to get out of this dead town."

"No, no, you don't have to go anywhere. No one'll bother you. I promise you, I won't bother you. Marry her, go ahead! Keep her! I'll give you all the money you need." Gwei Chang could not let him go away. Another blonde demoness—this one not dead enough.

"Keep your damned money." Ting An would not be bought. So Gwei Chang shoved the money at her instead. She was nameless and penniless enough to make the perfect target for him. She had no idea what the stakes were, so he bought her cheap—a nice house, car, a prosperous husband.

"But this warehouse is his warehouse," Gwei Chang told her. "He has to stay in Vancouver."

"Let us not move, darling!" she probably wheedled Ting An afterwards. "Vancouver has such nice weather."

They said that Ting An found her in a back alley. A fallen woman. He would have had to fish her out of a puddle. Gwei Chang didn't know that stray cats had got to be a habit with him. But how could he know, he hadn't ever bothered to ask Ting An if he wanted a wife. Gwei Chang had not noticed that Ting An's eyes never trailed after a woman, which was unusual for a man in Chinatown.

Now, all of a sudden, Ting An was set on marrying. One evening, he came to ask Gwei Chang for advice, his great eyes swimming around in a lovesick fog. Gwei Chang could tell that he had been drinking. Ting An had intentions of changing his name back to Chen, his mother's maiden name, as though it was very important that the slattern be properly titled. He had to consult Gwei Chang in case his birth papers had been bought or fixed, as many were.

Ting An sat on a swivel chair in front of Gwei Chang's desk, muttering, embarrassed.

"Sooo . . . I figured you must have given me the name Wong to make me look like a relative . . . or until you wanted to sell the name to someone else." Chinese bought and sold their identities a lot in those days.

"I am your father," Gwei Chang had to answer. "I gave you my name because you're my son." Ting An smirked at him.

"Don't you know that you are my son?" Gwei Chang asked.

"A Chang, you have always treated me like family," Ting An said hesitantly at first, then continued with too much deliberation. "All these years, I wanted to thank you for the protection of the Wong name, sir. I will always be very grateful to you for all that you have done for me."

Gwei Chang waited, but he could have waited a thousand years. Ting An refused to see the truth glaring at him.

After a while, Gwei Chang said, "Keep the Wong name. It is yours. Eventually, I'll find you a real wife from China. Marrying this female is absolutely out of the question for you."

"A real wife from China," Ting An repeated in disbelief. He shook his head from side to side, as though something rattled in his head. A suspicion perhaps, but he kept interrupting himself. His eyes narrowed at Gwei Chang, only to dart away a couple of times. Then a bewildered expression, as though he realized something for the first time in his life. Again, he looked away, but this time, his neck rigid, his face grim. Finally, he turned to Gwei Chang, his eyes wicked with hate.

"Like your real wife from China?" he asked. "Not a dirty half-breed, buried somewhere in the bush?"

The confirmation he needed was when Gwei Chang shut his eyes against the heat of Ting An's swollen rage. Gwei Chang hid his face in his hands. Ting An's fury seemed to throw him against the walls against his will. A shower of glass rained over Gwei Chang when Ting An threw a chair through the windows of the office. Shards cut Gwei Chang's brow, but he didn't move, he didn't look up. Even in this bloodthirsty rage, Gwei Chang knew Ting An would not come near him in any way. In fact, Ting An was desperately trying to escape, pressing away from Gwei Chang as if his eternal shame would contaminate him. Gwei Chang heard Ting An as he tore through the entire warehouse, wrenching what he could off the shelves. His sobbing surprised Gwei Chang, because all along, he'd thought . . . he didn't know what he'd thought.

KELORA CHEN

1894

Gwei Chang remembered that last summer. He and Kelora had travelled overland for two days, to help with the smoking of the salmon at her people's fish camp. The happiest, most elaborate harvest he'd ever been to; those indians had a rich life. Several villages worked together to harvest, clean and dry rack upon rack of salmon which had been caught downriver. The salmon-fish swam into fences built across a narrow part of the river, until the water teemed with tens of thousands. Then, they only needed to be lifted out by the netful. Back in the camp, they had to be smoked and cured over an open alder fire.

The sight of all this good food being hauled in got Gwei Chang very excited. It made him feel good to learn the indian ways, because they made him think that he might never starve like a chinaman again.

But Kelora told him that even with this abundance, her people faced famine later in the winter.

"The harvests haven't been as good as they used to be," she said, "there still might not be enough to eat."

Then a strange thing happened to him. Kelora looked up because she sensed a change. An icy silence perhaps. He stood over her on purpose, so that he could pour his bitterness onto her. Gwei Chang had often looked into the sallow face of famine. He could see how famine was the one link that Kelora and he had in common, but for that instant, it made him recoil from her as surely as if he had touched a beggar's squalid sore. The memory of hunger flung him back to that other world again, where his mother's wretchedness plucked at his sleeve and gnawed through his stomach.

In the next instant, he looked at Kelora, and saw animal. His stare hostile, as if he had just recognized her for what she really was. Then in that case, what was he except her prey—her trap so cleverly woven! He convinced himself that she had tricked him, and he willed himself to blot out those eyes of hers, already frightened and searching. She knew he was fighting against her lure; she knew that he had received a letter from his mother, pleading with him to come home and do his duty as the eldest son. Kelora probably also knew that he would abandon her long before he realized it.

GWEI CHANG
1939

"Would it help my dying soul to tell you that I love you, Kelora? Love like that only comes around once in ten lifetimes. And it's a love beyond death. You could spend the rest of your reincarnated lives searching for a love like that. So why did I leave you? I've never left you. You left me."

"So why did you spend the rest of your pitiful life feeling guilty?"

"O.K., I did leave you. In the gorgeous full bloom of our love, I left you and went back to China where my family beckoned. Yes, I surely did leave you. And to marry another, no less. I swore to you that I was coming back. So why did you die? You left me more than I left you. Why? Why did you have to weaken? Your spirit was fragile after all, when all along it seemed so strong! Ever since, I've lived a miserable life, grieving for your loss, bitterly paying. You told me that indians have another name for the eagle—the one who stays perched on a tree, who doesn't fly."

"Kelora, I lost your son," he told her. Funny, how he could just be sitting there and the feeling of her lips brushing against his would take him by surprise. The taste of her breath, sweet and faintly vanilla, would become more real than the feel of his sickbed against his tired back. But just for a second. Then it would be gone, leaving him to agonize alone. Funny, wasn't it, how she could still do that to him.

○

"You're just getting sentimental in your old age." A voice.

Something fleshy flitted across the corner of his eye. He turned his head, or rather, he tried to turn his head, but nothing happened.

"You've been haunting me all my life. Now, I need someone to talk to. So talk to me!" he said out loud.

Silence.

"I live with pain all the time now," he said.

"And heartache is the only thing that can chase it away?"

"I don't mean to whine."

"But you do."

"Kelora, I didn't mean to . . ."

"Never mind, the fire has gone out, the dance is over. There is nothing left for you to do."

"I can remember . . ."

The beating of clackers in his head. The front of him burning hot from the intensity of the fire, the back of him shuddering with cold. The frost of the night scratching along the edges of the ring. The smell of wood smoke on her skin. Kelora crouched on their cattail bed of blankets and hides, combing out her tangled hair. Her face relaxed, staring at the fire. The curves of her skin glowing, in shadows. He wanted to press his face into the mounds of her flesh with his eyes open, to feel the cottonlike lumpiness beneath the silken coverlet. His lips pressed against her breast, and she collapsed against him.

The shuffle of wooden rattles in his head. Her black cloud hair woven across his face, weblike, dreamlike. He looked up and saw smoke tendrils escaping between roof planks into the dark sky. Nudging and pressing against the stars, he soaring, she soaring. She, keeper of the fire, covering him with intense desire, he searing, they searing. She opened herself like a secret revealed; their bodies joined in dance, writhing with power. She, wet from tears, slick with lust, steeped in sweat; their souls keening, reaching for eternity. From another part of the village, a child whimpered and sighed. Other fires tended by other women glowed and murmured in the distance. He melting into her like molten gold, like sunset.

The steady rhythm of feet thumping in his head. The smell of snow; their burning hearts. They huddled together, legs a slippery tangle. Pure and naked, their juices still swift-flowing currents. The earth seemed to drift. He clung on, trembling; she reached out and pulled a blanket over him. Her cheeks beautiful, seductive, flushed. Her eyes still lewd; he wandered, helpless in their fiery depth.

He closed his eyes, the heavy chant of the storyteller turning to mist in his head.

International Women's Writing from Seal Press
Selected Titles

A WEEK LIKE ANY OTHER by Natalya Baranskaya. $9.95, 0-931188-80-6 An enthralling collection by one of the Soviet Union's finest short story writers.

WORDS OF FAREWELL: *Stories by Three Korean Women Writers* by Kang Sok-kyong, Kim Chi-won and O Chong-hui. $12.95, 0-931188-76-8 Three highly regarded Korean women writers are presented to the English speaking language for the first time.

NERVOUS CONDITIONS by Tsitsi Dangarembga. $9.95, 0-931188-74-1 A novel of growing up in Zimbabwe by a brilliant new voice.

CORA SANDEL: SELECTED SHORT STORIES. $8.95, 0-931188-30-X Masterful short stories by the Norwegian author of the acclaimed *Alberta Trilogy*.

ANGEL by Merle Collins. $8.95, 0-931188-64-4 This vibrant novel from the Caribbean introduces the remarkable voice of the Black poet and novelist Merle Collins.

TO LIVE AND TO WRITE: *Selection by Japanese Women Writers, 1913–1938* edited by Yukiko Tanaka. $12.95, 0-931188-43-1 An important collection spanning a twenty-five year period of change in Japan, during which women writers emerged as major voices in the country.

EGALIA'S DAUGHTERS by Gerd Brantenberg. $9.95, 0-931188-34-2 A hilarious satire on sex roles by Norway's leading feminist writer.

SEAL PRESS, founded in 1976 to provide a forum for women writers and feminist issues, has many other titles in stock: fiction, self-help books, anthologies and international literature. Any of the books above may be ordered from us at 3131 Western Ave., Suite 410, Seattle, WA 98121. Please include 15% of total book order for shipping and handling. Write to us for a free catalog or if you would like to be on our mailing list.